Only a Duke

Ladies Who Dare
Book Six

Tanya Wilde

ARE YOU SIGNED UP FOR DRAGONBLADE'S BLOG?

You'll get the latest news and information on exclusive giveaways, exclusive excerpts, coming releases, sales, free books, cover reveals and more.

Check out our complete list of authors, too!

No spam, no junk. That's a promise!

Sign Up Here

www.dragonbladepublishing.com

Dearest Reader;

Thank you for your support of a small press. At Dragonblade Publishing, we strive to bring you the highest quality Historical Romance from some of the best authors in the business. Without your support, there is no 'us', so we sincerely hope you adore these stories and find some new favorite authors along the way.

Happy Reading!

CEO, Dragonblade Publishing

Additional Dragonblade books by
Author Tanya Wilde

Wedding Fever Series (with Sara Adrien)
Dare to Tempt an Earl This Spring (Book 1)
How to Lose a Prince This Summer (Book 2)

Ladies Who Dare Series
Almost a Scoundrel (Book 1)
By No Means a Gentleman (Book 2)
A Knave By Any Other Name (Book 3)
A Little Bit of Hellion (Book 4)
Just About a Rake (Book 5)
Only a Duke (Book 6)

The Lyon's Den Series
Beauty and the Lyon

Chapter One

Ashford
Talbot residence

L OUISA TALBOT SHUT her eyes as she drew in the aroma of warm, honeyed milk. She could never get used to country hours. She had trouble sleeping so early. She had trouble sleeping, period. A warm glass of sweet milk usually helped. As did lavender-scented pillows, but she'd forgotten her favorite pillows in London and the ones the servants had prepared here lacked the same soothing potency. It was either mulled wine or milk tonight.

"It's good that I learned to heat my own milk," she mused. She'd done so almost as soon as she was tall enough to reach for a pot that hung on the wall. Not that she was allowed to back then, but she still loved to sneak into the kitchen to watch their cook prepare their meals. She'd even learned to bake bread at one time.

And she could fry an egg to perfection.

There was something magical about the kitchen at night, when not a soul roamed about, and candlelight cast flickering shadows over the well-worn surfaces. But more than meals, this was where all the gossip took root. Louisa herself had oftentimes stoked the flames of these little sessions. Until her stepmother had caught her and scolded the servants. After that, she'd abandoned their daytime teas.

Alas, she missed those times.

She held the cup with both hands, allowing it to warm her palms and she shifted more comfortably in her seat at the rough wooden table. The entire space smelled of spice, bread, and the last remnants of the evening's dinner.

Comforting.

Perhaps this was why she was drawn here. Of all the rooms in the house, no matter the estate, the kitchen held the most pleasant memories.

A kitchen *felt* like home.

And she could use a bit of homely comfort as her mind drifted back over her recent conversation with her friend, Theodosia King, who had visited to drop the stolen betting book of White's onto her lap. What on earth was she supposed to do with the thing?

Keep it hidden, yes.

But the Duke of Mortimer could come calling and request the book at any moment.

The. Duke. Of. Mortimer.

He was another matter entirely.

Louisa almost laughed.

A Cavanagh set foot in a Talbot residence? How spectacularly ridiculous. Their families were sworn enemies and had been for decades. Years and years of bad blood had spilled between them until it flowed like an unnavigable river dividing them into two territories. And to try to cross this river would mean being drenched in blood. Not that she kept up with all the accounts of wrongdoing and offense, but she'd heard her father bluster over that family's existence since she could remember, warning her to stay away from anyone bearing that cursed surname.

Plus, she'd simply rather not rub shoulders with a man such as him.

There were three sorts of men she avoided at all costs: fortune hunters, criminals, and men with great power—them most of all. Certainly the powerful included kings, princes, and dukes, but it wasn't limited to them. Thankfully, one could spot a powerful man yards away, which of course, suited Louisa since it made them easier to avoid.

Memories of a dark, enclosed space flashed across her mind before Louisa forcibly pushed them back down. She took two swallows of milk, willing her racing heart to slow.

"Botheration," she muttered. "Why did that memory have to resurface right now?"

Almost ten years had passed since her kidnapping on her tenth birthday. She could remember very little about that episode except the darkness—she recalled an abundance of that. And the memory brought along with it a rather harrowing feeling. It was also after that her struggle with sleep had started.

As the years crept by, she had glimpsed more of the world— her father's world—and the truth began to take shape, cold and inescapable. That night had never been about her. She had simply been a pawn. A means to an end. A hostage to their ruthless ambitions.

Such was the dark world of powerful men at times.

Men such as Mortimer.

Fortunately, their families were mortal enemies the likes of Shakespeare's Montagues and Capulets, though with only proverbial bloodshed. However, Louisa was no Juliet, and she doubted the duke could be mistaken for Romeo.

In all likelihood, His Grace would call on another heiress to collect the book from her in his stead. She needn't worry that he would cause havoc in her family by calling on her. Did she?

Urgh.

She already had more than enough drama with her step-mother's theatrics. Lawks, that woman should have become an actress. God only knew how Lady Camilla had beguiled her father, but Louisa could see straight past that woman's false smiles.

She took another sip of milk.

It wasn't that Louisa *hated* her stepmother. Though she

couldn't claim she loved her all that much either. The woman was . . .

Scheming.

Greedy.

Controlling.

Nothing could be done without her approval. The duchess even dictated Louisa's fashion. This was why when she, Lady Ophelia, and the heiresses rebelled and distributed copies of the pages of the betting book in a most public fashion earlier in the season, her stepmother's fury had nearly set their household ablaze.

If her father, the duke, had not been present . . .

Louisa shuddered.

Camilla always wore the look of a sweet, doting wife whenever her father entered the room. When they were not in the same room, her entire demeanor turned rigid and disdainful.

Hah! If it hadn't been for Papa, that woman would have married her off years ago. But Louisa refused to marry. Not while her brother Leo was still so young and easily influenced. Louisa couldn't say exactly what it was, but the way the duchess stared at her stepson . . . it set off a clamor of concern in her heart.

So, Louisa had taken it upon herself to make sure that her brother did not fall under the influence of their stepmother. Whatever her intentions—and she could sense intentions—she would keep an eye on the duchess. Luckily, Papa and that woman were attending several house parties for the next fortnight and she and Leo were here on their own.

Exhaustion tugged at her eyelids.

Lousia swallowed the last of the milk and placed her cup on the table. That should do the trick, shouldn't it? She reached for the candle and slowly made her way back to her room. Tomorrow, she had to decide whether she would keep that blasted betting book or send it to one of the other heiresses for safekeeping.

A sudden chill swept down her neck as she neared her chamber, sending the hairs at her nape to stand at attention. Then—a creak. A thud. A muffled oath.

She froze.

What on earth? Was someone in the house?

A servant?

No, the servants should be in their quarters.

Her fingers moved faster than thought, snuffing out the candle's flame. The dark unsettled her, but she refused to let it rule her. She rubbed her singed fingers together, her grip on the candelabra tightening.

Someone was in her bedchamber.

Should she scream?

No.

That might rouse her little brother, and who could guess what he would do if he were startled awake and frightened. He was only ten years old—she needed to protect him. So instead of retreating, she inched forward, heart pounding, lifting the candelabra, ready to swing. Hardly an ideal weapon, but it would do in a pinch.

She couldn't just leave. At the very least, she had to catch a glimpse of this intruder, even if just a fleeting one. Otherwise, she would never sleep again!

This is reckless, Louisa.

So be it. It wouldn't be the first reckless thing she'd ever done. She peered through the crack of the door, and her breath caught. A large, dark, male figure loomed over her writing desk, rummaging through the drawer. The very air stilled, her hands trembling slightly. The smart choice would be to retreat and hide with her brother, but her feet refused to move. They were rooted to the carpet as if some unseen force kept them there.

The dark figure suddenly straightened to his full height, pushing the drawer shut.

Tall.

So tall.

He tapped a gloved finger against his chin. Louisa couldn't

make out his features with only the moon giving her any light, and the cap pulled low over his face offered no help. Nothing about his attire gave his identity away either. From the little she could see, it seemed like plain, country wear. But from the shape of the man . . . it was plain that she wouldn't be able to protect anyone with this feeble candelabra!

Time to retreat, Louisa!

His head snapped her way.

Louisa started, and the candelabra slipped from her fingers. Time stretched impossibly thing as they stared at each other. The sharp thud of the candelabra hitting the ground jolted her from the spell and straight into action.

She turned on her heel and ran.

Away from the west wing. Away from her brother's chamber. And hopefully, away from *him*.

OLIVER CAVANAGH, THE seventh Duke of Mortimer, cursed.

Cursed his luck.

Cursed his choices.

And, at that very second, he cursed the table that struck his hip as he launched after Lady Louisa Talbot. A grunt of pain sprang from his lips as he dashed after her. It was bad enough that he'd broken into a Talbot residence, but being caught by Lady Louisa Talbot, in her bedchamber no less, was the most damnable thing.

He couldn't explain his actions. Well, he could, but he would sound stark raving mad since there were so many other ways he could have gone about retrieving the betting book from White's.

So many other choices.

None of which mattered at the moment because he hadn't made them. He hadn't even considered them.

And confound it!

She was whip fast.

He rushed down the hall, damning each thud of his boot on the rug. He descended the stairwell three steps at a time and still, it wasn't enough to catch up to her.

He pushed harder.

He didn't worry about being caught by the duke or the duchess. They weren't in residence. But Lady Louisa? She was a different matter entirely. He couldn't predict what she might do, and what he loathed most of all were things he couldn't predict. Variables with a question mark behind them. Always in reach, yet maddeningly out of grasp.

Her white nightdress flitted as she flew down the hall, slipping like a wisp of mist through a door he was certain led to the kitchen. Oliver clenched his jaw and tore after her. He could not let her slip through his fingers—if he did, an all-out war might erupt between the families.

More importantly, he couldn't afford for word of this to reach the woman he suspected to be the head of the secret women's organization—the duchess herself. Nor could he chance losing the strongest proof of their crimes—the coded secrets hidden within the wagers of the betting book. That single, complicated truth had kept the hair on his neck raised since the moment he entered this house.

Hostile domain.

Doubly so.

He chased her down another flight of stairs and burst into the kitchen after her, grunting when he knocked into something hard. Again. Faint silver rays filtered through the small kitchen window, offering the slightest guidance as she stumbled forward. Instinct, born of years facing danger, compelled him to draw to an abrupt halt, his hands shooting up in surrender, hoping she could tell he meant no harm. And he was right to do so, as the shadow of a sharp knife sliced his way.

"You have nothing to fear from me," he said, keeping his tone deliberate and unhurried. "You are in no danger from me," he repeated, deliberately lowering his voice more. "I give you my word."

"Your word means nothing to me, sir."

"Of course, you have no reason to trust me, but I promise, I'm not here to hurt you."

"Forgive me if I find that hard to believe after you've chased me through my home."

The lack of light offered him only the barest of impression of her—pale skin, wary eyes, perhaps a bit of a furrow between her brows. But he didn't need to see her clearly to sense the tension in her stance. Slowly, he lifted a hand to his cap. She still hadn't recognized him, but instinct told him the only way for him to gain any ounce of her trust was to reveal himself. "I'm going to remove this."

She didn't move an inch as he removed his cap, but the moment he did, she squinted at him, then her brow smoothed into astonishment. "You're the duke. The Duke of Mortimer."

He inclined his head. "I am."

Her mouth opened. Shut. Opened again. "Lawks! What are you doing breaking into our house?"

"The book."

"You mean the betting book? *This* is how you retrieve it?"

A flush of heat crept up his ears at the implied accusation of foolishness. "Can we light a candle? Then we can talk."

She flicked the knife toward the table beside him. "Light one yourself."

Oliver didn't argue. His gaze shifted to the tinderbox next to a candle and quickly lit a flame. More light was better than less. His gaze found hers once again as a soft orange glow spilled across the kitchen, just enough for him to catch the nuances of her expression. He also caught the cutting, dagger-sharp look she directed at him now.

"So," she snapped, "your candle is lit. Speak."

"I'll speak," Oliver said in a low voice, trying supremely hard not to react to the vision challenging him in nothing but her nightgown. "I know you've had a fright, but I need you to remain composed, Lady Louisa."

Her eyes narrowed, and she slashed the knife back and forth. She resembled a heavenly creature sent from another realm of existence, radiating righteous glory with curves that made all the other angels weep. "You are telling me to remain composed in a moment like this? And how am I not composed enough for you?"

Oliver tensed at her tone, his gut clenching in warning, as it did in all dangerous predicaments. "It is the only way to have a calm conversation."

"A calm conversation? For that, you would have had to start by knocking on the door for entrance, Your Grace."

"You are right. I made a mistake." A grave one.

Her eyes took on a goddess-like fire. "I don't know if you have learned this in all your years of life, but I shall warn you now, for the sake of your happy future, do not tell a woman waving a knife at you to remain composed in order to have a calm conversation. It may have the opposite effect."

"Rest assured, my lady, I don't plan on a repeat of this mistake." Never again.

The knife didn't lower in the slightest. "That's good to hear."

"That being said, are we still able to converse in a calm manner even though I did not knock on your door?"

Her look turned flat. "Well, seeing as you are already here, of course. However, it must be said that no matter our family differences, this is a bit extreme, is it not?"

"Those family differences aren't small," Oliver pointed out, his focus unwavering. "So please understand why I took such measures."

"A simple note would have sufficed." She lowered the knife, though her grip remained tight on the hilt. "After all, Theodosia informed me you might come to collect the book, though honestly, I did not expect you to. I also didn't expect *this*."

Oliver wanted to rake a hand through his hair but resisted, unwilling to make unnecessary movements while she still clutched the knife. The feud between the families wasn't widely known. At least, any rumors that might have existed when his father was still alive had already died down, though he knew the Duke of Talbot still bore him and all his family a great deal of ill will.

However, he *had* acted rashly. Almost *too* recklessly.

However, he hadn't anticipated Lady Theodosia handing the book over to Lady Louisa, or he would have intervened sooner. Lady Louisa had already taken to Ashford before Lady Theodosia left London for Brighton, book in hand. He hadn't thought it a problem—until he learned that she had detoured to leave the book with Lady Louisa, which had prompted his immediate rush.

He considered the angel before him. Her golden hair tumbled down to her waist in soft waves, a few tendrils falling over her shoulder. Full, rosy lips and a gently rounded jawline, framed by cheekbones that lent a hint of definition to her otherwise soft, youthful face. Bright blue eyes fixed on him with heaps of suspicion.

A beautiful tempest.

If her loyalty lay with her friends, he didn't doubt she would give the book to him. However, recent evidence pointed to the Duchess of Talbot, her stepmother, being the head of the secret women's club rife with illegal activities ranging from forgery of documents to the smuggling of various forms of antiques and substances. And as such, he couldn't completely rule out the possibility that Lady Louisa wasn't involved. Yet instinct rebuffed the notion each time it entered his mind. Even so, he couldn't discount the fact that the duchess might use or convert this angel in the future. It was a supremely precarious situation followed by an ever more perilous question: In the house of his enemy, could she be his ally?

"It's true that I acted rashly," Oliver admitted.

A brow rose. "Is that an apology?"

His gaze held hers. "Yes."

"Very well, since men find it hopelessly impossible to apologize properly and never actually say the words, I shall accept your assurance that this was an apology and let your *rashness* go. And do not worry, our family differences aside, I have no plan to keep the book from you." She finally set the knife down and picked up the candle. "Shall I go and retrieve it now?"

Oliver's lips inched upward ever so slightly. "I shall be forever grateful."

This was easier than expected.

Chapter Two

*T*HIS SCENT. THE soft richness of tobacco followed her as she slowly made her way up the stairs, taunting, teasing, and wholly unnerving her. *He* unnerved her. In what world was Louisa leading the Duke of Mortimer, of all men, *back* to her bedchamber?

Her family's nemesis.

Her nemesis?

She snuck a peek over her shoulder. He didn't walk beside her but rather kept pace behind her right shoulder, allowing her to take charge even though he knew very well the way back. She supposed she ought to be grateful for the courtesy, however misleading it may be. But this false sense of security from him bothered her less than his overpowering presence utterly engulfing her.

No part of her was *not* aware of his exact position, his exact movement, and even though his legs were so much longer than hers, he kept the perfect pace to keep the most exact distance between them.

Her nemesis?

Yes, and yet he impossibly also felt like a savior. And not least because he did look remarkably like a man who'd stepped out of a thrilling Greek mythology tale. Handsome to the point of sin.

She entered her chamber and didn't hesitate to stride over to the bed. She placed the kitchen candle on her small bedside table and lowered onto her knees to reach beneath the bed. She glanced at the duke—far too close—who took a spot right next to the source of light. She couldn't believe the man was in her bedchamber, looming over her with his towering height.

Very well, he wasn't *looming*. But he did take up space.

A lot of space.

The cap was back on his head, hiding his soft mop of russet hair. Her eye caught on the one freckle beneath his left eye, and she quickly glanced away. She also did *not* find that freckle rather adorable.

Focus, Louisa.

She pulled the case from under the bed and opened it, rummaging through the tons of bonnets and ribbons stored there.

Her brows furrowed.

Where was the blasting thing?

She rifled deeper.

And dug and dug until all the bonnets scattered around the case and only an empty space filled the thing.

This . . . was rather impossible, wasn't it? She motioned with her hand without looking at him. "Bring the candle over." Light bloomed over her mess as the candle was lifted over her shoulder. Had exhaustion claimed her sight? "What do you see, Your Grace?"

A moment of silence. "Nothing."

"So, I'm not imagining things." That was something, at least.

"The book is not where you placed it?"

Her gaze lifted to his face. "No." She could have sworn she'd hidden it here, hadn't she? No, she *did* hide it here. There could be no mistake. And yet . . .

"Is there another case?" he enquired.

"No." Her eyes drifted back to the case as she inspected every inch. "This is the only one." And no one else knew about the book.

"Are you certain you are not confusing this spot for another?"

She turned a glare his way. "I am not senile." But could she really have been mistaken? It wouldn't be the first time she misplaced something or thought she'd put an item in one place but found it in another. She would never admit that, of course. The man already sounded so annoyingly male with his light condescension.

She glanced around the room, her gaze falling on her writing desk. She rose and quickly padded over, motioning for him to follow with the light, hoping to find that perhaps she had put it there.

She hadn't.

Neither had she hidden it in her chest of drawers, armoire, beneath the mattress of her bed, or even the pillows. She inspected every corner of her chamber and came up with a rather puzzling loss.

Surely . . . this couldn't be?

"I suspect we have a problem," the duke remarked flatly.

Lawks! "Weren't you rummaging through my belongings moments ago? Why are you standing there as still as a tree now?"

"I searched in most of the places you did, my lady, and it wouldn't be proper of me to rifle through your belongings with you in plain sight."

"*That's* where you draw the line?"

"Most would commend me for having a line."

Louisa gave a derisive laugh. "What an arrogant thing to say for a thief who got caught."

He didn't respond to that. Instead, he said. "Is it possible that someone might have found the book and moved it? Like a servant?"

Louisa thought about it. Other than misplacing items, in the past she'd also dreamed or imagined she'd done something when in reality she hadn't, but then she believed she had. A rather strange occurrence, to be sure, though thankfully it didn't happen often.

However, could this be the case with the book?

If so, then had she simply left that cursed thing in the drawing room somewhere?

Ah, Theodosia! Why bring this curse to me?

She had never wanted to touch the thing. But the blasted book had been stolen from White's because, along with seven other heiresses, their best attributes and worst attributes were being tallied and their eventual marriages wagered over upon in its pages. Ghastly business. And she wanted only to put it and the comment it contained about her childbearing hips aside!

She scoffed inside.

Perhaps she could not remember where she placed it because her mind wished to erase the entire ordeal from its space. She wouldn't mind. Even so, the entry itself didn't bother her as much as the men who had written it. Honestly, was that the best they could do? Still, what had started only as the source of London's recent social chaos had now become evidence to bring down a criminal organization.

Urg.

I hate that damn book.

Had she carried it to her chamber and tossed it carelessly about out in the open? But then what had happened to it? No servant would take anything from her chamber. Had she truly left it in the drawing room, then? Wait . . . hadn't she browsed through the book the previous night by the light of a candle in the kitchen?

Louisa sighed.

Truthfully, at times, she found herself so exhausted from lack of sleep that she couldn't tell left from right. Those tired days went by at the pace of a snail, and a daze would settle over her for most of the mornings.

"I'm not sure," Louisa said after a moment. "I might have misplaced it more thoroughly than I thought." She didn't have to glance at him to determine what sort of look he made. "Yes, yes, I thought I hid it in the case, but I might have been a touch confused."

"I didn't say a word."

"No, but even the air surrounding you practically cried out in accusation."

"I'll admit, I am curious how a person could misplace such a book to such a degree."

"Rather easily," Louisa muttered. "If you must know, I have trouble sleeping, which at times, causes me to be a bit muddle-headed."

"Ah."

She sent him a dirty look, marveling at how much unspoken reproval could be infused in such a simple sound.

Only a duke . . .

She snuck a glance at him again. The Duke of Mortimer was more than a handsome man—he was a sculpture of perfection. On the outside. Chiseled jawline. Amber eyes that saw straight through a person's soul. Brown hair with a reddish tint that feathered his cheeks almost mischievously, even though she couldn't say one tendril of hair was out of place.

But now was not the time to observe a man's beauty!

A pinch of guilt made its way to her breast as she recalled the reason he was searching for the book. She shouldn't have been so careless with it, especially since its pages contained the evidence he needed to put away criminals.

"It's late," she said. "You should head back to your lodgings. I shall continue the search in the morning. I'm certain I shall find it when I'm more refreshed."

"You are absolutely sure someone has not taken it?"

"Who would do such a thing?" No one except Theodosia, that madman Saville, and the duke knew she even had the book in her possession. "I'll search all the places I might have taken the book. If one of the servants did decide to put it away, they might have taken it in my father's study or the library."

She could tell he didn't like that answer. Not that any of his facial muscles *moved* when he received the news—anything but *that*—but the tension in the room stirred, faint yet impossible to miss. A whisper of danger. It was a feeling she got rather than anything she could see.

"Do not worry," she tried to reassure him. "Our families might not get along, but I give you my word that I shall search for the book in the morning and send word to you when I find it."

Those hot eyes never left hers as he continued to observe her. "Very well," he said slowly. "I shall look forward to receiving your good news."

Louisa nodded. "By the by, where are you staying? If I am to send news, I should know."

"I am staying at the Bullheaded Inn."

The . . .? A bubble of laughter escaped through her mouth. If that wasn't an apt name for the man to call a temporary home, Louisa didn't know what would be! "An interesting choice."

"Will your parents be returning anytime soon?" he asked, ignoring that last.

"Do not fret; they are traveling about for a fortnight or so. They certainly shan't return on the morrow."

He gave a curt nod. "Then I shall be on my way."

Louisa watched him slip from the room with her brows deepening. If the light yet prominent scent of sandalwood hadn't remained, she might have thought this whole affair a dream. At least for this moment, she couldn't claim it was any form of her imagination. Would she still be able to claim such a thing in the morning?

She inhaled deeply.

Normally, she didn't care for this scent. But on the duke . . . he smelled rather wonderful.

It's best if you stop liking it altogether, Louisa.

The man was no friend to her family. Granted, she herself paid no mind to whatever grievances her father and whoever else had with the duke's family. However, that did not mean it would be the same for him.

She certainly couldn't tell what he might be thinking. He might truly detest her presence. She'd grown up with tales of the

Mortimer clan and had half expected the man to be cold as frost. Yet, while his countenance might as well have frozen over, heat still pulsed from his body.

She sighed, her gaze falling on the mess beside her bed.

What an impossible situation.

⟫⟪

NERVES HAD NEVER been an issue for Oliver, yet now they consumed him. He'd had the nerve to enter the Talbot residence. The nerve to gather information against one of his peers. And even the nerve to search a lady's bedchamber. But he had never once been nervous. *Those* nerves had always remained in check, carefully bundled and tightly controlled. A skill he had honed from an age he could scarcely recall. A discipline that hadn't been challenged. Until she brushed past him in the kitchen, their hands briefly touching. The smallest of touches, the faintest of scents.

And a bundle of those nerves slipped free.

Oliver chose a chair at the bar and sat down, signaling to the barman. "Tea, please."

The man arched a brow at him. "You are aware that you're in a tavern."

"I am. And I'll have that tea, if you don't mind."

The man shrugged. "Very well, but you'll have to wait a few minutes."

"Not a problem."

The man disappeared through a back door and returned moments later. He glanced over at Oliver curiously. "What ails you? Trouble with a woman, perhaps?"

Not exactly and yet exactly so. He clasped his hands together on the bar, trying to steady the storm brewing inside him. "Is it that obvious?"

"When a man visits a tavern with that look on his face," the man said, wiping the bar top, "it is usually about a woman."

"It's not the sort of trouble you might be thinking about." The sort that might plague a man in love.

Blue eyes flashed in his mind. A blue that could call a man to cross the ocean in search of adventure and more.

Confound it. He should never have told Lady Theodosia to hold onto the book. He should have seized it when he'd had the chance.

But he hadn't.

He'd been indulgent, yes, but he also knew that once word reached the duchess's ears that he was in possession of the book, she would likely retreat. And who could say what tricks she'd play after that. With the book still in play, he had a chance to lure her out into the open.

At least his gut seemed to have been right about Lady Louisa. She couldn't know about her stepmother's dealings, or she wouldn't have helped him search for the book.

Or was it all a ploy to throw him off?

He still could not be entirely sure about her. She was the daughter of his family's number one enemy—or rival, or whatever they were. That was troublesome enough. But at this point, he couldn't decide which was worse, their families' constant opposition, Talbot's petty schemes to block his every move, or the fact that he was relying on Lady Louisa for help that might implicate a member or two of the family that was his enemy.

She might also be supremely good at acting. But only observing her and waiting for time to reveal all her flaws would let him know if that was the case. For now, he could only rely on intuition.

And drink tea.

He nodded his thanks to the older woman who placed a pot before him along with a cup, a spot of milk, and some sugar. She disappeared through the back door again. He placed a coin on the bar top and pushed it to the barman.

"Enjoy your tea." The man swiped the blunt and nodded at

another customer approaching the bar.

Oliver nodded, pouring tea into his cup, forgoing milk and sugar. He took a sip, his eyes closing as the warm brew flowed down his throat.

This he *was* sure about.

Tea.

And also his instinct, which told him he could trust her where the book was concerned. After all, the theft of the betting book was an heiress thing, not a Talbot family thing. If she betrayed him, she would essentially betray the other women, as well. And she wouldn't do that.

But where the devil was the book?

Surely she couldn't be that absentminded to have lost it just like that? Was that even possible? He had never met a person who believed so wholeheartedly that they had placed a thing some-where only to discover that they themselves had been wrong, and that they could indeed not remember what they had done with it!

What horror was that?

His mother's words sprang to mind.

You are too meticulous, Oliver. Loosen up a bit, dear. Life is too short to be rigid. I blame your father for that in you.

He supposed it was true that his character and disposition had been developed over time due to his father's teaching, or lack thereof. Needless to say, his resolve to not repeat the mistakes of the late duke had also sprung forth during this tutelage.

He'd had no choice in his father. But he could choose his own beliefs, his own path.

Oliver swallowed the entire cup and poured himself another. "Let us not dwell on paths at the moment," he muttered to himself.

The barman glanced over, then chuckled. "If you are having problems with your lady just purchase her a gift and apologize. Not flowers—a necklace or a brooch. The opposite sex loves these sorts of trinkets."

"Thank you for the advice." Oliver took a sip while contemplating his beautiful nemesis. "But like I said, it's not that sort of trouble."

You did break into her chamber and rifle through her belongings.

But this regret he had already expressed.

Oliver grimaced when he recalled her remark about apologizing without saying the actual word. Perhaps he should sincerely apologize while saying the word? Perhaps purchasing a trinket or some such would help? No. Lady Louisa struck him as the sort of woman who appreciated sincerity above any form of flattery. Actions, not words.

Just let it go, then.

What else could be done?

Oliver glanced over to the barman. "The Duke and Duchess of Talbot." He waited until the man glanced over before he asked, "What can you tell me about them?"

"Not much." The barman shrugged, grabbing two empty glasses from the counter and placing them aside. "The likes of them will never set foot in this place."

True.

"But I hear whispers," the man said, sidling up to him.

"And what whispers might those be?"

"That the duchess beats her husband."

Oliver scoffed. Preposterous. A man such as Talbot would never take a beating from his wife. Few men would. "Forget I asked."

The man laughed. "I also hear they are traveling the coastal towns at the moment."

Coastal towns? Now that was interesting. A coincidence, perhaps?

Oliver made a mental note to send some of his men to investigate. It could be nothing, but given the secret women's club's proclivities, he had his doubts.

In any event, he still had to retrieve the book. A morning would give Lady Louisa more than enough time to find the book she'd lost. His gaze darted to the clock. An hour past midnight.

He hadn't left the house too long ago. How many more hours until he would receive word? Eight? Ten? Twelve?

Too damn long.

Oliver wanted to retrieve the book and then leave Ashford as soon as possible. He didn't want to wait around. If he got recognized and word got to Talbot that he was lingering in Ashford, there was no telling what the duke or duchess might presume—and, as a consequence, what they might do.

And Talbot would do something.

Like blocking another one of his initiatives in Parliament.

A thorn in his damn side. Prickly, itching, and one he couldn't seem to pluck out. True, he had his own connections to deal with these sorts of situations, but that didn't mean he'd actively go out of his way to aggravate this thorn.

He glanced at the clock again.

Should he just patiently wait for her note?

No.

Normally, Oliver prided himself on his patience. He was very good at waiting—that he could do. What he *couldn't* do was sit idly while he waited. *That* wasn't in his nature. What about Lady Louisa's nature? How would she react if she discovered these dealings of her stepmother's? How far would she go to aid him? A novel thought. An attractive one. She seemed to be the person best situated to help him get to the bottom of such things. She wouldn't be a bad ally to have on his side to search for more evidence.

And she didn't seem to loathe his Cavanagh blood like the rest of the family. But then, she didn't seem to remember who was behind her kidnapping ten years ago.

May she never find out.

Chapter Three

"WHERE IN THE heavens is that blasted book?"

Louisa straightened from where she peered beneath the last couch in the drawing room. Not that she ever believed the book would be under the furniture, but not searching there would have bothered her much more. If she hadn't looked there, she would have then been forced to endlessly wonder whether she *should* have looked if only to prove to herself that the book wasn't there.

No stone left unturned.

Her gaze flicked over every corner of the room with exasperation. One might think she had gone mad. The room was in utter disarray. She had overturned all the pillows of every sofa, opened all the drawers, and removed every book from the small bookstand in the corner. She'd even lifted the top of the pianoforte to peek inside, wondering if it might have somehow found its way there to keep company with the piano strings!

But no.

Nothing.

The betting book was decidedly *not* in the drawing room. Neither was it anywhere to be found in the kitchen, which had been the first place she'd looked, even though she and the duke had been in there mere hours ago and his hawk eyes probably wouldn't have missed it.

Louisa scratched her head.

"I should look in Papa's study next." She supposed if the book had been "put back in its place" by a servant, it ought to be her father's study. If anyone were to open the book to take a peek at its contents, it would be hard not to believe it wasn't a ledger of some sort, with its log of names and amounts. In other words, business. Of sorts. And business belonged in the study. If it wasn't there, then her only other place to search would be the library.

She glanced at the clock.

Drat.

The clock had already struck three in the afternoon.

A pair of hot, amber eyes set in a cold face filled her mind.

Undeniably attractive.

Stiff as a statue.

Papa would explode if he learned the Duke of Mortimer had been in his daughter's bedchamber in the dead of night. And even though her father would not direct his rage at her, it would give her stepmother the opportunity she'd wanted since Louisa debuted—to marry her off. It was fortunate, then, that no one would ever find out.

I should be more careful.

No one must discover the duke's presence anywhere near Ashford, either, which meant she must find the book before he made another nighttime visit. It would set any and all Talbots on alert, which was the last thing anyone needed at present.

Speaking of the man, he must be writhing on pins and needles waiting for her note. But Louisa hadn't risen until past noon, anchored to a deep sleep. For whatever reason, quite remarkably, she'd fallen into a slumber the moment her head had landed on the pillow. That hadn't happened in such a long time. Really, she shouldn't have gotten a wink of rest after finding a man—the duke of all people, and a mortal family enemy of her family— snooping in her chamber. Yet, she had slept as though she had years to make up for. And she probably had.

Might it be because of the warm honeyed milk? The lingering

scent of the duke? Or had the stimulation of last night exhausted her to the point where her brain had shut down?

She couldn't say.

All of them could have played a role. But was it too much to hope that sleep would come easy again tonight? If it did manage to happen, then she could rule out the duke as a contributing factor. But if not, could she ask him to sneak into her chamber again?

What are you even thinking, Louisa?

She shook her head at her musings and strode to her father's study. She'd best locate the book first. Not only for the duke, but for herself and the other heiresses. Theodosia had entrusted her with the safekeeping of the thing, so misplacing it was out of the question.

She stopped in the middle of her father's sacred space, her shoulders slumping when her gaze landed on his messy desk and all the cabinets filled with ledgers atop ledgers. What's more, several piles of books were stacked on the floor beside the desk.

This is going to take a while.

Another small tendril of guilt curled in her belly. How could she have misplaced the *betting* book of all books? She must have been in a fit of complete senselessness!

Lawks. "Might as well start at the desk and then work my way outward." She harbored no doubt that if she didn't find that book today, there would be a man in her chamber tonight. And while she might indulge in ridiculous thoughts about the situation, she still couldn't have a repetition of last night.

"Well! Let's get to it, then." She sprang to work, lifting each book on her father's desk, not happy until she had touched every single one to confirm that it wasn't the betting book. She didn't want to miss it because she hadn't been thorough or paid enough attention. Again.

Finally she cast the desk one last dirty look and plopped onto the chair to survey the room at large. Servants wouldn't haphazardly clean the study or disrupt the flow of her father's mess. If they hadn't placed the book on the desk, she didn't think they'd place it anywhere else.

However, she couldn't *not* search every inch of this room. It would drive her to Bedlam. It would also be yet another reason to lay awake at night.

Louisa let out a begrudging sigh, her gaze drifting to the tall windows overlooking the sweeping gardens. Her brows furrowed as she caught sight of a man standing amidst the lush greenery of blooming roses and neatly trimmed box hedges, observing his surroundings.

Louisa blinked at the sight.

Why did that rigid posture look so familiar? She squinted, her eyes raking over every inch of the man. Broad shoulders. Long legs. Hah! That was because he *was* familiar!

Mortimer!

Lawks. There was no mistaking his build.

She leaped to her feet and strode over to the window, peering hard through the glass. Was he . . . dressed as a gardener? He might be wearing the clothes of one, and they might be well-worn and dulled by sun and soil, and they might even have belonged to a gardener, but they did not belong to *him*.

Louisa suddenly laughed.

So much for waiting patiently until she sent word to him. She should have known! That man wasn't capable of standing aside without lifting a finger. Given the lengths he had gone to sneaking into her house, *this* could be considered almost nothing.

But it wasn't good either. What if someone recognized him and told her father?

No, no, no. This wouldn't do!

How can the man be so blasted confident? He didn't look anything like a gardener. No amount of humble clothing could hide the fact that he was a man born of station. A high station. He stood too straight, too assured, more like a man accustomed to giving orders than one who spent his days bent over flowerbeds.

Authority bled from every one of his pores.

If he wanted to look the part, he should at the very least try to act the part.

Dig up a plant, Duke!

Her stepmother ran the household with an iron fist. She received reports from her servants about all the other servants. This gardener would be reported, Louisa was sure.

She strode to the door, intent on sending a duke home. She would toss him bodily off her property if she had to. In fact, the picture that formed in her mind held a wealth of appeal. But as her fingers curled around the doorknob, a question stirred in her mind, unbidden. One Theodosia had asked her recently.

When would you not *marry a man?*

Louisa pulled a face. Right. She wouldn't marry a fortune hunter, a criminal, or a man with too much power. She needed to stay strong.

She yanked the door open.

Now was certainly not the time to be thinking about men— least of all a duke. Especially one who still oozed power, despite dressing in unattractive, outdoor clothing.

⇻⟫⟪⇺

OLIVER'S GAZE TRACKED over the garden, the house, and the little boy who exited the side doors of one of the drawing rooms. This must be the Talbot heir, Lady Louisa's brother, the future duke.

Ah, to be young and still at such an age. Oliver could scarcely recall such a time of his own life. Of course, his father hadn't allowed him much of a childhood. He certainly didn't recall himself ever possessing such innocent, rosy cheeks when he was young. This must be because of *her* presence.

His gaze returned to the house.

The young lord would probably not give him a second look, so he needn't worry. He had a man at the front of the house as well, so he would know if any servants or Lady Louisa left the house. There had been no movement so far.

He wished he could have disguised himself as a footman and been *inside* the residence. But servants were quite quick-witted amongst themselves. He'd have been caught in no time. A gardener, on the other hand, was a bit easier to overlook. In fact, the moment Oliver had learned of the duchess's possible involvement in the organization he was hunting, he'd placed one of his men here in the household as a groundskeeper. Today, he'd simply taken his place.

He hadn't actually been able to get any of his men inside the house—a pity. The duchess was meticulous when it came to hiring new servants for their residence. It almost made him surprised that she'd been so lax with the gardens. No one had questioned his presence yet.

The boy's eyes landed on him, narrowed, before he strode straight over to him. Oliver didn't so much as twitch.

Interesting.

The boy stopped before him, craning his neck to meet his gaze. "Who are you and what are you doing here, sir?"

"What do you mean, young master?" Oliver inched the corner of his mouth upward. The boy was sharp. "I'm the gardener."

"You don't look like a gardener."

"Oh?" Oliver said, half amused. "And what does the young master think I look like?"

The boy raked him up and down with a thoughtful look. "An imposter."

Perceptive and blunt. "If I were to be that, should you be talking to me, an imposter? Would that not be dangerous?"

"A respectable point." The boy pursed his lips. "But it's too late now, is it not?" His eyes narrowed more. "You still cannot be a servant. I don't recognize you."

"Would you recognize me?" Oliver questioned the lad curiously. Most boys of his age and station wouldn't give much thought to a servant. "I am but a humble gardener."

Suspicion filled the youth's eyes. "That can't be. I know all the servants, including the gardeners." His chin lifted a bit. "Their names *and* designations."

Amusement filled Oliver. Quite commendable for a child his age—and certainly something he should be proud of. "What a smart young master you are."

"Are you mocking me, sir?"

"Of course not," Oliver said with a hint of a smile infused in those three words. Not many tricks would work on this child, but he thought he knew one that might. "Your sister hired me."

Suspicion turned to outright skepticism. "Louisa hired a gardener?"

"The young master makes it sound as if she would never do such a thing," Oliver remarked. The excuse would have to do.

The boy lifted his hand to his chin in a thoughtful manner, a gesture clearly borrowed from some adult he knew. He probably considered himself an adult as well. "It's not that she wouldn't, but it's also not something she would. She certainly wouldn't hire a gardener who just stares at the garden."

"I was merely contemplating what to plant in that corner over yonder." Oliver nodded to a patch that had no plant or flower. "Something that would resemble the lady herself since she has given me this opportunity."

"My sister doesn't like flowers."

Ah. So that was why the young heir thought Lady Louisa would never hire a gardener. "Is that so? I didn't realize."

The boy nodded proudly. "I know her best."

"I thought all women loved flowers."

The boy instantly shook his head furiously. "Not all women are my sister. She sneezes at the mere sight."

"I see." Oliver swept his gaze over the garden, the roses blooming all around. He bit back a smile. So, the lady didn't like flowers . . . "Well, young master, I am thankful for your insight."

"Didn't she tell you this when she hired you?" Suspicion crept back into his voice.

Oliver wanted to laugh. If all lawmen could be as skeptical, perceptive, and sharp as this boy, England's criminals would be in sorry shape. "She must have told me, but I was so captivated by her beauty, I must have forgotten."

A moment of silence before the boy slowly nodded. "That does make sense. Men usually act all strange when they first meet her."

Did she point knives at those men as well?

"All her suitors have brought her flowers," the boy went on. "She tossed them all away."

Poor flowers. "Does she have many suitors?" Oliver asked in the spirit of inquiry. He imagined she had, and yet she had forsaken the activity of the London season to retire to Ashford. Far be it from him to understand the workings of the female mind.

"Of course. She is an heiress, after all."

Oliver nodded, all too aware of that fact. "Then perhaps you can help me once more and point me in the direction of what she might enjoy?"

"Why would I tell you such a thing?"

Fair question. "I wish to show her my gratitude for . . . hiring me."

"Oh." The boy rocked on his heels. "In that case, do a good job and do everything she wants you to do. That will make Louisa very happy. She loves bossing people around."

Of course she did. He was off to a bit of a splendid start, then. His very presence here went against everything she wanted. "What else does your sister like?"

"Scolding me."

That brought a smile to Oliver's face. He almost laughed outright. He could easily imagine Lady Louisa scolding her brother for some mischievous act. They even bore a striking resemblance. The boy had the same blue eyes, the same pale skin, and the same sandy hair. They could have been twins, were they born in the same year.

"I believe that is a sister's job—scolding you." Oliver caught movement in the corner of his eye. "You shouldn't be speaking to me right now, should you?"

The boy's brows knit in confusion "Why not?"

"This is just a guess, but I suspect your sister might scold you."

The boy's lips parted to retort but was interrupted by Lady Louisa's, "You are right about that!" She strode over to them, her brow furrowed deeper than a scholar puzzling over ancient Greek scrolls. "What are you doing, Leo? Are you distracting the servants from their work again?"

The boy puffed up at the reprimanding questions. "Your gardener was just standing about like a garden sculpture."

"So? Does that mean you must accompany him in doing so?"

The boy scowled. "How come you hired him, then, if this is all he'll do? Don't you hate the outdoors?"

"When have I ever disliked the outdoors? I enjoy the outdoors very much!"

"Liar," the boy muttered, his chin not dropping an inch.

Oliver bit back a smile.

"Who is the liar here?" Lady Louisa demanded, hands on her hips. "Didn't you tell your governess you were going to read in the library? What are you doing outside fraternizing with the servants, heh?"

"I did read. Now I'm taking a break."

"Seems to me you are just making excuses." She pointed to the house. "Go find Mrs. Shire and report your reading."

The boy pulled a face—almost like a small pout—but obeyed, casting Oliver a brief glance before striding back to the house at a leisurely pace, head high, arms clasped behind his back.

"Bright boy. Promising future."

Her sharp gaze cut through him, eyes hot—no, blazing—with annoyance. "What, pray, are you doing here?"

Oliver arched a brow. "Keeping an eye on my interests."

Her breath hitched, nostrils flaring. "What a provoking thing to say!"

Amusement, and a hint of *temptation*, unfurled in the center of his chest. "Offering my protection, then."

She rolled her eyes. "The only person I seem to need protection from is you."

"Then you shouldn't have hired me as your gardener."

"I didn't hire you as my gardener!" She pressed her fingers to her temples, shooting him another annoyed look before darting a quick glance around. "We can't talk here."

"We can talk while you show me about the garden you so love." As he thought, the boy had been exaggerating about her sneezing at the sight of flowers.

Her chin lifted. "Stow the mockery, it's not appreciated."

He suppressed his chuckle, though the edges of his mouth still twitched. "I take it you haven't found the book."

Her lips pursed, voice turning sour. "I am still searching."

"Did you get some sleep?" His eyes flicked over her face, noting no shadows beneath her eyes.

"Surprisingly, yes."

That was good, then. He knew the suffering that came from lack of sleep. However, a hint of impatience clawed at him. As expected. That hint, however, wouldn't disappear until he had the book in his hands and was no longer standing on Talbot property. Fortunately, Lady Louisa was nothing like the other Talbot family members he had dealt with over the years. Nor was her brother. They were different. A breath of fresh Talbot air. Perhaps, there was hope for the two families.

Then he thought of the Duke of Talbot.

Past sins.

Not a chance. Some resentment ran too deep.

Still, there was something about the day that seemed a bit brighter, in spite of it all. He gave into temptation and stepped closer, his voice soft, "You should smile, or it might look to others that you are scolding me."

Her eyes widened.

So did his smile.

Challenge lit her whole face. "So, what if I am?"

Chapter Four

L OUISA GAVE A fake grin to the fake gardener, which, come to think of it, might look stranger than actually scolding the man! But, Lawks, this duke deserved a good scolding. He didn't say anything. However, that smile—so vexingly *knowing*—remained. It amazed her how a mere stretch of lips could convey so much more than words.

And then there was Leo.

That her brother and the duke were having a conversation hadn't surprised her. Leo loved slipping away from his governess to keep the company of their servants. She had been the same when she was young. She was still the same. She herself enjoyed conversing—gossiping—with the servants. They knew *everything* in and about town.

What worried her was that this was Mortimer.

She didn't believe the duke lacked honor, but she couldn't ignore the fact that the man was still an enemy of their family. Who knew what nonsense he would whisper in her brother's ear, given the chance? If the duke had designs of his own beyond the book, she and her brother could become pawns in a dangerous game. She wanted to avoid that at all costs. It wasn't just this man's presence she feared, it was the influence he could have if he lingered too long. The havoc he could wreak.

Had she let a wolf into the den by playing along with him and not clubbing him over the head with a candelabra or stabbing him with a knife?

Please, Louisa. You would never stab a man.

Well, she did possess a vivid imagination.

She dispensed with the fake smile and sent the man A Look instead.

Where on earth is that deuced book?

All her worries would be solved if she could just find the book.

"Your brows are furrowing," he murmured. "This might be stating the obvious, but I gather you are not pleased by my approach."

"I applauded your observation." She opened her arms in a display of confusion. "From a thief to a gardener? You are a man of many talents."

"I am."

She scoffed at that simple admission. "I should have known you wouldn't be able to wait leisurely for my missive. Is it because I am a woman or a Talbot?"

"On the contrary, I am simply not a man of leisurely pastimes."

Louisa didn't care to dwell on what sort of pastimes he might prefer. And heavens, this close, why did the man still look so maddingly handsome dressed in such drab clothing? Where had he even gotten such clothes?

Not the point, Louisa!

"Do you take all your disguises so seriously?" she muttered.

"Of course. Would you not?"

That innocent tone with an *innocent* question truly riled her! Louisa used the most sarcastic tone she could muster. "Is that really the point here?"

"If not, what is?" Another "innocent" question.

"It is that you are here at all! Right now! Dressed as a gardener!"

"Are you certain? Is it not that you lost the book?"

Louisa inhaled a deep breath. Very well. She had stepped straight into that jab.

"Lady Louisa," the duke began, but paused, having the good sense to look a bit—a tiny smidgeon—sheepish. But that look only lasted for one brief second before it vanished beneath a cold shield of indifference. Was this a mask he wore? He wore it well.

But then, did all men not wear one? Women too. Even she lifted a smile for her stepmother while inside her chest her heart scowled. Mortimer should be no different. What did it matter? It had nothing to do with her. *He* had nothing to do with her.

"The book . . .?" he said, bringing her back to the present and leaving the question itself unspoken.

Yes, that blasted book. "*Well*, I was searching my father's study when I caught sight of you through the window."

He gave a nod. "Which distracted you."

"*Which* reminds me, you still haven't told me what you hope to accomplish by acting as a garden statue." Acting all suspicious.

"I am not here to cause trouble, Lady Louisa. I am merely making it easy for you to deliver the book once you find it." Those sharp, amber eyes searched hers. "It's rather a mystery, the book's lack of presence."

You don't have to tell me that, Duke.

He didn't trust her, that much was clear. Still, if he wanted to dress the part so he could stay close, he should also act the part. She jabbed at a nearby shrubbery. "These bushes could use a good pruning."

The duke adjusted the cap on his head and stepped up to the closest, already neatly trimmed shrubbery, catching a small leaf between his fingers. The corner of his lips inched upward. "Pruning, you say? It's true that like many things in life, if not pruned regularly, the most beautiful of shrubs starts to grow waywardly and recklessly. Though perhaps not daily."

She glanced between him and the hardly wayward greenery. "What are you getting at? Is this your way of getting out of gardening duties?"

"Not everything benefits from a quick trim."

Lawks. Also, do not *fight* with dukes, highwaymen, or criminals! "Since you are the gardener, prune it. Some. More. Lady's orders."

"No." Resolute. But why did it seem like his eyes were laughing at her? He picked another leaf. "I respect a craftsman's touch, and also my limitations."

"That remains to be seen. However, did you truly have to go this far? Did you have to come here?"

He didn't hesitate to nod. "Yes."

Very well, fair answer. It was hard to believe a whole criminal enterprise was being run through the wagers in that book—at least some of them. If Theodosia hadn't enlightened her as to its secrets, she would have dismissed it as utter hogwash, but she had been persuaded. And Mortimer had been hunting for the book from the start, which was telling in itself.

Drat, she had misplaced no ordinary ledger.

This mysterious organization wasn't just in need of a pruning, but rather it was a weed that needed to be plucked from the earth altogether. But first things first. "We should show some interest in more of the garden so we don't raise any suspicions." Her stepmother's eyes were everywhere.

"What about that tree? Perhaps we could be discussing it." He pointed to a huge tree whose branches and leaves hung down to the ground.

She smiled. "Ah, yes. This weeping willow is my favorite tree. As a little girl, I would hide from my governess here." In fact . . .

Louisa marched toward the tree, parting the branches with ease as she entered the shelter within. Inside, it felt like a second realm, one separate from the world beyond its shelter. A good spot now for a private conversation.

The duke entered after her, his voice cutting through the rustle of leaves. "You must have hidden a lot."

She turned to him, smiling. "How did you know?"

"A feeling in my gut."

"You are right." Her gaze flicked to the sky of leaves, then back at him. "Even to this day, I still enjoy reading my books in its branches."

He glanced up. "In its branches?"

Louisa stepped up to pat a particularly sturdy branch jutting out from the tree. "It's thick and low enough to enjoy without the fear of falling to one's death."

"Fair."

"It should also provide enough shelter to talk for a moment." She met his gaze. "You must be wondering how I could not yet have found the book."

"I am curious, yes."

Louisa brushed her fingers against her cheek. "I am curious about it, too. I cannot rightly explain it myself." It was driving her rather mad, to be honest. A light breeze parted the curtain of leaves, and her eyes caught on a scene beyond the duke. She gasped and took a few steps forward to get a better view, stopping beside him. "Are they *kissing?*"

He turned to follow her gaze. "Who?"

She pointed between the leaves of the hanging tree, parting them slightly. "There, don't you see them? It's Milly and John! Dear lord, they are kissing in our garden. In broad daylight!"

He ducked his head, tilting it toward hers. His breath brushed her ear, "Ah, indeed. It is rather shocking behavior."

Louisa's whole body went taut. *What's more shocking is your proximity!*

He was *so* close.

She took a quick step to the side. "Must you lean this close?"

A brow arched. "Didn't you want to show me the two servants kissing?"

"That's . . ." She hadn't expected him to look so closely! "Never mind." What was the point of trying to reclaim a respectable distance when nothing about their encounters was respectable?

A short pause before amusement laced a simple question,

"Lady Louisa, are you embarrassed?"

"Are you not?" she retorted, suddenly a bit breathless. "Asking me such a question!"

Their eyes locked, and the devil danced in his. "Why be embarrassed about young lovers embracing?"

"You need an answer for that?" Lawks, why was she so riled by this man? Her heart drummed almost painfully, but she couldn't help herself. "I am an innocent lady!"

"Would innocent ladies proclaim it so ardently?"

Louisa narrowed her gaze to slits. "What are you saying, Duke? Are you saying I'm not innocent?"

"Merely that the term can be debated."

"Well, I have never kissed a man before. That makes me innocent, no?"

A lofty brow lifted. "And yet you know enough about kissing to recognize that it's inappropriate for your servants—and you— to do it so publicly. Some might claim that to be innocence lost."

"So I am not completely innocent because I am aware of what it means to be innocent or not?"

He shrugged. "It's a debate to be debated."

Blast the man. She was outdoors but somehow still needed air. And distance. And possibly a large stick. Hah! She would rather debate with a fence post—it was sure to prove less vexing.

INNOCENCE.

A term that should be as clear in its definition as the cloudless sky, yet much like the sun rising within its domain, there were various degrees to it. It was a term that didn't quite suit Oliver in many ways, and yet he himself could claim innocence in certain areas. Like dealing with crafty females such as Lady Louisa. No, dealing with crafty females was not the same as dealing with Lady Louisa. His mother could be considered crafty. In fact, all the females in his family could be considered so. Lady Louisa was something altogether *more.*

He was out of his depth here.

His gaze dropped to her plump lips and quickly whipped up again. What the devil was that? An "innocent" glance? His mind filled with curses. He blamed the kissing scene he had just witnessed.

The corner of his eye ticked.

He retreated a step, averting his gaze. "Should the leaves be trimmed a bit?" He supposed he ought to snip a few so as not to draw too much suspicion to him. "I don't have a tool with me, though."

A scoff. "Forget my earlier comment. Trimming my weeping willow leaves would be blasphemy. You are not a very good gardener."

Oliver couldn't blame her for wanting the tree to remain untouched. He would also be reluctant to do anything that would ruin the shelter of this magnificent tree, much like the shelter he had found in the ruined cottage on the ducal estate in Kent. He would retreat there as a boy whenever he wanted a moment of quiet, a moment to collect his youthful thoughts. They had this in common.

He looked over to her. "Do not worry; I shall try not to be so obvious in my lack of skill and try to live up to my disguise."

"I think it best if we change your position."

Curiosity filled Oliver. "Change it?"

"Why be a gardener when you can be a footman?"

A footman? She would let him into the house? While this surprised him, the prospect was undeniably intriguing. However, "I don't think that will work."

"Why not?"

"I won't have much freedom as a footman." And he needed freedom. Eventually he would have to slip away with the book while drawing as little suspicion as possible. Servants tended to notice servants, and he would never go unnoticed.

How one woman could be so forgetful, and create a situation

that required his presence in the first place, still baffled him. However, he also knew how exhaustion clouded the mind and slowed the body. She'd said last night she needed to search the study and the library, and she'd already been working at least on the study, apparently. He would allow her more time to complete her search of those two locations. He could pretend to be a gardener for a while longer. If the book wasn't found *there* . . . She would not be able to convince him something else wasn't afoot.

Her brows scrunched in thought. "What about my personal footman and a driver? I shall make it clear to Mr. Hall, the butler, that you only take orders from me."

Her brother's words came back to him. "You truly do like bossing people around, do you not?"

She flashed a grin. "I do."

"Be that as it may, most of the servants likely already saw me in the garden."

She waved a dismissive hand. "Well, *I*, your employer, have decided you are not gardener material. You are much better suited to be my right-hand man of sorts."

"And why would a lady need such a right-hand man of sorts?"

"Good question . . ." She tapped her chin with a finger, a glint sparking in her eyes. "Oh, I know—I have a harasser."

"Are you referring to me?" Oliver said flatly.

"Well, that I cannot say. I only know that someone broke into our home. There are also the wagers." She smiled at him. "I'm afraid I have a shadow pursuer who harbors unknown intentions."

Oliver's jaw ticked. "To be clear, you don't really have a shadow pursuer who harbors unknown intentions, do you?" That would not only be concerning, she would also require actual protection.

"Who is to say I have, who is to say I haven't?"

Crafty female.

"Very well." He didn't waste time considering the complications of his decision, only that he would feel more comfortable searching alongside her. "I shall act as your footman, driver, protector, right-hand man."

"Very good, I shall have some livery procured for you."

There was still one thing . . . "What will your father," and stepmother, "do when he learns of this?"

"I daresay Papa will applaud me for my foresight."

"The foresight of handling matters on your own without informing the head of your family that you are in trouble?"

"How patriarchal of you." Her tone turned sour. "Why are you siding with my father before he's even had the chance to say a word?"

"I'm merely pointing out minor flaws in your plan."

"Well, I can handle my father. Anyway, why should it bother you what he thinks? Aren't you supposed to be mortal enemies?"

"We have our differences." To say the least.

A loud snort of disbelief. "I believe it's more than that."

"What about you, Lady Louisa? Are you my mortal enemy?"

"You have not given me a reason to be, Duke."

He nodded. "That is good to hear."

She stepped up to him, forgetting her earlier outcry against closeness, and said in a low voice, "I find this all rather thrilling if I'm honest."

Oliver's brows furrowed. Were all women so impossible to comprehend? "Do you mean consorting with the enemy?"

She flashed her teeth. "Of course."

He thought so. Nothing about the heiresses this season was *normal*. Oliver thought of his mother. Just last month she had helped a lady escape marriage merely because the chit didn't wish to be leg shackled so soon. Yet at the same time, she scolded him for not yet taking a bride.

How was he to understand this logic? He didn't want to marry so soon either.

Perhaps in another twenty years or so he would revise his thoughts. Presently, the very word "marriage" held nothing but notes of suffocation. Why were mothers so interested in their children's prospects, anyway? Oliver knew his duty, knew what needed to be done. But there was still plenty of time to do it. And if he did, for whatever reason, fail to see his duty of producing an heir through, well, there was always his cousin who could rise to the occasion. Apparently, he was actually quite fond of rising.

Besides, he had a mission at the moment: to put a stop to this secret organization. He also wasn't so arrogant as to believe that cutting off the head of a snake like this was enough to prevent another from appearing. If all went to plan, his goal was to capture the head and shed light on the body, ensuring they could long longer operate in total secrecy.

There would be eyes on them.

Watching, waiting.

Perhaps after this hunt, if a bloody miracle were to change his mind, he would give his mother what she wanted most. A daughter-in-law followed by a grandchild. But such a thing was hardly likely.

His gaze flicked to Lady Louisa.

She reminded him a bit of his mother. Not in a strange way, but she had the same pluck only a few women possessed. Only a scarce few ladies, in his view, were bold and brave enough to stand upon their own views and stick to them. It didn't mean they all rebelled against society exactly. But they knew what they wanted, and they didn't compromise.

He admired that in Lady Louisa.

But the book had become problematic. Since he'd captured Lady Ridgeland, who was still being detained at the moment and out of communication with her associates, he had assumed that because one of the heiresses possessed the book, it would remain safe, for the time being at least. No word should have reached the Duchess of Talbot about the finer points of his actions or his aims. But the moment his role was revealed, the moment his mission came to light, who could say what the secret organization would do to thwart him?

He had to be smarter from here on out.

"Shall we start today then?" Oliver asked Lady Louisa. "The role of footman, driver, protector, and right-hand man."

She nodded. "Follow me." She parted the curtain of leaves and strode across the grounds to the door she had exited from earlier, Oliver following in her wake. The moment he stepped over the threshold, a sense of foreboding skittered down his spine.

A warning.

Of what, Oliver couldn't say.

But he had entered the lion's den with the lion's cub. There were sure to be consequences.

Chapter Five

I N THE SPACE of an hour, they were back in her father's study. Mr. Horace Hall, the butler employed by her stepmother, hadn't been happy to hear that Louisa had hired a new servant who would serve as her footman, driver, and right-hand man. She had, of course, omitted the protector part. That would only come into play if they were caught.

Camilla would undoubtedly learn of this hiring the moment she returned. But hopefully by then, they would have found the book, the Duke of Mortimer would be long gone, and Louisa could explain away her new servant by claiming they had caught a shadowy pursuer and that she was once again safe from harm.

But how could a book simply vanish into thin air?

She rifled through all the books on the desk once more.

"It's not here."

Louisa glanced over at the duke. He was scowling at a pile of books stacked on the windowsill. Even from this angle, where she could only glimpse his side profile, there was no denying the man was handsome. Too handsome.

Especially in livery.

Had a servant ever looked this delightful and dashing?

Stop it, Louisa. You ought not to be admiring his comeliness!

It would be reckless to take note of anything concerning the man. She was aiding him not out of personal interest, but because it was her duty not to hinder his pursuit of criminals—and out of loyalty to Theodosia, who had entrusted her with the book and sworn the duke could be trusted with its secrets.

She tore her gaze away and swept the room, and her brows furrowed at all her father's messiness. "I suppose you are right. If the book had been placed here, it would have been atop the rest, but I had to be certain, else the doubt would have plagued me endlessly."

She stole a glance at him, only to find him staring straight at her, causing her fingers to tingle with an awareness that stole her breath. Goodness! Why did he have to gaze at her as though he could see through to her very soul?

She cleared her throat. "Shall we head to the library?"

He nodded, tapping his finger on one of the books, an accounting ledger of sorts, if she were not mistaken. "It feels rather strange, standing in your father's study like this, in disguise."

Dear Lord. "Please don't use this to act against him."

His brow furrowed slightly. "Why would I make a move against him?"

"Because you are adversaries."

"Just because we are adversaries doesn't mean we have to go out of our way to harm each other, or is that the sort of man you believe me to be?"

No, she didn't. But a simple fact remained. "I do not know enough about you to believe anything, good or bad. Also, I don't have any enemies, so I cannot begin to grasp the inner workings of your mind." Did Camilla count as an enemy? If she did, well, perhaps Louisa might have the faintest inkling, but certainly not on the scale of mortal foe. Not yet.

"I cannot argue against that, Lady Louisa."

Indeed! She could hardly imagine how he and her father could attempt to undermine each other. Such matters were certainly not her forte, and she had no desire to delve into the reasons behind this feud. Leave it to the men.

But she was curious about something else. "How did you

even learn of this club if they are so secret?"

He propped a hip against the windowsill. "A person can learn many things when they observe and listen."

Right. "Like a phantom."

"Exactly like a phantom."

She leaned back against the desk, both hands curling around its edges. "So you heard *something* about *something* and became curious?"

"Became suspicious," he clarified. "Bow Street already had their suspicions about a secret organization and their dealings, but because it involves the gentry, everyone had to tread carefully."

"And you help Bow Street with their cases? You? A duke?"

"A man must have his hobbies."

Of course, but, "It seems like an odd hobby for a duke."

"On the contrary, it's rather stimulating."

"And dangerous," she appraised him from head to foot. "But I suspect you enjoy the thrill of the chase."

"The thrill of the catch," he corrected. "The stimulation of the chase."

How supremely male. "I shall take your word for it. It all sounds rather tiring to me."

He mirrored her personal assessment, dragging his gaze from her head to her heel and back up again. "Then what would you consider a hobby? Reading in trees?"

"Just so." She scrunched her brows. "Also, gossiping with servants, looking after Leo, and trying my hand in the kitchen." Plus, keeping Leo away from the direct influence of Camilla . . . but she couldn't tell the duke *that*.

"Interesting that your brother is your hobby," he answered, then gave a slow nod. "But strangely, it aligns with my perception of you."

"Yes, well," her cheeks heated a bit, "why should he not be?"

"No reason at all. But what happens when he grows up?"

"Not all hobbies last forever." She hadn't thought that far. Didn't want to think that far ahead.

The corner of his lips lifted at this. "You are remarkably insightful. And it seems you have a great affection for your brother."

"Is *that* strange as well? He is my brother, after all."

"It's not strange to care, no. I am quite envious, in fact."

She started. He was? Why did that make her heart feel all warm? "Well, if there is anything that rivals your passion for solving cases with Bow Street, it is my devotion to ensuring my brother receives the upbringing and guidance he merits."

A line formed between his brows. "It sounds as if you are worried about that."

Louisa's senses went on alert. If he'd managed to guess that from her tone, then she had already revealed too much about her family situation to a family enemy. The man was too perceptive for his own good. He would most likely weigh each and every word spoken and draw conclusions from them.

Accurate conclusions, no doubt.

"Worry is only natural," Louisa said. "He is a boy who still requires love and guidance."

"What about your father? School? You can't be with him all the time."

"I am aware I cannot be with him at all times, and I'm not worried about my father or school. In any event, once he is all grown up, I shall be at peace." She paused.

Fabulous, Louisa. What happened to being careful with your words?

His arms folded across his chest as he studied her. "You have no intention to marry then? Or will you simply steal him from your father if you do?"

Louisa almost choked. Marry? The question stung on numerous scores. Perhaps she had wanted to marry when she was a little girl. Mayhap she had harbored childlike hope for a grand love that transcended time. But that dream had slowly been buried after her kidnapping, and furthermore, once her father married Camilla, she had begun to view a different side to love. A darker side.

Not the love for a person.

But the love of whatever could be gained, a greedy version of love.

However, steal Leo from her father? A grin spread at the thought. What a marvelous idea! "If I do marry, I might just do that, yes. Thank you for the advice."

He stiffened. "It wasn't advice."

"Are you sure?" Louisa teased the duke. "It sounded like advice to me."

"You spoil him."

The note of objection rang clear in his tone, but her brain refused to allow that note to enter. "You seem awfully interested in my brother."

He shrugged. "I am merely trying to understand you."

"And you believe you can understand me by questioning my care for Leo?"

"Is there a better way than this?" He averted his gaze to the garden beyond the window. "How else can we truly understand a person, if not by what lies in their heart?"

"Do you not gain this with reciprocity?"

His gaze returned to her. "In other words, you're asking what there is in my heart?"

Her pulse stuttered. She couldn't deny that she was curious. "Quite so."

"Intention."

Louisa scrunched her brow. Intention? Did all hearts not harbor this? What else would there be in a person's heart if not their intentions? Wasn't this the very foundation of every single action ever taken? Her own intentions were born of a desire to protect her brother from the darker intentions in another person's heart—Camilla's.

As vague answers went, this one was unsettlingly evasive. Also, very much in line with the man before her. Elusive. Mysterious. Entirely questionable. Yet every line of his posture was indeed imbued with a sense of *intention*, of purpose. But what purpose was it?

"If you didn't want to answer," she said, her tone dry, "you need only have said so."

"That would have been rude."

Louisa bit back a retort, deciding for the sake of her sanity, to let it go. "Well, let us take our intentions to the library." Speaking on matters of the heart with the Duke of Mortimer was anything but heartening. It was terrifying.

She must not forget that while they were allies at the moment, in the grander scheme of their lives, their families were at odds with each other. Most importantly, she had to remember that whatever she revealed in these moments together could very well be used against her in the future.

"Very well." A rare smile touched his lips.

She froze, caught off guard by the blinding sight. "Why are you smiling? My suggestion couldn't have been that amusing."

The corner of his mouth inched upward further. "Am I smiling? It must be because I find you fascinating in this moment."

Was this a tease from the *duke*? Surely not! Her fingers gripped the edge of the desk. "It's as if you're laughing at me."

To think she had found him handsome in that livery. Urgh. Deny, deny, deny! From the very start, he was a vexing man. There was no way she would ever think of him as anything more than the Duke of Mortimer, enemy to her family.

She glared at him, and he chuckled before his face resumed his usual cold mask.

That was better.

That was familiar.

OLIVER TRACED THE shelves of the library, his mind only partially occupied with hunting for the book they sought. The other part was occupied by *her*. No movement escaped him. No sigh. No grunt. No vexed stomp of her foot.

A touch of amusement struck him once more.

Oliver had never been a petty man, but standing in the duke's library brought a sense of roguishness to his bones. The sense that he, Oliver Cavanagh, had a secret. A secret the Duke of Talbot didn't know. Would never know. Would probably have several fainting spells over if he did know.

His sense of devilishness quickly disappeared. For it wasn't the only secret he possessed. He also had a dark one. And it was far from amusing.

Best he focused on the book.

His *intention*.

However, it was becoming all the more apparent that they would not be finding the book here. He outwardly dragged a hand through his hair while inwardly tugging at it. Hard. He wanted—no, *needed*—to find that book fast.

His shoulder blades were still scarred from the sharp looks Mr. Hall, the butler, had sent his way. As for the rest of the servants, in his brief time within the residence, those he had passed either ducked their heads to avoid attention or smiled too brightly.

He was doomed.

This disguise, doomed.

He turned to check on Lady Louisa's progress, and his gaze followed her finger, trailing over every spine of the books she passed.

She had lovely hands.

There was no diabolical bone in this woman's body. He couldn't help but believe her claim that she had only misplaced the book, not hidden it from him or given it to someone else. She truly appeared distressed and frustrated that she could not find the book.

The betting book wasn't here. He *knew* it in his gut. The book wasn't anywhere in this house. It was gone.

He pinched the bridge of his nose. But how? The duchess?

One of her servants? If the duchess's people found the book, would they know the significance of it? If the book wasn't anywhere to be found, then its absence itself might hold the answer.

"Unbelievable," Lady Louisa muttered. She had stopped her progress around the room at the tall windows overlooking the garden.

"I beg your pardon?"

"They are at it again."

"Who?" Oliver strode over and stopped beside her, following her gaze to where a couple could partly be seen frolicking. They were behind a tree, and while most of their bodies were hidden, you could still glimpse enough from this view to understand what they were doing. "Your family certainly employs passionate servants."

"How laughable! Here we are searching diligently for a book and they are equally diligently romping about!"

He caught himself before he smiled. "When the master's away, the servants get up to all sorts of mischief."

"I ought to applaud their bravery, then."

"Or leave them be. They are up to mischief. We are up to mischief. You could pretend not to see them."

She threw him a sidelong glance. "You surprise me, Duke. But who can pretend not to see people kissing? Lord, I can't *not* look." Her gaze whipped back to the garden. "They are inviting my gaze."

"Perhaps you are so intrigued because you have never been kissed," Oliver said, the words rolling off his tongue before he could stop them. Confound it. He'd never been one to speak so boldly to a lady. With her, however, he was constantly challenged. In every shape and form a challenge could take.

Her gaze flew back to him. "I beg your pardon? What sort of remark is that?"

Don't ask him, he didn't know either. He rubbed the back of his neck. *Ah, you fool. You already started, might as well finish.* "A simple one," Oliver said. "You seem awfully curious about kissing."

A fierce scowl knitted her brows.

"That's because I am curious." She paused. "I was once told I look rather intimidating to men. Perhaps that is why no man has ever dared to steal a kiss and I have been unable to satisfy my curiosity."

"Whoever told you that is a fool."

"Tell Leo that when next you see him."

Of course. He almost laughed. He could imagine the scene. "I daresay once you have experienced the marvel of a kiss, you shall be able to look past lovers stealing them in a garden."

Her whole face turned incredulous. "The marvel of kissing?"

He froze, cursed himself. "I misspoke. There is nothing to marvel about with regard to kissing."

"*Really?* Are you sure? I wouldn't have guessed that you'd have such a romantic view on the subject. You seem more the sort who would kiss for calculating reasons such as distracting a woman or using the kiss to get something in return."

Oliver hated how he couldn't exactly refute that. "You have keen observational skills."

She grinned. "So I'm not wrong."

"You are not."

A chuckle. "Have you ever heard of *denying?*"

"Should I have?" Oliver asked. "Why should I deny the truth when it has already been caught?"

"The truth can be caught?" She tucked a curl behind her ear, smiling. "What a clever way to put it. In any event, it certainly will not put you in a favorable light amongst the ladies."

Oliver nodded at that, somewhat amused. "I suppose it won't." His gaze dropped to her lips, and before he knew it, he was leaning very close—drawn by an impossible pull, as if some invisible force was guiding him closer. Yet she didn't flinch, didn't avert her gaze. She simply stared at him, unblinking and unmoving.

"What are you doing?" she breathed.

"I don't know," Oliver offered truthfully.

"Do you intend to steal a kiss?"

Did he? Someone else seemed to have taken over both his body and mind. "It wouldn't be stealing anymore if I did, now would it?"

"Since I caught the truth of your intention?"

"Correct." He straightened, suppressing the urge to succumb to a temptation he had no desire to entertain. If he did steal a kiss—or simply kiss her—it would not be out of noble sentiment. Rather, it would be to vent his frustration that the book had once again eluded him. "The book isn't here."

She let out a sigh he couldn't interpret, leaning back against the windowsill. "Don't say that. We haven't searched the whole library yet. There is still that section," she pointed to a row of shelves. "And that section."

"We won't find the book in either of those sections." He was sure of it.

"How do you know if we don't look?"

"My gut."

"And that is something you can trust more than your eyes?"

Indeed it was. "If it's going to bother you endlessly, look if you must, but I'm telling you, the book isn't there."

"Where else would the book be? It *must* be in the library."

Where else, indeed. He watched her proceed over to the books, the defiant set in her shoulders almost making him smile. Lady Louisa was determined to prove him wrong. He welcomed her to try.

The question, however, should be raised—could the duchess already have the book in her possession? That would not be good for him. Should he tell Lady Louisa about her stepmother? She appeared unaware of the duchess's involvement, or was she actually all too aware, he wondered.

Devil take it. He hated this doubt. This uncertainty.

But he also trusted his instincts, and they told him the book wasn't here, and that Lady Louisa didn't know about its connection to her stepmother. But that brought on even more questions. Would she help him if he told her? Would she be surprised? Outraged? Would she worry about her brother? Would she question her father's involvement? Would any good come of knowing the truth?

His gaze caught on a small head peeking into the doorway. Oliver cocked his head to the side, studying the boy, who stared at his sister before turning to him, visibly starting when their eyes met.

Ah.

A key element fell into place.

This was why they couldn't find the book.

Little Leo Talbot.

Not only was Oliver now certain that the boy knew about the book, his whole face told Oliver that this young master was enjoying watching them search for the very object he'd had a hand in hiding.

"Lady Louisa."

She glanced over her shoulder. "Did you find something?"

"No, but I do have a question. Did you give the book to anyone else to page through?"

Her brows scrunched. "Why ever would I do that?"

"A feeling." Oliver arched a brow at the boy, motioning him to come over. The boy hesitated, then his head disappeared again.

"A nonsensical feeling. Why not just help me search the shelves?"

"I have a better idea," Oliver countered. "Let us ask your brother about the book's whereabouts."

She turned to him. "Leo? Why?"

"He's outside the library door, eavesdropping."

"What?" Her whole body swiveled to the door. "Leo! Are you there? If you are, you better show your face right this instant!"

A few seconds ticked by, then a small body filled the doorway. The boy directed a disdainful glare at Oliver. "What is *he* doing here?"

"*He* is my servant."

The boy pulled a face. "Was he not a gardener a few hours ago?"

Oliver arched a brow again. For a child, Leo Talbot was not that easily fooled. He could sense Oliver was no ordinary servant. His perceptiveness was most impressive. In some ways, he reminded Oliver a bit of himself at that age.

"And now he is my personal servant," Lady Louisa announced.

"Why do you have a personal servant?"

Lady Louisa's hands settled on her hips as she retorted, "That is not a matter to concern yourself with, Leo."

Her brother looked over to Oliver again. "If you have a personal servant, then I want a personal servant, too."

Oliver pursed his lips. The boy had spunk. Just like his sister.

"You do not get to have a personal servant."

"Why not?"

"You are still a child. Once you reach my age you can have as many personal servants as you want." She suddenly paused. "Actually, I suppose you do get a personal servant."

His eyes brightened. "I do?"

"Yes, and you already have one: your governess."

Oliver almost barked out a laugh.

"Now tell me," Lady Louisa went on. "What are you doing here, spying on us when you should be in your schoolroom going over your studies?"

The boy looked away.

"Leo Talbot! Tell me you didn't hide the book I am looking for!"

"What book? I do not know what you are talking about."

"You are the worst liar. What did you do with it? Hand it over right now!"

Oliver rubbed his chin as he studied the two siblings. His instincts prickled again, warning him this was no simple matter.

And he was about to be proven right.

Chapter Six

WHENEVER HER BROTHER eluded her, Louisa silently applauded him. She also—deep in a corner of her heart she would never expose!—felt a secret pleasure when he outwitted his governess. It reassured her that he might, when darkness loomed, evade its clutches. Though perhaps not the most prudent of sentiments, it was the truth of her feelings.

Granted, evading darkness in the real world was not as simple as evading one's tutor. One must master the delicate proverbial footwork and precise proximity required for a waltz, so that one could leverage these artful steps to navigate and escape the scheming or dangerous situations in society.

She had learned this lesson ten years ago and in a petrifying way, no less. Vigilance was armor in the presence of powerful men. It was why Louisa felt the urge to laugh even as she burned with frustration at her brother's antics!

The moment he dashed from the library, he disappeared like a puff of smoke.

The little brat!

While she had possessed the same skill for eluding her governess when she was his age, she didn't know every hiding place on the estate. She'd only ever concealed herself within the sheltering boughs of the weeping willow, and she had managed to preserve that hiding spot precisely because she had never been discovered.

Her brother, on the other hand, often sought the company of the servants, so while the duke searched the house, she would ask the servants Leo loved to converse with.

She strode into the kitchen, smiling at the cook who was busy kneading dough. "I'm looking for that rascal of a brother of mine. Have you perhaps seen him?"

"Can't say I have, dearie. Why? Has he given Miss Hale the slip again?"

Louisa glanced at the other servants present, several of whom doted on her brother and indulged his whims. "Indeed. Then, do you perhaps know where he might choose to hide if he were hiding from her—or me?"

"Can't say, dearie," Cook said, kneading away. "But perhaps he has the same mind as you."

"The same mind?" Louisa raised an eyebrow, clearly skeptical. "Meaning?"

Cook shrugged. "The young master is always following you around."

Her? Surely not. "You mean he is always keeping the staff from their duties."

Cook smiled. "And you always catch him, dearie."

Precisely!

Wait . . . she *did*.

Did that mean . . . "Are you saying Leo bothers the household closest to where I am at any given time?"

The two maids standing to the side bobbed their heads furiously, and Cook chuckled. "It seems you finally understand."

Louisa stood flabbergasted.

She had never noticed the connection. She always believed she was simply at the right place at the right time to catch her brother in his mischief. So, then, he had deliberately positioned himself to be caught by her.

For her attention?

Was that why he had taken the book?

That blasted book . . .

Chaos had reigned when Ophelia Thornton, one of the women on the list in the book, had slipped into White's dressed as a man and stolen the thing. After they'd shared copies of the book at a ball, many of the women of the *ton* began revolting against their male counterparts. One member of White's, a lord Digby or something, if she recalled correctly, had all but started a witch hunt.

So much trouble.

And now the book was connected to a criminal organization?

Double the trouble!

Honestly, Louisa just wanted to find the book and be done with it. The tall, stately man in livery flashed in her mind.

Make that triple the trouble.

Well, he certainly brought a measure of thrill to an otherwise dreary Ashford. Bothersome man.

But returning to her brother, if he were to follow her patterns, could it be possible that he had chosen her usual hiding spot? The weeping willow tree?

Could it be as simple as that?

"Thank you," Louisa said to Cook, nodding at the housemaids before striding from the kitchen and making her way to the gardens. Halfway there, she broke into a run until she burst outside and her slippers touched the soft grass. She slowed, padding over the lawn until she came to a stop a few feet away from the tree. She couldn't see anything through the leaves at this time, but she could hear the soft murmur of voices.

Her brother.

And . . . the duke?

"How did you find me here?" Leo was asking.

"My observational skills are top notch."

"Is that *all*?"

"Of course, there is nothing else required."

Louisa almost snorted. Nothing else required? She could just imagine the duke catching sight of her brother traipsing down the gardens and slipping through these hanging branches, and now he claims masterful observational skills?

But then again, he did possess a keen mind, and those eyes missed nothing.

At least they had found her brother. That was all that mattered. Now they would find the book. She stepped forward to part the branches and make her presence known, but her brother's next question stopped her in her tracks.

"Will you tell my sister?"

Louisa furrowed her brows. What was she to do with that wretched question? She already knew! Should she retreat and pretend she'd heard nothing? Also, was this truly her brother's hiding spot as well? Was it even a hiding spot at all when it seemed the servants also knew about it? That Leo had known? Had it ever been a secret?

She shook the thoughts off. It didn't matter anymore. If her brother didn't want her to know, then let Mortimer retrieve the information from him. She retreated slowly, but the duke's answer brought her to a halt again.

"She already knows."

"How?" Leo asked with a note of bewilderment and a smidgeon of consternation. "Did she send you here?"

"No," the duke answered. "I told you, I possess exceptional observation abilities. They alerted me to the fact that she is standing beyond the curtain of branches, eavesdropping."

Eavesdropping! Eavesdropping her arse!

Louisa swiftly parted the drooping branches of the tree and stepped into the shelter of the inner sanctum, her vision filling with a scene of a small boy and a large man kneeling before him. She came up short at the subdued sight.

"Sister!" Leo exclaimed, jolting.

She crossed her arms over her chest. "I'll have you know, I was not eavesdropping."

"Then what would you call it?" that sly duke asked.

"Hesitation."

Leo furrowed his brows. "Hesitation? You? About what?"

Why did she have to explain herself to them? Still, she said, "Whether to reveal that I know my brother's hiding spot, of course!"

"How *did* you know?" her brother asked.

Her chin lifted a notch. "I realized something about my brother." Man and boy stared at her, and she narrowed her eyes even further on the smallest one. "You are always following me about."

"I am not!" her brother instantly denied.

"Oh? Then why am I always catching you dilly-dallying with the servants? If you were clever, you would do it far away from me."

"That doesn't prove anything!"

"No? Then why are your cheeks so red?" Louisa asked. "Are you feeling guilty about something?"

"I am not!"

"And I don't believe you." She lowered her hands to settle them on her hips. "Which means you weren't far away when Theodosia called on me that day and also handed over a certain book into my care, were you?"

His cheeks flushed, but he remained silent. Louisa knew her brother well enough to recognize that when he dug in his heels, nothing but a miracle would move him unless he wanted to move. It rarely happened, but when it did, it was quite a sight.

But this was no ordinary matter.

It was an extremely important one.

"James Leonard Talbot!" Louisa exclaimed when her brother moved to dart away again. "Where do you think you are going?"

The duke was faster and grabbed her brother by the scruff of his collar and pulled him back. He straightened to his full height. "Perhaps we should take the matter inside."

Louisa nodded, glancing at the overhanging branches. While this spot served well for a bit of a retreat, it was apparently no secret, and anyone close enough could overhear their conversation. Though—she glanced at the duke—they would have to get past his masterful skill of observation first.

Did he have to look so irresistible and striking standing there, tall, commanding, and undeniably impressive?

Lord, Louisa.

She must be going crazy. Why else would she be so attuned to this man? A man her father would never approve of. A man *she* didn't approve of. A man who didn't approve of her.

Best they found that book and parted ways as soon as possible.

OLIVER STUDIED THE boy intently, his gaze following the faintest flicker of emotion. They were back in the library, and none of them had yet exchanged a single word. That look—the one now on Leo's face—was all too familiar. He had worn that very expression countless times in his own youth when faced with questions *he* would rather not answer. He knew well that little could persuade the boy to loosen his tongue.

Nothing had ever persuaded him.

But this boy was not him—he had a weakness. Oliver glanced at Louisa. The young heir had a spirited sister, a dynamic presence he had never known as a boy. If he had, perhaps the same nervous look now appearing in the boy's eyes might have mirrored his own.

"You won't be in trouble if you tell us," Oliver said calmly.

The boy's eyes shifted to him before he crossed his arms over his chest. "And who are *you* to promise that?"

In other words, *you are nothing but a mere servant unable to promise anything.* Oliver nearly smiled. That the boy hadn't called him a mere servant to his face was quite something. Other lads would have been quicker to remind him of his place. It was clear that Lady Louisa's influence had already left its mark.

The lady in question snorted, pursing her lips to hold back a smile, no doubt. "He has a point."

"What if I am no mere servant?" Oliver asked the lad.

The boy glanced at Lady Louisa before looking back at him. "You look like a servant and you dress like a servant. Therefore, you are a servant."

Lady Louisa chuckled. "Well said, brother."

"Did you not call me an imposter earlier?" Oliver asked him.

"That was then, this is now."

Amusement filled him. Even his own right-hand man had remarked that he could dress like a servant but would never deceive anyone into thinking he was one. Apparently, ducal arrogance couldn't be concealed by livery or even potato sacks. His attention turned back to Leo.

"So then, I am correct in saying that you, little lord, perceive me as a servant?"

The boy nodded.

Oliver smiled then. "Let me ask you this: Do servants look like me?"

The boy started, but then considered him, carefully trailing his gaze over every inch of him. Slowly, he shook his head. "They are not as big."

"Just my size sets me apart?" What a strange conclusion to draw. He was tall, but so were many other people.

"And you are rather insolent." The boy pursed his lips. "If you are not a servant, who are you?"

"I am someone your sister brought here to protect her."

Leo's eyes widened, and Oliver felt heated blue eyes light upon him.

"Protect my sister?" The boy swiveled to Lady Louisa. "Are you in danger?"

"Of course not!" Her burning look turned into a glare she directed his way before she softened and reassured her brother. "I am not in any danger, Leo."

"You are not lying to me, are you?"

"No, I . . ." she started but Oliver cut her off.

"Not imminent danger, but that doesn't mean there is no

danger at all." Saville, Lady Selena, and Warrick were proof of that, given what had happened back in London. There had been blackmail in abundance, and the two men had even been kidnapped, leaving it up to Lady Selena to rescue them.

"Will you stop!" Lady Louisa hissed at him. "He is just a child!"

Leo stepped forward, fisting his hands at his sides. "Does this have to do with the book you are searching for?"

"Correct," Oliver said bluntly. "Did you hide it from your sister? Perhaps as a prank?"

"Yes, out with it, Leo!"

Leo wrung his hands together. "They said the book was dangerous. They said if I retrieved it for them then they would make sure it's danger didn't touch our family. They also gave me sweets."

An exclamation of shock left Lady Louisa. "Who are *they*?"

Oliver tensed, every muscle coiled as a jolt of foreboding gripped him. He kneeled before the boy when he wouldn't meet their gaze. "Do you know who those men are?"

The boy shook her head. "There were two of them. They looked terrifying with scars on their faces."

Louisa joined Oliver, lowering to look him in the eyes. "Where did they approach you?"

"At the bookshop when Miss Hale took me to purchase books," he answered honestly. Then he hastily burst out, "It wasn't her fault! She was busy speaking to the shopkeeper about a book we couldn't find!"

"We are not blaming anyone," Oliver said steadily, trying to reassure the boy. "We merely want as many details as possible."

Oliver's mind raced. Could it be their stepmother's henchmen? But according to what he understood about the secret organization, they only hired women, and the men who were involved were limited. The evidence seemed to indicate that it stretched no farther than their husbands and sons. However, Lady Ridgeland had kept a hulking man at her side back in

London, so he couldn't completely disregard the possibility.

"Is there anything else you can remember about them?" Lady Louisa asked her brother.

Her brother bit his lip and looked away.

"Leo," Lady Louisa said softly, "we need to know."

"They said the book is dangerous. Is that true? Did I make a mistake?"

Oliver felt sorry for the child. None of this was his fault. "No, you are not to blame. You didn't approach them. But we do need to find the book before it falls into the wrong hands."

The boy looked at Oliver. "You are our protector?"

"Yes, I am." And he would be, no matter what.

"Just who are you?" Leo asked with a bit more confidence now that he'd been reassured. "I don't even know your name."

"He is a man from Bow Street." Lady Louisa inserted. "His name is . . ." She glanced at him, prompting.

"Oliver, and yes, you could say I am from Bow Street." It wasn't a lie. And it was best if they didn't reveal too much of his identity—too many eyes and ears in this house. And the boy himself, depending on the influence of his father, might clamp up if he learned the truth. "I've been looking for the book for a while now."

"Why? It's just a bunch of strange entries."

Oliver nodded. "They are wager entries, but many of them are written in code. It's evidence that I need to capture a group of bad people."

The boy's face suddenly paled. "Do you mean that I gave the book to the criminals you are trying to catch?"

"Not exactly." Though he could not honestly say. "The people I am looking for are women. You said you gave it to two men who had scars on their faces?"

The boy nodded enthusiastically. "They were big. One had a nasty scar cutting through the left side of his lip. The other man's scar lined the right side of his jawline." Leo traced the pathways of their scars on his own face. "They both had dark eyes. Almost black. Black hair as well. Brothers, they looked like."

Oliver's blood chilled.

"Oh, and the one with the scar on his lip had a very low voice. Almost scratchy. And they didn't wear fashionable clothes. But they weren't commoner clothes either. They wore everything in black. And decent boots. Polished."

His blood turned even colder. "I see."

"Do you know these men?" Lady Louisa asked.

"I can't say for sure." And he couldn't, though everything in him roared that his fear was right. A scar that split one of the men's lips, dressed in all black, dark features, brothers, along with interest in a book tied to an organization that smuggled goods . . . If his suspicion proved correct, this whole affair had just spiraled into something far worse than he'd expected.

"When did you give them the book?" Oliver asked.

"The day after my sister's friend visited," Leo admitted. "They said they would be watching, and I should put the book in a satchel and place it on the street. They would pick it up."

"Did they say anything else that you can remember, anything that might give us a clue to where they are from?"

"One of the men was impatient. He wanted to get back to the Brighton."

Brighton.

Bloody hell.

He had hoped against hope that his blooming suspicion would turn out wrong, but that didn't seem to be the case.

If what the boy said was correct, they were not dealing with any ordinary men. They were dealing with a group of brothers that might even be worse than the duchess and her female organization.

The Bastards of Brighton.

Or so they were known. They ruled the underground of Brighton. It was even rumored they owned more than half the buildings and shops in town. Nothing happened that they weren't aware of.

"You do know, don't you?" Lady Louisa asked. "And it's not good, is it?"

Oliver had hoped that she wouldn't be as perceptive with her brother about, but her senses were as sharp as ever. "It's not good. But it's not necessarily bad." Maybe. It certainly wasn't hopeless. At least it hadn't been the duchess's people.

"What does that mean?" Lady Louisa demanded from him.

Oliver rose to his feet. "It means I may have an idea who they are." It also meant his time in Ashford was over. He had to get to Brighton, post haste.

She rose as well. "And?"

"They might hand over the book, they might not."

"Surely, you jest."

"I assure you, Lady Louisa, I do not." Not if these were the men he believed. They were unpredictable. Difficult. Dangerous. No jesting about that.

"That's not reassuring at all." She pinched the bridge of her nose. "How did they ever learn of the book's whereabouts?"

How, indeed. And did they know that the Duchess of Talbot was the head of the female organization? They must suspect. They must have had their eye on the betting book from the very start, as well.

Oliver glanced at the boy, his mood darkening. "What did they give you in return? Just a promise that your family would no longer be in danger?"

Leo nodded, wide-eyed.

Oliver scowled. He hadn't known this little boy for long, but a protective instinct as old as time rose within him. Like a lion sensing hyenas closing in on his cub. It didn't make sense, but he didn't need it to.

Those blackguards.

Playing on a boy's fear of his family being harmed and handing him some sweets. If they had approached a Talbot once, they could do so again, especially if the duchess's involvement became known and they wanted more leverage over this family than a book. Then it might not just be an object they took, but a person.

His gaze found Lady Louisa.

Or two.

The danger for them hadn't passed because they no longer had the book. He was afraid it had just begun.

"Lady Louisa—"

"You are going to Brighton, aren't you?" Her back straightened. "I'm coming with you."

Instant resistance welled. "No, you are not."

"I'm the one who lost the book. I shall help retrieve it."

"You didn't lose the book, and it's best if you stay at home with your brother while I handle this matter."

"Why?" Her eyes narrowed on him. "Because you're a man?"

Yes. "Because I'm experienced in such matters."

"Who says I'm not?"

Oliver arched a brow.

"Well, you can't know until you experience it, can you?"

What reasoning. "The answer is still no." He bowed. "I shall take my leave."

His back prickled as he strode from the library. It wasn't until his feet cleared Talbot property that the tension unraveled from him—and only then did he realize how tightly it had coiled around him in the first place.

Around her.

But now it's all over.

Chapter Seven

The next morning

IF THE DUKE of Mortimer believed this was the end of the matter, he was about to learn a valuable lesson! Did he honestly believe she would just sit back and do *nothing*?

How arrogant!

Louisa might be many things, but it wasn't in her nature to be a shirker of responsibility. The book had been swindled from them on *her* watch, and her brother's actions were her responsibility as much as they were his. More even—since he was just a child, she would take full responsibility for them. Besides, she intended to look those men who had approached her brother in the eye and make it clear she was not the sort of woman to shrink from a few scars and menacing faces. Men like that—men who wore darkness like a cloak—had no business speaking to a child. The very idea of them circling Leo like vultures made her blood run hot. If they thought they could frighten her family, they were gravely mistaken.

Let them try to cow *her* with their shadowy threats.

And the duke was hiding something from her.

Something important.

She could tell by the way . . . the way he . . . She could just tell! Call it instinct or intuition or a woman's unique senses, but she was sure of it. But Louisa also knew that powerful men like the Duke of Mortimer, once they made up their minds about something, would not change them easily. Therefore, she could only resort to craftier ways to get his attention.

Such as sending a threatening note to his lodgings to wait for her, or else she would travel to Brighton alone.

Grim satisfaction clawed up from her belly. She could just imagine his face, and what a face it was. Let him seethe. Let him fume. Because like it or not, Duke, she was coming.

Louisa leaned against the carriage, staring at the door of his establishment. Her brother's head popped out of the carriage window. A tail she hadn't been able to shake no matter what. Stubbornness seemed to run thick in all Talbot blood.

"What if he doesn't come?" Leo asked.

"He will." Or he would have already left. In which case, Louisa would set for Brighton after on her own just as she had promised in her missive. She had suspicions. She wanted them confirmed.

"You know that Papa will turn so many shades of red when he learns about you and the Bow Street Runner."

"Oh, I think the color will deepen considerably if he learns about you and those scary men. Shall we make a wager?"

Leo's mouth clamped shut, and then after a few beats, ventured again, "It is best if we keep this between us."

Louisa curled her lips into a smile. "What a smart boy you have become!"

He pouted. "You are mocking me."

"Only a little bit." Louisa's senses leaped to attention when a tall man strode from the establishment with a familiar, cold look on his face. What a delightful sight.

His gaze moved from her to Leo. "What is the meaning of this?" It was the tone of a man who always got his way. Lord, it should repulse her, honestly, but instead, her pulse leaped, and challenge rose in her chest.

"I am waiting for you." She pushed away from the carriage, pushed Leo's head back into the carriage, and opened the door. "Shall we set off?"

Amber eyes bore into her, hot and cold at the same time. He said not a word, only nodded once, but she caught the slight tick in his jaw. Without a word, he strode to the carriage. Only then did Louisa glimpse two men emerge from the shadows. One disappeared around the corner and the other entered the establishment. They must be Mortimer's men and would probably follow in their wake.

She turned and started to find the duke simply standing at the door waiting for her to enter. She smiled at him. "After you."

He gave her a long, inscrutable look before entering the carriage. She followed after him, pleased as punch. Also, rather surprised that man would give in so easily.

"You brought the boy."

"Why wouldn't she bring me?" Leo asked before she could respond.

The duke arched a brow, but his gaze turned to her for an answer. What a morning grump! She almost repeated her brother's response but thought better of imitating the duke's surliness. "He refused to be left behind. I daresay he would have found a way to follow if I hadn't brought him."

"Like sister, like brother."

"Of course," Louisa said.

Leo gave a curt nod. "I must take responsibility for my actions."

"That is commendable," the duke answered, his expression unchanged. "So long as you keep out of danger, we won't have a problem."

"Oh, he shall do exactly as we say," Louisa reassured. "Right, Leo?"

Her brother nodded. "I only wish to accompany you."

Louisa caught the duke's lips twitching. It wasn't exactly in amusement, but she chose, in the spirit of smoothing his feathers, to interpret it that way. "Do you find something amusing, Duke?"

"No, indeed." He followed her lead. "I was only imagining how my youth would have been if I'd had a sister such as you."

Louisa jolted.

A sister like her? She shivered at the prospect, her mind immediately rejecting the idea as she shifted her gaze to her brother, seated next to her and opposite Mortimer. Much better to have a younger brother! "Be glad you did not have one like me."

He shrugged before his whole countenance turned all serious again. "Since you've taken charge of our arrangements, do you have a plan?"

Louisa paused. "I rather thought you had one. I just planned to join you."

He suddenly chuckled. "Very well."

Was he teasing her? No, *mocking* her? The rascal! "Well, I also have another motive for wishing to accompany you, but I shall only tell you once we arrive in Brighton."

His brows furrowed but smoothed out again. "I look forward to learning this motive, then."

"Me too," Leo piped up.

"You shall learn nothing but patience," Louisa retorted, her voice stern. "And perhaps more importantly, why you should never indulge strangers or accept sweets from them!"

"What would you have done, Louisa?" her brother exclaimed. "They said the book was dangerous. I . . ."

"It's all right," Louisa shushed her brother, patting his head, regretting her tone.

He was not to blame here. She was the one on that ridiculous list that derided her childbearing hips. *She* was the one who had played a part in what transpired in London. *Her* friend had entrusted the book to her.

"I would have done the same as you, Leo." It was the only reassurance she could give her brother. Who was to judge another's reaction in fright? Certainly not she. If anyone was truly to blame, it was the duke. Waiting so long, waiting until the book came to her. He should have known better.

"That's right, Master Leo," Mortimer murmured. "You were never in the wrong."

The duke's features almost turned sheepish. No, that couldn't be right. Sheepish? She inspected his face. He returned her gaze with a magnetic one of his own.

Why on earth do I find it breathtaking instead of alarming? And why don't I find it alarming that I don't find it alarming?

She supposed alarm was a relative term at this point.

But he did possess some sort of pull . . .

"Intrigue." If she had to describe that pull, it would be summed up in *that* one, punchy word.

"I beg your pardon?" Mortimer asked, shifting back into his seat.

"Oh, do not mind her," Leo answered for her. "She does that sometimes."

"I do what?" Louisa questioned.

Her brother gave her an odd look, as though she'd gone mad. "Mutter single syllables or words that make no sense."

I beg your *pardon.* "I don't do that!" Heat flushed her cheeks.

Her brother's brow arched alongside the duke's.

"Whatever you are speaking of, it's called a slip of one's tongue." Perhaps several slips, but did he have to make her sound like a madwoman?

"You talk to yourself," her brother said. "Admit it, Louisa."

"Why should I ever admit to that?" That *would* just be madness, and she wasn't mad.

Her brother huffed out a breath and looked away. Heh! She should have left him at home, the cheeky brat. And yet, she'd come to accept the undeniable truth: she was one of those sisters who doted on their brother beyond reason.

She caught Mortimer's gaze. She couldn't decipher what she saw in their depth, but the flush on her cheeks spread through her whole body.

Louisa quickly averted her gaze.

Why was her heart pulsing in her chest, her belly, and her throat all at the same time?

OLIVER LEANED AGAINST the outside wall of The Trotting Horse, observing as Lady Louisa chastised her brother for a misstep. Little Leo had followed a stable hand into the stables without so much as a word to her, or to him—and without either hesitation or suspicion. Too trusting, this lad. He lacked the skill his father should have taught him—awareness of the dangers that might lurk in his surroundings. Ill intent did not always wear a villain's sneer. A wandering child, unaware of the risks, was an easy mark. A boy of his station, even more so.

Lady Louisa certainly recognized the danger, and he couldn't fault her for reprimanding her brother. The boy needed to learn that trust given too freely could lead to consequences far graver than a scolding. That still hadn't stopped the young man from acting haughty afterward at breakfast, prompting another reprimand.

These two were truly amusing to watch.

The trip to Brighton had proven far more uneventful than Oliver expected. The angel had been surprisingly well-behaved and even unusually quiet during their trip. Not that he wanted it any other way, but he couldn't help but wonder when the next blow might land.

It was sure to leave a mark when it did.

A stuffy feeling entered his chest. It rather felt like he was traveling with family, and not the daughter and son of his family's enemy. He could just imagine Talbot's fury if he ever discovered these events.

Not that he wanted to tempt fate.

Talbot's ire would be bad for him. And he didn't have the time or the inclination to fight off Talbot. He'd rather fight battles worth fighting. Family feuds, however, weren't so easily unraveled—grudges had a way of sinking deep. Old dogs didn't just hold onto their grudges, they guarded them, nurtured them, passed them down like heirlooms. It would be up to the younger generations to break the cycle—if they weren't already trained to carry it onward.

And speaking of families that held grudges, Oliver hoped again that the Fury brothers wouldn't make things too difficult for them in Brighton. He wanted to get those bickering Talbots home as soon as possible.

A small girl with a teary face overlapped the image of Lady Louisa in his mind. How many years had it been since his father had stolen that little child away? That single act had ignited the feud into an all out war at the time, sealing the bad blood between their families. Talbot had put a hole in his father's shoulder, but the old man had lived.

And yet, Lady Louisa showed no visible repulsion toward him as a Mortimer. No wariness. No lingering hatred. Fear. Almost as if she were unaware.

Had she blocked the events from her mind? Or had it never been revealed to her who had been behind the deeds ten years ago? That must be it—in all likelihood, her father had never informed her. Perhaps to spare her more distress.

She suddenly turned to him, and their gazes collided. Oliver's muscles tensed, and his spine straightened as if bracing for impact. But the blow had already landed.

One smart brow rose, and she called out, "Are you just going to stand there the whole day, or are we setting off?"

Oliver strode over, nodding at his men. The angel was better off forgetting the anguish of the past. Forgetting about him. Since she didn't remember him from back then, let it stay that way. "Are you always this lively in the morning?"

The young Talbot heir cast a miserable look his way. "Yes, she is."

"Little brat, that is only because of your brattish comments."

The boy pouted. "What's so brattish about wanting steamed fish for breakfast?"

She poked his forehead. "You don't even demand steamed

fish for breakfast from our own cook! How can you demand it from the innkeeper?"

"Didn't you once say a person should enjoy the things outside that you can't enjoy at home?"

"Whenever did I say that to you?" She asked, eyes wide.

"You didn't say it to me." Leo lifted his shoulders in an innocent shrug. "I heard you and your friends speak of it before you slipped out of the house to go to an alehouse."

"That . . ."

Alehouse? A particular one came to mind. One owned by her stepmother. Oliver patted the boy's head. "You do make a valid argument, and so does your sister." To Louisa, he said. "A tavern called The Rose perhaps?" Her heiress friends had been there a time or two while Oliver had been doing surveillance of the establishment, but he had never spotted her there.

"No," she said. "It was called something else, but I can't recall."

Oliver nodded, motioning to the carriage. "Shall we?" This time he didn't wait for her, he snatched up the boy by his waist and entered the carriage in one swift motion, placing the "brat" beside him.

Lady Louisa entered with a dark look but didn't comment on him forgoing his manners. "We should talk about what happens when we find the men who approached my brother. Brighton is a popular town. People will recognize us."

Oliver rested his hands on his legs. "Which is why we shall board with a friend of mine on the outskirts of town."

Her gaze flashed with surprise. "Who is your friend? He won't mind if my brother and I join as well?"

"You won't know him," Oliver said. "I sent a man in advance to inform him of our imminent arrival."

"I see. Well, I thank you."

He picked at his sleeves, withholding a smile. "Since you came to pick me up, paid for the lodgings, and orchestrated our travels, I could do at least this much. How would you wish to proceed?"

She blinked, then cleared her throat. "Well, since they have a gentleman's club book but seem rather ungentlemanly, I suppose we should start at a teahouse."

Oliver arched a brow. "A teahouse? Why?"

"Gossip runs rampant at teahouses. The servers know about everything going on in town."

"And how would *you* know this?"

"How else?" Leo piped up from beside him. "She enjoys gossiping with the servants."

"You as well, little brat," Lady Louisa shot back.

Oliver cocked his head in thought. Just what did a lady gossip about with the servants? He couldn't imagine such a thing. Well . . . he thought about the scowl of his valet, also a man of— *secret*—affairs, riding his horse alongside this carriage.

Very well. He *could* form a picture in his mind.

But they didn't gossip. It was only ever pure business. Mmm. They did speak of other people's business. Could that be considered business gossip?

Were he and Owen gossips?

No.

"We shall arrive in a few hours," Oliver murmured in an effort to prevent the two from falling into bickering again. "You and your brother are friends of my family traveling with me."

A snort came from Lady Louisa's bench across from him. "Friends of your family? You are surprisingly humorous."

He caught the teasing note and smoothly asked. "Shall I introduce you as an enemy then?"

The lad waved a hand. "Friends are fine."

Lady Louisa leaned over to pinch his cheek until he yelped. "Why do you think you are in charge here?"

The boy sat straighter. "I am the highest ranking here."

She threatened to give him another pinch. "Until you reach the age of eighteen, age trumps rank, brat."

Oliver stared at the young heir. Their resemblance was uncanny. The boy reminded him too much of Lady Louisa as a little ten-year-old girl. How old had he been back then? Barely a man himself. Another memory clutched at his mind, sharp as a hook. A small girl clinging to his neck, sobbing in fright.

A prickle ran along his hairline, and he rubbed the back of his neck, trying to shake the sensation off. He should never have entered her home nor the carriage when she'd appeared again. The former he'd thought a necessity given the circumstances. But the latter . . . How could he explain his feet taking on a life of their own? It was as though a cord had wrapped around every one of his limbs and pulled him forward.

The same had happened when their gazes had locked earlier.

"My friend shall be asking around already. Let us see what he uncovers. If his information is unhelpful, then we shall go to your teahouse."

Her gaze shifted from her brother to Oliver. "As you wish."

"So amenable," Oliver murmured. Again, that feeling of expecting the next blow to land at any moment moved along the edges of his nerves.

A childish snort came from Leo. "She's amenable because she doesn't have a better plan."

"What is the definition of a better plan?" Louisa retorted. "The better plan is the one that succeeds, and you don't know which one that is until it succeeds."

Oliver leaned back in his seat, watching the two.

Bickering again.

It was almost nostalgic, this back-and-forth.

Soothing.

Chapter Eight

LOUISA STEPPED FROM the carriage, her gaze sweeping over the cottage before her. It was by no means grand, not by any stretch of the imagination, yet neither could it be considered anything near rundown. Ivy climbed along the sides, and a few flowerpots sat by the windows with bright flowers. It was oddly delightful.

But its true allure?

The view.

Lawks! Louisa wouldn't mind waking to a view of such a breathtaking scene as this every morning. The cottage looked over the beach, where the sand met the sea in an endless stretch of blue.

"Your friend lives *here?*" She glanced at Mortimer. Even the duke took on a different aspect with this place as the backdrop. He appeared a touch more serene. Even dressed in plain clothing, though she would have loved to see him again in his livery! If she were to have to choose between that sight and this view, it would be a truly difficult decision!

Mortimer didn't dawdle, he only nodded and led the way, all commanding and authoritative. She almost snorted, thinking about how he had "led" the way into the carriage earlier. Well, she had started it, but she couldn't help but muse at how the man played along, as though it had always been in line with his own authority.

She trailed after him, bemused at the enthralled expression of her brother as well.

A tall man—almost as tall as Mortimer, but leaner—stepped from the house, grinning when his gaze fell upon the duke. "As I live and breathe, when I received your missive, I thought the heavens must be playing a trick on me."

Louisa blinked when she heard the duke's low laughter. The man always presented as a stiff, cold figure, so discovering this carefree laughter was quite startling.

"Thank you for helping us with lodgings," Mortimer said.

The man waved his comment aside, but his curious gaze settled on Louisa and her brother. She stepped up to him and held out her hand. "Louisa Talbot. It's a pleasure to make your acquaintance."

He hesitated, but only for a fraction of a second before shaking her offered hand. "Talbot, you say. *The* Talbot?"

Oh, drat. Should she not have introduced herself with her real name?

"It's a long story," Mortimer answered the question his friend didn't ask.

"I'm Leo Talbot," her brother announced, following her lead, not noting anything amiss.

The man shook Leo's hand as well. "It's a pleasure to meet you both. I'm Michael Helgate."

Louisa paused. Michael Helgate? Why did that name sound so familiar? She also didn't miss the *what are you bloody doing* glance Mr. Helgate shot Mortimer.

Well, she couldn't fault his curiosity or skepticism. Their families were not on good terms, and apparently, he knew it. A pinch of regret filled her. She should have shown more interest in how and why their families were actually feuding. She'd always understood it to be a sort of struggle between two ducal powers. To others it might seem rather ironic that she, the daughter of a duke, would want to steer clear of dukes. However, she couldn't choose the family she had been born with, but she could choose the family she would spend her life with—the husband part of it anyway.

But the look Mr. Helgate leveled at the duke sharpened her curiosity about the many layers to their feud.

"Come inside," he gestured to the house. "I've just boiled water for tea. Miles will be by later to cook. A silent fellow, you probably won't notice him. He does the chores at the house."

How intriguing. "We thank you for your hospitality."

"You are still using Miles as your personal servant?" To Louisa, he clarified, "They served together in the war, and Miles is the only one who worries endlessly about this one's bad habits."

Mr. Helgate laughed. "What bad habits?"

"You are getting lazier by the day. Still having Miles cook your food? Draw your baths? Get a wife and give the man some peace."

"What would a wife do with me?" Mr. Helgate said. "The only one who will put up with me is him."

"I quite share that sentiment about a wife," Leo piped up.

Louisa flicked her brother's forehead with a finger. "What do you know, little brat? You're only ten years old."

"I'm old enough to know about the ways of the world."

Mr. Helgate let out a deep chuckle. "I like this lad."

"He is quite entertaining," Mortimer agreed.

His friend cast a glance at him. "Much like *you*."

Louisa stared at the two men's backs as they strode into the house. In this setting, conversing with a friend dressed equally humbly, while he still possessed an air of strength, the duke seemed more like a mortal man, rather than like the eternal, impervious god-like presence he projected at times.

She rather liked this duke.

"The lady and her brother can share the first room to the left upstairs. You are the one across from them," Mr. Helgate informed them, gesturing to the staircase.

Louisa inclined her head. "Thank you."

"I'd rather room with our gardener," Leo announced, folding his arms as if bracing for a fight.

Mr. Helgate arched a brow, his gaze shifting to Mortimer. "Gardener?"

The duke merely grunted in answer.

Louisa, on the other hand, narrowed her eyes on her brother. "You cannot sleep with him."

"Why not?" Leo demanded.

"Because you will disturb his sleep," she said, hands on her hips.

Her brother pulled a face. "I don't want to room with a girl."

"You had no trouble rooming with me last night."

"I was asleep when you took me to my room. Today, I'm not."

A true brat.

Although, Leo did have one hell of a kick in his sleep. Also, terrible sleeping posture. She flicked a glance at the duke. *Well.* "If our gardener allows it, who am I to disagree . . .?"

Leo puffed out his chest. "I shall not take no for an answer."

The duke stared at them, as if summoning patience from the depths of his soul. "So I do not get a say in the matter?"

Louisa lightly lifted her shoulders in a helpless shrug. "What can I do? The brat wants what the brat wants."

Leo nodded, satisfied.

Mortimer arched a brow at her brother. "Why aren't you pouting or protesting being called a brat?"

"Because it serves my purposes."

Mr. Helgate burst out laughing. "If he doesn't want you, lad, you can room with me."

"No," Mortimer said. "I'll take him."

"The offer stands." Mr. Helgate motioned to a drawing room with windows that overlooked the beach. "How about some tea or sherry? I have bread and cheese if you are hungry."

Louisa's ears perked up. "Sherry shall be wonderful. Leo will have some tea."

"Sister!" Leo protested.

"What? You don't believe I would actually give you sherry? Would you rather have some milk?"

He scrunched up his nose. "Fine, I shall have tea. Only children drink milk."

Louisa shook her head at his distaste. "I'm not a child, and I still enjoy milk."

"To sleep. There is a difference."

She caught the duke's curious look. He must be recalling the first night they met. She hadn't been in bed when he snuck into her chamber like a burglar. Come to think about it, would he have rummaged through her drawers if she'd been sleeping? Just where had he thought she was on discovering her gone? Clearly the bed had been unmade.

He must have guessed at her thoughts because his lips suddenly curved, not quite a smile, but close to it.

This sly duke.

She wouldn't be surprised if she'd walked right past him that night without realizing. A rather unsettling thought. But then, was a person's presence ever so tangible that one could sense it without seeing them? Had the hair on the back of her neck prickled at some point that night? She couldn't recall. But at that moment, a shiver traced down her spine.

Mortimer.

You are a dangerous, dangerous man.

OLIVER AVERTED HIS gaze and stepped to the windows overlooking the ocean. A slight breeze from an open one carried in a salty freshness, cutting through the sweetness of Lady Louisa's scent— but only for a moment. Soon, as if defying the wind itself, it fused with the crisp sea air, teasing him before the next gust granted him another fleeting breath of relief.

When it had started, he couldn't say, but somewhere between Ashford and Brighton, he'd begun noticing a faint trace of her. Soft at first, but as time wore on, it grew bolder and impossible to ignore. It was something inviting. Something intoxicating. Something undeniably *hers*.

Disarming.

He should have been able to ignore it, yet every time, it caught him off guard.

Helgate poured them each a glass of sherry and quickly disappeared before returning with young Leo's tea. A wry curve tugged at Oliver's mouth as Leo accepted the cup, his posture resembling that of a king more than a child.

The sweetness grew stronger.

His gaze shifted to Lady Louisa.

She had settled herself with her hip resting against the windowsill beside him, sipping her sherry, lost in the view. He let out a low breath. There was no escaping this. He still couldn't tear his thoughts away from the impossible reality of the moment. That she was here. Lady Louisa. With him. The entire scene seemed like a dream.

"So, you wish to approach the Fury brothers," Helgate said as he poured himself a sherry and joined Oliver.

He wrenched his gaze away from Lady Louisa and nodded his head. "Yes."

It was no secret that the Fury brothers ran the criminal side of Brighton. One wouldn't think that Brighton would have such a thing, but it was the main route for most of the smuggling operations in England. It was also close to several coastal towns and estates where nobles took to during the season. The Furys were no secret.

Unlike the *other* organization.

However, few dared to utter the Furys' names. Their power ran too deep in these parts. Bastard sons of the late Duke of Crane, they were the half-brothers to the current duke, though, if the whispers held any truth, there was little love lost between them.

"Just who are these men?" Louisa asked, looking at them. "They sound rather fascinating. All mystery and intrigue."

Oliver frowned. "They are dangerous, not intriguing."

"Yes, yes, and where do we find these rascals who approached my brother?"

Oliver glanced at Helgate, who answered, "If the description of the scars you described in your missive is accurate, you are looking for Maxen Fury and Dagger Fury. But there are seven of them altogether—byblows who took their own name and built an empire on it. They are not easy men to deal with."

"*Dagger* Fury?"

Oliver sighed, then gave a low chuckle. The fascination in her tone had returned tenfold. "A nickname, I gather?" he directed at Helgate, who nodded.

"Many of the Furys go by a nickname rather than their real names."

"Well," Lady Louisa said. "Unfortunately for this Maxen and Dagger," she smiled again, "we are not easy to deal with either."

"Do you have a plan?" Helgate asked, glancing between the two of them. "I hope you have a plan."

Oliver nodded. "Request nicely."

"A marvelous plan," Helgate said flatly. "When do you plan to ask nicely?"

"I vote for sooner rather than later," Louisa said, setting her sherry aside. "And after you've asked nicely, I would like to give them a piece of my mind for approaching a young child to do their dirty deeds."

Oliver's gaze locked with hers, and he inwardly sighed. He had expected this. Lady Louisa wouldn't tag along merely for the sake of tagging along. A wolf had approached her cub, and she now wanted to meet that wolf eye to eye. He would rather she not, but he also wasn't that worried. He'd be there every step of the way. He supposed that was worrisome in its own right—him indulging her to such an extent—but not so much that he wanted to dwell on the matter.

"I would not dare stop you," Oliver reassured when sudden challenge lit her gaze, as though she expected him to put up a fight. With anyone else, he would have.

"What about me?" Leo piped up.

"You, I dare stop," Oliver said without hesitation. One Talbot was enough.

The boy pouted, looking at his sister for help.

Louisa's lips twitched as she shrugged. "The man wants what the man wants."

"How about I take you fishing?" Helgate offered, tipping his head toward the shore. "We can have Miles cook the fish you catch."

The boy's eyes lit up. "Truly?"

Helgate pressed his hand over his heart, solemn as a judge. "Truly."

"No matter what the fish?"

Helgate paused, and so did Oliver. "We can cook any fish you catch, but I make no promise that I shall eat it."

Leo lifted his head a bit. "Very well. I shall stay and put food on the table since I am the provider in my father's stead."

"Right you are," Louisa agreed before she returned her gaze to the shore with a chuckle. "I cannot get enough of this view."

Oliver agreed. She was.

Helgate sent him a probing look, his voice dipping low, but not enough for it not to be overheard. "Do you know what you are doing?"

What a question. He wanted to say yes. He normally did. But he couldn't claim such a thing this time. It would be a lie. "I am addressing each circumstance as it presents itself."

Helgate arched a brow. "Since when do you deal with circumstances individually without thoroughly planning for them? Damn near drove me crazy with it in the past."

"Since recently." Oliver couldn't pretend he hadn't had much of a choice, because he had. He had made his choices, one after the other. He could have done things differently from the very start. "Be that as it may, what's done is done."

"Well, Godspeed, then."

Lady Louisa turned to them, amusement in her expression. "Godspeed? What a thing to say. You are talking about me, aren't you? I am one of the 'circumstances,' am I not? Good heavens, am I a harridan that the duke requires divine intervention?"

"No, my lady, but your family and,"—he cast a glance over Oliver—"and his aren't exactly what you would call friendly."

"Why aren't they friendly?" Leo asked from the sofa, setting his empty cup on the table. "Aren't you here to protect my sister? Her hired hand acting as a gardener, recently turned footman?"

Helgate burst out laughing. "Hired hand? My friend, you must have made quite the sacrifice. What did it cost you—your pride or your soul?"

Lady Louisa merely lifted her sherry to take a sip.

Oliver ignored his friend as well as the urge to ruffle the lad's hair. "When you're older, you can join the conversation about our families. For now, focus on how you can catch a fish."

Helgate scoffed. "Don't answer the question, then. You'll find the people you seek at The Raging Stag, a tavern in Brighton run by the brothers. Their lair of sorts."

"Not exactly subtle."

Helgate shrugged. "Hiding in plain sight. You can take my curricle. Your vehicle is too . . . notable. Word might reach Talbot if you are spotted exiting a carriage with his crest on it."

Oliver inclined his head. "Much obliged."

His friend turned to the young Talbot. "Care to see my stables while we ready the carriage? I have a mare that just gave birth to a foal."

The boy jumped to his feet. "Yes! I love baby animals!"

Oliver watched the two strode from the drawing room. It was the first time he'd glimpsed the pure delight of a child in that boy. He even had a slight skip in his step.

He turned to Lady Louisa. "You enjoy the beach?"

"I can't say I do, I can't say I don't," she answered thoughtfully. "I've never taken a walk on it before. But the view is quite breathtaking."

"You've never taken a stroll on a beach?"

"Well, no." Her gaze flicked to him then back at the ocean. "I've never had the urge, honestly. Now, I might develop one."

"Then I shall accompany you for a stroll," the words left his mouth before he could think better of it. He cleared his throat to cover the growing discomfort. "Sometime."

Her smile gave way to a light chuckle. "All right. But only after we retrieve the book for you."

He leaned against the window pane and crossed his arms. "You could have washed your hands of the book. There was no need to join me, so why did you?"

The smile slipped from her lips, and a moment of silence stretched before she said, "That's right, I do have a reason, and I would like some answers from you. I had almost forgotten about it. Camilla. My stepmother."

Oliver stilled. "What about her?"

"You made a comment about her. Subtle, but the more I think about it, the more I think you are hiding something from me."

Ah, yes. He had done that. He hadn't thought she would catch it. What else had she picked up on? Was she aware of her stepmother's secrets? Did she know more than she let on? "I am not hiding anything, Lady Louisa. I simply choose not to tell."

"Which, of course, is your right, but when it comes to my stepmother, I want to get to the bottom of every nuance."

You and me both, angel. "Understood."

"Well," she pressed. "Are you going to tell me or not?"

Oliver hesitated. If he told her, it would be yet another gamble. "The truth may not serve you well. She is your stepmother, after all. Your father's wife."

"Be that as it may, I should still like to be the judge of that."

As she should be. But what about *his* judgment? It seemed every moment in her presence whittled away at it. Still, he chose to admit, "The betting book is proof of a criminal organization with dealings in smuggling and will reveal the involvement of many aristocrats."

"Yes, I already know that. The secret women's club." Her eyes widened. "Are you telling me my stepmother is involved in that organization?"

"I believe she is the head of it."

Her mouth dropped open.

Oliver couldn't help but flash a grin, and he leaned in close to ask, even though he already saw the truth reflected in her eyes. "Tell me, Lady Louisa, are you with them as well?"

Chapter Nine

LOUISA STEPPED INTO The Raging Stag, still irked at the irksome duke who questioned whether she was in collusion with her stepmother. She inwardly snorted for the hundredth time. How ludicrous! On some level, she knew he had been teasing her, but she couldn't help being bothered by it. She would rather chew glass than be cut from the same cloth as that woman!

She glanced at Mortimer.

Lawks, the man was tall. And aloof. And impossibly vexing. His facial muscles rarely moved. She supposed that hunting criminals as a duke, it was a rather good skill to possess. If one could even call it a skill.

"Keep close," Mortimer said in a hushed voice.

"I shall be fine."

Sharp eyes flicked over her face. "I suppose you are right. Nevertheless, don't storm the castle's soldiers."

What is *that* supposed to mean? But she had no time to dwell on it for immediately she felt the prickle of four shrewd gazes falling on them.

"Well, well, well, what do we have here?" One of the men with a scar slashing through his left brow said, rising from his seat at the bar to his full height. "A little bird and a hawk."

Louisa's eyes widened to saucers before she caught herself and smoothed out her features. Goodness, that man was even taller than the duke! Bulkier too. Big and scary, just as Leo had said. Her eyes narrowed on them. So, these were the men who approached a small boy? She understood now why her brother had done what these men told him.

Scoundrels!

"Gentlemen," Mortimer greeted.

"There are no gentlemen here."

Lord, spare her the dramatics. Louisa narrowed her eyes at the man. Since he was the one who rose to speak, she focused her attention on him. "You are right, clearly there are only dogs. Were you one of them, sniffing around the boots of my brother?"

The man suddenly gave a low laugh. "The lady chirps."

"Reaper," the man behind the bar said. A scar split his lip, just like Leo had described, but *big* and *scary* did not do his presence any justice. The man looked nothing short of menacing. Deadly. "What brings a duke and the daughter of a duke here?"

And they knew who they were.

"Good," Mortimer spoke up with a low drawl. "There is no need for an introduction. You must be Maxen Fury."

The man didn't smile. He also didn't confirm or deny the duke's assertion. "You won't get what you came here for."

"Hah!" Louisa exclaimed, annoyance flaring. "You resemble the likes of big, bad brutes, and yet you had to resort to browbeating a boy to get what you want."

Those dark, almost black, eyes settled on her. "We still got what we wanted, didn't we? And we merely asked the lad for a favor. He provided."

"Then, do *you* owe him a favor now? This is how your world works, no?"

The man called Reaper laughed. "I quite like this one. If only she weren't one of *them.*"

"One of whom?" Mortimer stole the question from her lips.

"That pesky women's club or whatever they call themselves," Reaper bit out with a scowl.

"I am not part of that club," Louisa snapped, irritation surging anew. Of the four brothers present, he was the most talkative, and the most infuriating. Every word from his mouth seemed designed to prick at her patience, like stepping barefoot onto a bed of thorns.

Reaper's eyes bore into hers. "Your mother, on the other hand, is very much the bane of our existence with her club and their shenanigans. Do you really expect us to believe you are not also part of it?"

"*Step*mother," Louisa pointed out through clenched teeth.

"Same thing."

"They are not the same thing, you simpleton, and I don't rightly care what you believe."

"Reaper," the one called Maxen interjected. To Louisa, he said. "Forgive my brother. His tongue is sharper than his head." Reaper growled at that, but Maxen continued, ignoring him, "This book is something the duchess wants, so when we heard it fell into your hands, we had to retrieve it."

"How do you even know if *fell* into my hands?"

"We have been following the book's trail since it disappeared from White's."

"You mean you've been following the heiresses," Mortimer said sharply, and Louisa sensed his displeasure.

Maxen said nothing.

Dear Lord, had they been spied upon from the very start? "How? You couldn't possibly know who had the book at any given time."

Reaper shrugged. "How else? A strategy as old as time."

"Servants," Mortimer muttered.

Reaper grinned. "And a bit of luck."

Honestly, could you not trust anyone in this world?

"What's done is done," Mortimer said, his indifference back. "But we do require that book to deal with the matter of the secret women's organization."

"Well, what do you know, *Duke*?" Reaper said. "We needed it for the same reason."

"I refuse to accept we are at an impasse," Mortimer said. "There must be a sort of compromise we can come to?"

Louisa nodded. She was not leaving Brighton without the book. No matter what they had to do. Lord, what if Mortimer decided to break into these men's property to find it next? They weren't the sort of men to merely brandish a knife without drawing blood, were they?

"Maxen," a voice came from the shadows. Another bulky man, but his face was partly obscured by a cap. Louisa couldn't make out his features.

The brothers shared a brief look before Maxen inclined his head. "We shall exchange the book for something else."

Louisa folded her hands over her chest, not the least bit surprised that she wasn't surprised. There was always *something* with men like this. "Whatever it may be, you still owe a favor to my brother."

"If you can deliver this," Maxen responded, his dark eyes meeting hers. "Even though I never promised one, I don't mind owing the future Duke of Talbot a favor if it's within reason."

Heh. Within reason. As if approaching a young boy to steal a book from his sister was within reason! "What do wish to exchange?"

"A ledger from the Countess of Havendish. It will most likely look like a brown leather journal of some sort. If you get it for us, you can have the betting book."

Louisa paused, frozen, which drew a look from the duke.

"What is it?" he asked softly.

Her head tilted to him, meeting his gaze. "My father and stepmother ought to be at the Havendish estate in Worthing at the moment."

"I see."

"Why do you want this ledger?" she asked Maxen. "Is it the same as the betting book?" It had to be as useful—if not more so—if they'd exchange the book for it.

"More or less," the man answered. "At least we won't be at a loss trading the book for the ledger."

In other words, they'd still have their leverage over the women's club. Perhaps even more. He didn't say it outright, but he didn't have to. The answer rested plainly in what he left unsaid. Her gaze returned to Mortimer.

"Is there a problem with this exchange?" Reaper's annoying voice came.

Louisa ignored him, her mind racing. She didn't know how to feel about this request, or demand, she should say, but one look at these men . . . They weren't going to give in, and she and Mortimer certainly wouldn't be able to pry the book from their beefy hands.

To her shock, Mortimer asked her, "What do you want to do?" He stared at her steadily, and although those facial muscles—which she just wanted to pinch and poke and pull apart—remained smooth, she perceived the earnestness underlying his question.

"We . . ." she broke their gaze and turned to Maxen, "shall do it. You have a deal." And if they couldn't find the ledger in question, they would just forge one for the book. Or steal the book back in some way or the other. That shouldn't be a problem given the duke's capabilities and connections. Probably.

That brute turned his gaze to Mortimer and raised a brow. God bless his soul, Mortimer didn't hesitate to say, "As the lady said, you have yourself an arrangement. The book for the ledger."

Louisa snuck a peak at Mortimer. Why did it seem another meaning lay beneath his agreement? An edge slightly veiled.

Maxen nodded. "One last thing."

Louisa scowled at the man.

"We'll want collateral," the man finished.

"For what purpose?" Louisa snapped.

"So you keep your word."

Why wouldn't they keep their word, for Heaven's sake? They were the ones that wanted the book! Something seemed off here. "And what about your word?" she countered. "What collateral do *we* have?"

"I'll send a man with you."

Honestly! "That's not collateral—it's intimidation. And just what collateral do you want exactly?"

"Your brother traveled with you, did he not?"

Louisa stiffened, and almost immediately a hand circled her wrist gently.

"You can send one of your brethren with us," Mortimer's unaffected voice came. "But we are not handing the young heir over to you. If you must, you can send another brother to him at Helgate's estate. I trust you know where that is already."

Louisa's head whipped to him. He didn't return her probing gaze, yet she could feel his decidedness, and for some unfathomable reason, she did not resist. The fingers on her wrist squeezed slightly.

She trusted him.

For some reason, she believed deep within that this man would not disappoint her. And he would never let any harm come to Leo. Whoever they sent to Mr. Helgate's cottage . . . God save *his* soul, for that person's life would be on the line if anything happened to her brother.

Maxen arched a brow. "Helgate? Are you sure it's fine to have one of our men go to his residence?"

"He'll have no problem with it," Mortimer said.

"That still doesn't seem fair," Louisa said. "So you have my brother *and* the book. What do we have?"

Maxen motioned to Reaper. "You get him."

"Like I said," Louisa muttered. "What do we get?" This stinky man? They were most definitely at a disadvantage here while the Furys got to keep a close eye on them.

Reaper narrowed his eyes to slits. "Can you handle it, little bird? One of my dog brothers will be approaching yours again."

Louisa snorted. "My brother is better dealing with dogs than I am, it's true."

Mortimer chuckled.

And that low laughter seemed to reach within Louisa and latch onto her bones. Why did it feel as though she had reached the edge of a cliff, and she had no other recourse but to jump?

Early the next morning

"A PENNY FOR your thoughts," Oliver asked Lady Louisa. Worthing was about ten miles west of Brighton, and they had been on the road for about an hour and had one more to go before they reached their destination. And the angel hadn't said one word in all that time.

She parted the curtain to peek out of the carriage window to where the Fury called Reaper was following on horseback. "It's like they don't trust us at all."

"They don't."

"Well, I am thinking if they want that ledger so badly, perhaps we should keep it." Her gaze met his. "You owe me a penny."

A penny suddenly felt fascinatingly scandalous. Her idea was also intriguing. "Double cross the brothers? And here I thought you were worried about your own brother."

"You had them send a Fury to Mr. Helgate. There must be a reason for this. And as you saw, he enjoys fishing. I don't imagine he's even missing me. I'm more concerned about my father. Since the betting book is evidence, it must mean the husbands of the women in the club are involved, correct? Only men would be able to make entries in White's betting book, after all."

Oliver nodded. The women didn't have access to the betting book. But whether the Duke of Talbot specifically was involved, he couldn't be sure. He would only be able to tell once he had the book in his possession. Quite frankly, he should have gotten the book from the heiresses much sooner, but he had been content to know that he could retrieve it at any time.

That was his biggest mistake.

And it wasn't like him.

However, he couldn't deny that he had been rather amused at the heiresses' behavior and, if he had to be further honest, had been indulging the antics. Since the investigation had been slow, and he had found the secret club's tavern, he had thought he had a bit more time before the contents of the book would become necessary.

She lowered her voice suddenly. "Back to those blasted beasts. Think about it. What can they really do? And who knows, this ledger might help you better in your investigation, no?"

Oliver nodded. It pleased him that she trusted him to the degree that she did. There were multiple times she could have lost her calm, but she had never lost it once. "Depending on the contents."

"Do you believe the ledger has something to do with the women's club?"

"Most definitely." Of that, he had no doubt. Otherwise, they wouldn't trade their only leverage for it. Only, while the betting book was evidence of the club's illicit dealings with the *ton*, the ledger likely contained true accounts of some sort. Perhaps it logged details revealing contacts or shipping routes. If that were the case, it would be invaluable for his investigation—and would also implicate the Havendish family.

Her brow scrunched. "I suppose we shall have to see."

"You want to teach them a lesson that badly?"

"They irk me." Her gaze met his. "Do they not irk you?"

"I've faced worse."

"I can imagine," she said with a nod. "Speaking of which, what shall happen to my stepmother if she truly is the ringleader and she is caught? Is it your objective to march her down the streets of London and into a trial?"

Oliver's lips briefly tugged upward at the vivid picture that filled his head. "Is that what you want?"

"I mean," she began with a devilish glint in her eyes, "I'm not opposed to the idea."

He wasn't either. "Unfortunately, what happens depends on Bow Street as well as your father. He has many connections, and this is the kind of scandal that could ruin your family's name." The fact of the matter was that the duke could probably crush any trial against his wife and deal with her on his terms if he wished to do so. He had enough clout for this. But punishment wasn't Oliver's purview. "My objective is to bring the conduct to heel."

"The Talbot family name will survive the scandal. We are a sturdy bunch." She peeked out of the window again. "What about those Furys' conduct? They are criminals, too. Will you go after them next?"

Oliver shook his head. "They are none of my concern."

"That's rather biased, is it not?"

Well, he was rather biased, honestly. His gaze met her curious one. "I am assisting in this matter because my mother asked me to help dismantle the club."

"Your *mother*? How surprising." A short pause. "Wait! Do not tell me she was a member?"

"No," Oliver denied. "One of her friends, on the other hand, was very much involved but wanted to withdraw. When she tried, her son was beaten within an inch of his life and her life was threatened."

"Holy stars, what happened to her then?"

Oliver shrugged. "They fled to Scotland to hide. My mother followed to keep her company. The entire affair is unacceptable."

"Well, you certainly are a good son."

"I didn't have much of a choice in this regard," Oliver said, recalling the last letter he received from his mother. "She is standing her ground alongside her friend in Scotland until this club is destroyed. I also find their actions unacceptable."

"Brave woman."

Oliver stared at Lady Louisa, his gaze tracing the smooth skin of her cheeks. Yesterday, in The Raging Stag, he had been impressed by her mettle. This angel had a backbone that few ladies possessed. *She* was a brave woman.

"Shall you be joining the house party," Lady Louisa jolted him out of his thoughts, "as a duke or servant?"

"Servant," Oliver said without hesitation. Talbot was at the party. Showing up the same day as his daughter might not be the strongest strategy since the man was suspicious by nature. At least, from what Oliver had seen so far.

"That is probably for the best."

Her knee brushed against him, and a ripple of awareness trickled along his spine. His fingers twitched. He hadn't been this aware of a woman in a long, long time. In fact, had he ever been this aware of a woman before?

He shrugged off the thought.

Naturally, he would be aware of Louisa Talbot. She was a *Talbot*. Every nerve, every instinct he possessed leaped to alertness with every movement and every word she spoke.

"You had your reservations about the duchess before I told you of her involvement. May I ask why?"

A moment of silence fell before she answered, "I'm not sure. It's more of a feeling I get whenever I'm in her presence. She is also a different person in front of my father than she is else-where."

Oliver nodded thoughtfully. "It makes sense. If she is the true head of this organization then I would imagine she would be rather good at manipulating people. She is also blessed with a fair, innocent face, which must help."

A snort. "There is nothing fair and innocent about that wom-an. A conniving and scheming person. My father must be blind as a bat or . . ."

She didn't need to finish the sentence. He understood. Or her father might very well be part of the organization. "Will your father question your sudden attendance?"

She shrugged. "I shall tell him I was bored and decided to join when I heard Theodosia would attend. She is the reason I'm in this pickle, is she not?"

Oliver arched a brow. Her brother was the real reason, but he decided not to point that out. "Is she attending?"

"No, but I shall then claim I must have gotten it wrong."

"They might not wish you to leave until the party is over." Best be prepared for anything.

"Oh, no need to worry about that. My father is rather lenient with my whims. Otherwise, I would have been betrothed the moment the heiress scandal lit up all the gossip pages."

Ah, right. "Yes, I heard chatter that he might marry you off."

"All bluster."

"Well, if it's any consolation, I do not believe your father would stoop to outright criminal activities such as smuggling."

"Unless we became paupers and required blunt."

"You don't sound optimistic."

"I have learned that when it comes to powerful men, one cannot rule out anything." Her gaze met his. "Men such as you."

Her words hit like a blow. "You don't like men such as me?"

"I don't."

Ever so blunt. Oliver couldn't blame her. She'd been abducted when she was young as a means to gain the upper hand in a dispute over property. Rather disheartening, that.

"You know, ever since we met that night you broke into my chamber, I've found a sense of familiarity come over me from time to time when we meet gazes. I wonder why."

Oliver flinched. "Perhaps you have heard so many Cavanagh horror stories over time that you now feel a certain amount of recognition when we meet."

She sent him a skeptical look. "I'm not sure. I've never really lent my ears to Cavanagh horror tales."

She hadn't? "Is that why you do not regard me as a family enemy? Even to the point of traveling with me to Brighton? Bringing your brother along?"

"The enmity is between you and my father. I, for one, don't have the energy to fret about such things."

"I doubt your father would be happy to hear that," Oliver pointed out. Talbot might even challenge him to a duel in the future if he discovered Oliver had traveled alone with his daughter through the countryside.

"Then, he shall never hear it. Once my stepmother is dealt with, we shall go our separate ways and none shall be the wiser."

So, optimistic, this angelic creature. "Your brother is the wiser."

"Leo lives for secrets. He shall keep this one. If all goes well, this family feud shall die with you and Papa."

A man could hope.

Chapter Ten

LOUISA STEPPED INTO the drawing room the footman led her to, filled with the women who were guests of the party, as well as the host, Lady Havendish. She'd left the duke at the stables with the carriage and their horses. As well as that rascal called Reaper. The duke, however, had instructions to rest the horses but to have them ready to be harnessed again as soon as possible.

The plan was clear.

She'd find a time to search the house, locate the ledger, then they would leave post haste back to Brighton.

However, the more she thought about it, the more flawed this plan became. For one, she'd be leaving after she found the ledger. Would this not cast immediate suspicion onto her when the ledger was then discovered to be missing?

Also, she had pretended it was not a problem before, but it *would* get her into a spot of trouble with her father. Even if she weren't suspected, or if the ledger weren't found missing soon after she left, it would still be rather rude to join a party and leave the next day without so much as a by your leave.

Louisa decided she'd slip away like a ghost in the night. She'd thought of other ways, but she couldn't merely claim something like illness, for then they'd expect her to recuperate here.

She stared at the ladies, who all turned their heads to stare at *her.*

This part was the worst. She really didn't want to be here!

Perhaps she would use Theodosia as an excuse to leave, since that was her excuse for coming and Theodosia clearly wasn't here. Another course of action could be to leave word that she'd received a message from a friend that they needed help in an urgent matter, though if someone did a thorough check of that one, she might be caught in the lie.

Would it even matter, though?

Hopefully, by then, the truth would be out about this blasted women's club, and everyone would have forgotten about her rudeness.

Why then, did her heart flutter like a trapped bird??

"Louisa?" The Duchess of Talbot's gaze widened in what Louisa could only assume was true disbelief and false delight. "What are you doing here?"

Louisa's gaze swept over the drawing room, brushing past the silent scrutiny, before falling on her stepmother again. "I've found myself in the mood for some company."

"Well," Lady Havendish said with a smile, "you are most welcome. Come sit. You are quite on time. There is a masquerade ball tonight."

Masquerade ball?

Louisa's mood cleared a bit, as she lowered into an empty chair. That was indeed quite perfect! It may even benefit Mortimer, who could use the cover to sneak into the house. Then again, seeing how he was dressing like a working man these days, she doubted he would come as himself. The corner of her lips inched upward. Would she be able to see him in livery again?

With a mask?

She could just imagine the dashing figure he would cut. He'd be able to move a bit more freely in the house, while she would use the masked ball to slip away and search her host's bedchamber. That should be the likely spot to hide an incriminating item of value. It was where she would hide it if she were part of a secret club and kept a private ledger.

"I do so enjoy a masquerade ball."

"Indeed," the duchess said, her smile tight. "It seems this must be fate."

"Fate?" Louisa said with an equally tight stretch of lips. Her stepmother's tone put her instantly on guard. "Why?"

"Since you are here, there is someone I would like to introduce you to tonight," the duchess answered with a gleam that put Louisa further on edge.

Lawks, this would not be good. In fact, this could be really, really bad. "Oh? And who might that be?"

"The Earl of Westbridgeson."

Curses she would never utter out loud flew across her mind.

"Ah." Louisa fought to keep her smile in place. All eyes turned to her reaction, so she took a page from Mortimer's book to keep her countenance as cool as a fresh, crisp breeze. "I am sure he is an interesting fellow." *With your nails dug deep into him.*

Considering what she'd recently discovered about her stepmother and presumably her stepmother's friends, every single woman in this drawing room took on a suspicious aspect.

She could not trust anyone in this house.

"And quite handsome," Lady Havendish said with a smile that didn't quite reach her eyes, yet her gaze held some sort of excitement in them, nevertheless.

Louisa shivered.

One of the other women, Lady Keening, poured Louisa a cup of tea. "Have some honey tea, Lousia. You must be weary from your journey."

"Oh, it wasn't that far," Louisa said lightly, willing her heart to stop throbbing in her ears. "The journey was quite uneventful." If you could call sharing a carriage with a man who exuded raw power with one mere gaze and constantly stole small increments of his companion's breath uneventful. Stole *her* breath.

But she preferred *that* over *this*.

Honestly, Louisa!

She accepted the cup from Lady Keening, a beautiful woman who could be considered in her prime. If only she didn't have ties to her stepmother and their host. Her gaze flicked over the other ladies who were chatting away in all corners of the room, most not paying her any attention anymore except for the occasional glance.

So, this was how it felt to enter the den of predators. Like a pack of hyenas, each gaze glinted with cunning, always assessing, and always calculating.

They would sense the smallest weakness.

But so long as Louisa revealed no weakness and did not challenge these gazes, no teeth would be bared her way. Fortunately, her only weakness was in Brighton. *Unfortunately*, a wolf had already entered *that* den.

She brought the teacup to her lips and took a sip. Lawks. No sugar. Smile, Louisa! Her composure was her strength! She set the cup on the table. "I would very much enjoy some rest before the ball tonight if that is possible?"

"Of course," the duchess said as if this were *her* household. "I shall inform your father of your arrival when he returns."

Lady Havendish nodded.

"Where is Papa?" She hadn't glimpsed any gentlemen yet.

"He is out hunting today with the other gentlemen."

In Worthing? What on earth would they be hunting? Birds? An inward snort. Hyenas? They need not look any further than this room. In any event, it seemed everyone at the party was on the hunt in one way or another.

At least she was not being scolded for joining the party without notice.

What was Mortimer doing at that moment? Not to mention that man, Reaper. Hopefully, they were both staying out of sight. There was no way she'd be able to explain her "hires" to her father, and never mind that scarred Fury, the duke would recognize the other duke instantly.

"It's a shame the earl went hunting as well," Lady Keening said. "The two of you could have taken a delightful stroll in the garden."

Delightful? *No, thank you.*

"And we have a lovely conservatory," Lady Havendish added.

What did that have to do with her? She enjoyed greenery but not enough to idly wander in a conservatory with a man she had no interest in. She dipped her head politely at Lady Havendish. "I'm sure there shall be ample time to view the gardens and conservatory."

"The masked ball shall have to do for now," her stepmother said. "I hope you have brought your best dress."

Ah, no. She hadn't.

Lady Havendish nodded. "Yes, tonight is special. We will present a marvel from the depths of the ocean, and tomorrow, that marvel will grace our plates as a rare delicacy."

How . . . delightful.

Louisa gave a slight nod, her mind racing over her belongings rather than fixing on this rare delicacy, whatever it was. She had packed for the trip—a trip to Brighton to see criminals—but nothing extravagant. Nothing the duchess would approve of. In fact, she had a dress with her that Camilla would absolutely hate.

Her grin turned inward.

She lived to displease her stepmother.

And it wasn't as if she wanted to shine her brightest for this earl they wished to introduce her to, either. "I have just the dress in mind."

A simple black day dress. Thoroughly out of fashion, since it was one of the dresses she always wore on the anniversary of her mother's death, as well as the anniversary of the day she was taken captive. It would do perfectly.

Which reminded her . . .

What day was it today? If she was not misplacing *time*, that bittersweet day was tomorrow.

Lawks. It *was* tomorrow . . .

Her twentieth birthday.

And the ninth anniversary of her mother's death and the tenth anniversary of her abduction. Birthdays were not days she usually enjoyed celebrating. Her most terrifying and saddest memories had happened on them. Yet somehow this year, she'd almost completely forgotten. Well, then, she'd just have to make the most of tonight, wouldn't she?

"THERE IS A masked ball tonight."

"I know." Oliver stared at the neat scrawl on the note from Lousia, not bothering to lift his head to the Fury who had followed them. He cursed his inability to observe and act fast if something were to happen out of his control. He wanted to be inside that house. He wanted to keep an eye on the angel who could turn impulsive at any moment.

Discomfort gnawed at him.

He despised the sensation. It made him feel weak. Powerless. Had he made the right decision? Sending her into that den of vipers without him? Send her in at all?

He almost barked out a laugh. What decision had he even made? She had all the power here.

His gaze swept over the corner of the stables they occupied. He had his own matters to attend to. The men had gone hunting and would return soon, so they would have to keep out of sight as much as possible.

He stretched his legs, shifting on the small stool beneath him.

"Are you attending?" Reaper asked, dangling a mask from his fingertips.

Oliver frowned at the swinging item. "Are *you*?"

"And what if I'm considering it?"

"The moment you set foot in that house, I'll alert everyone of an imposter with a scar on his face."

Reaper tossed the mask at him. "This damn scar," he said, mockery thick in his voice. "Always a damn hindrance."

"Then you shouldn't have gotten cut there."

The statement earned him a menacing look. "What about you, cavorting with the enemy's daughter? That might leave a scar of its own."

Oliver's jaw tightened. No need to tell him that. He could feel it with every passing moment—each second with her dug deeper into his flesh. "At least I don't browbeat ten-year-olds."

"As my brother said, we asked, and he provided."

Oliver scowled at the man. "He provided because he was a boy trying to protect his family. That lad took one look at you and saw danger. I wouldn't be surprised if he even saw adventure."

"You cannot fault us for *that*."

"Why not?" Oliver challenged, his gaze steady. These men were rough but not fools. They had even offered sweets. "I can fault you on many things."

Reaper plopped down on a patch of hay. "But you are not going to, are you?"

Oliver shrugged, his shoulders stiff with annoyance. "Only because I don't wish to waste my breath on vermin."

"We might be vermin, but we are still the vermin people need."

Oliver arched a brow at the man. "And what people are they?"

Reaper leaned back, crossing his arms over his chest as he studied Oliver. "People below the notice of a duke."

"There are no people beneath my notice."

"I find that hard to believe," Reaper retorted, biting down a piece of straw. "You are but one man. We serve the majority, those below the consideration of you privileged few."

Louisa called her brother a little brat, but this Fury . . . What a bloody *brat*. "Stop taunting me and do what you came to do."

"I came to keep a watch on you."

"Does keeping watch require you to use your mouth?"

"What can I do?" The man shrugged. "My mouth moves on its own, I don't have any power over it."

Oliver laid the full weight of his gaze on the man, who could be a bit younger than him, or at least the same age. "I went along with your brother's requests, but do not believe for one moment that I need to."

"Same here, Duke." The man studied him, chewing his piece of straw. "So you choose to go after this organization because it is run by your ladies. What about us bastards? Will you come after us next?"

Oliver caught the dark note of curiosity in that question. "Trust me, Fury, you don't want my eyes on you. For now, we need each other, after that, I don't care what you do so long as you don't care what I do."

"Being the smart man you are, you must have figured out our plan, why we want the ledger."

"You plan to absorb their routes."

"Will you try to stop us?"

"Why would I do that?" He didn't plan, nor did he want, to start a war with the likes of the Fury brothers. Some battles were better fought by those who had less to lose. "Do what you want."

The man's features turned disbelieving. "Aren't you a man of self-justice?"

"I'm not that polite." Oliver glanced at the crest of the carriage he guarded. The angel's. He had taken on this battle because of his mother, but he would finish it for her. "I am very much a man of self-interest."

Reaper chuckled darkly. "A true peer."

Oliver shrugged. What could he say? "Yes."

"So bloody blunt. Annoying."

The corner of his lips lifted in a wry smile. "Is this not our strength, staying true to our nature?"

Reaper's lips curled in a derisive smile. "True to our nature? Maybe for you. For the likes of me, staying true to my nature means you end up with a knife in your back. Aren't you happy I'm steering clear of this 'nature'?"

"Not untrue."

"Then why does it sound as though you do not agree?"

"I don't know if I agree, I don't know if I don't," Oliver replied coolly. "But perhaps your nature is not as menacing as you think."

"You mean I'm a puppy, not a wolf?"

Not a puppy, no. Oliver shrugged, not answering. Let the man draw his own conclusion.

"Hell. I wish Maxen were here to hear that. He'd have a good laugh." He gestured to the mask. "So, will you let your little swallow fly in the lead, or will you spread your hawk wings and follow?"

Oliver glanced at the mask disregarded on a patch of hay. Truthfully, he didn't mind taking the lead, he didn't mind following hers either.

A first.

An absolute first.

He snatched up the mask, his finger running over its edges as he inspected it. "What if we don't hand over the ledger when we find it?"

"Then you will never get the book."

Oliver lifted his body from the stool, his gaze meeting Reaper's. "I already have the book."

The man scowled, spitting out the straw in his mouth. "What are you saying? We have it."

"You have the original. Copies of the pages were made ages ago."

Reaper unfolded from the hay and slowly rose to his feet as well, his body rigid with displeasure. "Then what the hell are we doing here?"

"The original book would be ideal, but maybe this ledger would be a bit more ideal for me."

"My brother is with the heir of Talbot's dukedom."

Oliver straightened out his arms and shoulders. "You have not met *my* brothers, blood or not. Nor have you met Leo Talbot. I wouldn't stack the odds against the lad."

"You've grown fond of your nemesis's offspring, especially the little bird."

Had he? He certainly could not deny his body's response, nor his mind which could not help but constantly drift her way. Yet none of that held much bearing when weighed against the facts of their situation. And he . . . had kept some important ones from her.

Himself.

That one word—himself—echoed back and forth in his mind. Him? No matter how fond he'd grown of her, he couldn't be anything to her, whether friend, acquaintance, or more. And the fact that *more* even existed in his thoughts right now . . . But it could never be him. His family had caused too much trauma. There were still nights—very rare, but they came—when his dreams filled with her cries.

If she ever discovered the truth, she would finally see his family for what they were: foes, even though he himself didn't consider them as such.

In any event, it was all moot, since he was merely testing the man's response by threatening to make off with the ledger. And Reaper, except for a scowl and a growl, didn't seem all that bothered.

Arrogant.

The man cleared his throat loudly. Oliver glanced at him. "What?"

He laid a set of neatly folded livery on Oliver's stool. "You might need this."

"Where the devil did that come from?" He'd only disappeared for a short while before returning with the mask, and he hadn't seen any clothes. "Are you that confident I won't back out from our understanding?"

Reaper shrugged. "Even if you do, we have our ways."

And Oliver had his.

This was why he didn't care to challenge the brothers. They would destroy each other in the process. Leave that to Bow Street or the constables who enjoyed the fight.

"If you don't want to go, I don't mind if I do," Reaper said lazily, plopping down on the hay again.

"I'll go," Oliver replied, fishing out Lady Louisa's note from his pocket and trailing a thumb over the ink.

"I thought as much. So eager to reunite with your lady."

He was, but not for the suggestive reasons Reaper implied. Even so, the last sentence of her note that had caused his jaw to tense the moment he'd read it. Apparently, her stepmother was intent on introducing her to the Earl of Westbridgeson. It was written as a complaint but . . .

He didn't like it.

"I need a favor."

Reaper lifted his brow. "You want me to do something as horrible as enter as a servant, don't you?"

"No," Oliver said. "I need you to go visit some taverns in town and ask about Lord and Lady Havendish's routines and if they have met with anyone that stands out."

"Why?" Reaper asked skeptically.

"Call it a feeling I have." Which had nothing to do with Lord or Lady Havendish or their ledger.

But everything to do with *her*.

Chapter Eleven

T HE MOMENT LOUISA stepped into the ballroom, her eyes were drawn to the buzz of activity caused by the eccentric display set up by their extravagant host. In the center of the room stood a large, delicately constructed glass tank, slightly foggy with condensation. Inside, a single writhing octopus moved sluggishly, its tentacles trailing through the water. So this was the marvel from the depths of the ocean Lady Havendish had spoken of earlier.

Louisa could hardly believe her eyes.

An octopus, here, at a country ball? She didn't know if she should be fascinated or horrified, since the creature itself was fascinating, yet it would grace their plates tomorrow. This was a reminder to the guests of the host's richness and the hard truth of the lengths some would go to entertain their guests.

She shivered.

She'd rather skip that meal. Another reason to find the ledger quickly and leave tonight. She much preferred the ocean view from Mr. Helgate's cottage.

Louisa slowly made her way over to the tank perched on a table. The creature clung to the glass, its tentacles splayed, each movement sending small ripples through the tank. Laughter and whispers crackled around her. Some found the octopus grotesque, others exotic. She felt a pang of pity for the creature's plight. It would not be able to escape its fate in this life.

Little octopus, you shall undoubtedly be the talk of the county for weeks to come.

A prickling sensation at the nape of her neck stiffened her spine. A presence. Unseen, but unmistakable. A shadow fell over the octopus, and her gaze lifted to meet a pair of eyes staring at her from the other side of the tank through a black mask.

A frisson of awareness traveled down her back.

Mortimer.

She would recognize those eyes—that gaze—anywhere. She couldn't look away. He seemed to pull her into an unfathomable daze, one of which she found impossible to describe. This man, from beginning to end, captured her fascination. And she could not deny that part of this fascination might stem from the fact that they were not supposed to be in contact. That at any moment, if her father were to discover their connection, a storm would be released, and a reckoning would follow.

She lifted her hand and placed it on the glass separating them. A flicker of something unreadable passed through his expression.

"Lady Louisa."

Louisa blinked, brought out of her daze by an unfamiliar voice. She turned to the gentleman who approached her, her brows furrowing. "I'm sorry, have we met?"

The man smiled. "No, we haven't been properly introduced, so forgive my boldness." He bowed slightly. "I'm Lord West-bridgeson. I saw you standing here and grew quite impatient for our introduction."

Oh, it was him. "Lord Westbridgeson, how did you recognize me?"

"I've been aware of you for some time, and a mask could never hide your Talbot beauty."

He'd been aware of her for some time? Did that mean he'd been watching her? Louisa touched the mask Lady Havendish provided. She didn't care for this man approaching her so boldly, especially given who desired to introduce him.

She resisted the urge to shoot a glance at Mortimer. "I am flattered, my lord." Repulsed, more like, but she swallowed it down with a smile.

He glanced at the octopus. "Remarkable creature, is it not?"

Louisa's fists clenched before she forced them to relax. "Rather pitiful, I believe."

"You do not enjoy the sight?"

Her gaze moved from Lord Westbridgeson to the tank again, but the figure on the other side had already disappeared.

Wait a second!

Had he been dressed in the Havendish *livery*? Ah, well, she would get a better look later. For now, she had to rid herself of this eager lord, who carried himself with the quiet assurance of a man who had never doubted his place in the world. A man who didn't doubt his inevitable introduction to her. Glancing around to avoid looking directly at the man, she could see her father and Camilla hadn't arrived yet. In fact, she hadn't once caught sight of her father since she'd arrived, as the men had returned from their hunting while she'd been resting. That might be a good thing. She didn't know how well her composure would hold up if she did meet him here.

She suddenly wanted to slip away as soon as possible.

"Lady Louisa?"

She blinked at the octopus. "If you must know, I can't say that it's all that appealing. I think it's a rather cruel sight."

"Because the animal is caged?"

"Because it's on display while caged, almost taunting the poor creature that its fate is no longer his own." Her gaze returned to Lord Westbridgeson. "A beautiful creature. A lonely fate."

"His fate was never his own to begin with, my lady."

The words chilled her blood, and something unpleasant trickled down her spine. The words seemed almost to possess a meaning that stretched beyond the octopus. Fortunately, she, Louisa Talbot, was not an octopus.

"Speaking of which, how *did* you become acquainted with

my stepmother?"

The question seemed to startle him. "I was introduced by Lady Havendish."

"I see." She studied him for a moment. "Are you and Lady Havendish close?" She remembered the way Lady Havendish's eyes had glinted when she'd spoken of this man. They should be more than close if that was any indication.

"We have been friends for a while. Same with her husband."

"I see." Louisa doubted he was on the same terms with Lord Havendish as with Lady Havendish. Call her mad, but it was just a feeling she got—all was not what it seemed. Her entire body bellowed for her to run.

The orchestra struck up the chords of the next tune, and Lord Westbridgeson extended his hand. "May I have this dance?"

Dancing all around the octopus tank? Their hosts sure knew how to put on an act for the guests. Refusal was not an option, for he would surely report back to Camilla or their host. She didn't wish to unnecessarily raise any suspicions. She'd dance and then she would slip away.

She placed her hand in his. "Of course," she said, allowing him to lead her onto the dance floor.

Louisa usually enjoyed dancing, but this dance, she found herself rather distracted. Her gaze couldn't help but sweep across the crowd, looking for a tall servant figure with a familiar masked face, but with no luck. Where had Mortimer gone? Had he left? Was he still watching? She despised the flicker of disappointment at the thought that he might not be.

The moment the dance concluded, she excused herself before Lord Westbridgeson could find any other excuse to stay by her side or, God forbid, her father and stepmother arrived and she would have to engage in further pleasantries.

Now should be the perfect time.

She quickly made her way across the room, sweeping one last glance over the room and the poor octopus, before slipping away. No one would be very likely to suspect anything at this point or question her leaving. This was the fortunate thing about country house parties where the guests resided on the same premises as the party. She also couldn't truly explain the sudden urgency that drove her to act fast if she were pressed.

Lady Havendish's chamber was in the west wing. She'd already asked the maid who had helped her dress all sorts of things that had slowly revealed the location.

Where on earth was Mortimer?

She hadn't told him where she would be searching at any given time. Of course, she could be wrong in her speculation, so it was probably best if he went off to search on his own. He must have his own thoughts about where this ledger might be hidden. If Lord Havendish was involved along with his wife, there might be a chance that the ledger was in the man's study.

She strode past a maid, head held high.

The girl didn't even give her a second glance.

Louisa smiled. All she had to do was walk the corridors with confidence and she wouldn't look suspicious. She was dying of curiosity to see what was so special about this ledger that those frightening brothers wanted it. No doubt they were in some sort of power struggle with the women of the club. That was the only thing that made sense to her.

They should most definitely copy the pages before handing it over. Come to think about it, they still had copies of the betting book of White's. Well, Ophelia still had them, if she hadn't thrown them away. Would that help Mortimer? If so, they might not need to hand over the ledger to the brothers at all.

How satisfying that would be!

They had dared to approach her brother. Let them dare to try again! Of course, one of those brothers was keeping an eye on Leo now, so if they did decide to take this route, they'd have to tread carefully.

Louisa padded along the hallway where Lady Havendish's chamber was located, her steps light, her pulse steady. Finally, she reached the door and quickly, quietly, slipped inside, gasping when she felt the presence of a chest pressing up against her back.

The door clicked shut.

Warm breath brushed her ear.

"Lady Louisa."

THIS WAS FOOLISHNESS. Utter madness.

Oliver pushed into the chamber with Lady Louisa, his chest pressing into her back. Whatever madness possessed him to do so had begun the moment he'd caught a glimpse of her entering the ballroom. A vision in black silk, she had appeared like an angel of death, ready to claim what she had come for, and at that moment, it felt as if she had claimed him. He had planned to remain in the shadows, but his feet wouldn't obey his command. And when their gazes had locked through the octopus tentacles in the tank . . .

She had touched that tank as if touching him.

And then another man had appeared at her side.

A strange, unfamiliar sensation had twisted his gut. He didn't like it.

So, he had retreated and kept to the shadows, yes, but he followed her the moment she'd slipped from the ballroom.

She whirled to face him. "Lord, you scared me!" she exclaimed, her hand flying to her chest. "What do you think you are doing?"

"I am following you."

"Why? Do you not have somewhere else to search? No, wait, that's not even the point. Step back, let me see you." Her gaze dragged over him, slow and deliberate, from top to bottom, a bold flash of appreciation sparking in her eyes before she said, "You still look much more dashing in Talbot livery."

His ears caught fire, and Oliver abruptly turned to lock the door, sealing them in the chamber alone. "I didn't plan on following you to search at all, but I changed my mind."

"Oh? Why all of a sudden?"

"I found it impossible not to keep an eye on you," he admitted.

The grin she sent him could have sweetened any bitter potion. "Really? That is your excuse?"

He shrugged, his gaze dropping to her mouth before meeting her eyes again. "I was also annoyed by your," a cough, "our companion."

"Ah, Reaper. No that, I do believe."

Oliver cursed inside, striving to gather his deuced wits. "It would be much more enjoyable to leave without him."

"He does have a way to dampen the mood, does he not?"

"Exceedingly."

She gave him an arch look. "That and my sole company is much more preferable, is it not?"

His lips twitched. "Immeasurably."

She chuckled, turning toward the desk, but he caught the way she bit her lower lip between her teeth. "If we find the book tonight, we can leave right after."

"Of course." The sooner they departed, the better for all. "So let us find that book."

She paused, glancing at him over her shoulder. "Wait, Reaper is keeping watch over our carriage, isn't he?"

The corner of his lips lifted. "I sent him on an errand." He quickly explained what happened.

She let out a delighted laugh, eyes brimming with devilry. "Serves the man right! Let us hope my instinct is correct and that the book is here."

"It will be here," Oliver said confidently. He believed in her.

She cocked her head at him, amused. "How can you be so sure about that?"

"Because you are here."

She blinked and, for a moment, simply stared at him. "Are you telling me you've placed all your trust in me? I am honored beyond words."

He took a step closer, lowering his voice. "I believe the word is faith."

"Lawks," she exhaled a laugh. "Well, no pressure to find the ledger then."

The corner of his lips lifted. "None at all."

She turned her attention back to the chamber, scanning the room. Her gaze bounced over the bed, the nightstand, the sofa, and the writing desk. "Now, if I were Lady Havendish, where would I hide a secret ledger?"

"Beneath the bed in a suitcase filled with old bonnets?" Oliver offered, the scene from the other night filling his head.

Louisa smiled. "Probably not."

Her gaze returned to the writing desk nestled against the wall. "It shall be a place where I can retrieve it quite easily to add to the entries."

"That seems plausible."

She strode over to the writing desk, her skirts brushing against her legs as he followed close behind, close enough to once more catch the faint scent of sweetness. "Many of these desks have hidden compartments." She felt around it. "There must be a latch."

He stared at her face, obscured by a black mask quite similar to his. It fitted perfectly with her dress. "That was lord West-bridgeson earlier, correct?"

She spared him a glance over her shoulder. "Oh, yes." Her lips curled in annoyance. "Can you believe he approached me without an introduction?"

Oliver arched a brow. "One could argue that I did as well."

"You are different." She suddenly chuckled. "Honestly, it feels as though I have known you all my life."

Oliver's raised brow lowered again and joined the other in a furrow, an indescribable feeling entering his chest. He brought the subject back to the earl. "If your stepmother intended to introduce you, then she must have wanted to do so for a reason."

"You are quite right," she said, still fiddling with the desk. "Apparently he is to be considered a good match for me."

He was most decidedly not. "What do you think?" Oliver asked her.

"I think it's poppycock," she answered instantly, then scoffed. "Ours would be a good match for the duchess, but not for me."

Oliver bit back a smile.

Clever angel.

He thought it was poppycock too. If the match was desired by the duchess, there must be something more to it, but even more importantly, the man did not suit Lady Louisa at all, even without the worry of criminal intent. Just from watching them dance, he could tell it would be a match made in the chambers of hell.

They did not look good together.

In fact, to his eye, they looked quite mismatched.

"It's best to avoid him in the future," Oliver agreed.

"Yes, I intend to do exactly that." A latch clicking into place made both of them jerk. She shot him a grin. "Well, well, well."

"Let us hope there is a ledger." He hoped to God there was.

She laughed, lifting a thin wooden panel from the inside of a drawer. Moments later, she pulled out a brown leather journal. "No hope needed!" She lifted the thing up to her face. "This looks like a ledger to me."

Oliver took the book from her fingertips, flipping through the pages.

Sure enough . . .

The back of her head filled his sight as she leaned close to peer over his hand. Delight laced her words. "How lucky are we! But I'm rather surprised at how easy this was."

Oliver would have to agree, but he was not the sort to question good fortune. "Not everyone chooses the best hiding spots. Shall we go?"

She straightened, nodding. "Yes, now would be the perfect time to slip away."

Good. "What about your father? Should you leave a note?"

"No," she said, scratching the tip of her nose. "I've yet to see my father, so I've decided to disappear as though I never came in the first place."

Oliver didn't comment. It wasn't his place to interfere with her family, and he also wanted to leave this place as soon as possible. "Very well."

They left the bedchamber without incident, and it wasn't until they slipped into the garden that the sudden approach of voices alerted them to people turning the corner. Oliver sprang into action. He grabbed Louisa by the waist and pushed her up against a nearby tree. He leaned over her, bending his head to hers until their noses brushed over each other, their lips hovering an inch apart, as though this closeness would help them go unnoticed.

"Oh!" A voice suddenly exclaimed.

Damn it.

Two hands gripped the front of his jacket, and Oliver moved his body, pressing in as close as he could, so that he covered Lady Louisa completely, hiding her from any prying eyes.

"Morti—"

His lips pressed against hers.

Nothing else. They just rested against hers, cutting off any sound.

"Let us go," a male voice said. "Give the couple some privacy."

Their footsteps faded, and it wasn't until Oliver was certain they had left completely that he lifted his head, slowly pushing away from Lady Louisa.

"Are you all right?" he asked softly.

She blinked once. Twice. Then let out a slow breath. "Am I all right?" she echoed, her voice a touch higher than usual.

Oliver stretched into a slow grin. "You must have gotten quite a fright, being so speechless and all."

Her brows furrowed. "Speechless?"

He laughed now. "Do you know where you are, Lady Louisa? Or have you been thoroughly swept away—"

She swung her fist, landing a solid punch in his gut. He coughed out another laugh. "That's more like it."

"How bold of you, Mortimer!"

"What else would you have me do?" Oliver asked. He'd acted out of instinct, but he still didn't regret his actions. He'd do it again.

"I don't know, but a *kiss*?"

He straightened, fingers circling her wrist and pulling her towards the path that led to the stables. "It was but a peck, if it can even be called that."

"A kiss by any other name is still a kiss!"

True. "A necessary evil."

"Lawks, I cannot believe you just referred to a kiss as a necessary evil."

Neither could he. The woman scrambled his brains.

Every single time.

Chapter Twelve

THEY WERE ON the road within a quarter of an hour. However, Louisa had never known time to pass in such a slow, daze-like pace. She could scarcely remember how she had gotten to the carriage, her head busy replaying detail for detail the brush of Mortimer's lips on hers, his hand clamping around her wrist, him pulling her all the way towards the stables without letting go.

A peck, he had said.

What peck?

That made it sound as if it was nothing. A small little thing of no consequence. Nothing to dwell on. But if lips brushed lips, what else could it be called but a *kiss*? A. Kiss. And what's more, that was her first kiss.

Louisa couldn't claim she had been obsessing over her first kiss and how it would occur since she was a little girl. She hadn't. However, she had at least known to some degree if it should happen—when it did happen—that it would be special. Meaningful. *Breathless.*

Very well.

It *had* been breathless.

But what about meaning?

Fine, if she had to nitpick, then she supposed it did have meaning, since if he hadn't kissed her, *pecked* her, they might have been caught. She just didn't care much for this meaning. And special?

She shot him a narrow look.

Well, it was a little, very tiny bit special.

Because it was *him*.

"You can hit me more if you like," he murmured, his voice low and laced with something infuriating that made her heart quicken.

She scoffed. "One punch was enough." Quite honestly, she didn't know if she could lift her arm *to* punch the man again. Both of them seemed to have gone rather numb. She handed him the ledger instead. "Oh, I recalled that we still have copies of the betting book. I would keep the ledger if I were you."

The eyes that met hers glinted. "I recalled the same thing earlier as well. Do you have copies of the whole book?"

Louisa turned over her answer carefully. "I believe Ophelia might, though I'm not sure how complete her copies are or if she has done away with them. However, they are also all over London."

He fell silent, then said, "There are other betting books the club should have filed away after they were filled, but I'd rather use the most recent one. And if my suspicions are correct, they will not use the same method again."

Louisa nodded. "That makes sense. Then shall we copy the ledger?"

He nodded. "That is not a bad idea, Lady Louisa."

"Please, drop the *lady* and just call me Louisa. I feel strange every time I hear *lady* coming from your lips." *Moreso now that they've touched mine.*

He inclined his head, lips quirking. "Very well. Call me Oliver, then."

Louisa couldn't help a chuckle from escaping.

"What's wrong? Do you not like my name?"

"No, it's not like that." She pursed her lips before saying, "It just seems like such a boyish name for a man such as you."

"And what sort of man is that, Louisa?"

She shivered at the simple, clear, deliberate use of her name. "A formidable man."

His amber eyes probed her. "Perhaps I am not that formidable."

"Let us agree to disagree on that score, *Oliver*."

A hint of a smile formed on his lips. "Let us do that, then."

Heh. They truly were an unlikely pair, were they not? "No one recognized you, did they?" she asked, returning to more serious matters. Safer matters. Though, in themselves, they probably couldn't be considered much safer. Especially if he had been recognized.

He shook his head. "No, no one that I could detect."

What a relief. "Good. Papa is going to be so angry when he discovers that I came and then vanished before he could see me. Oh, yes—what time is it?"

He pulled out a pocket watch. "A few minutes before midnight."

"Good, good." Her mind spun. "Perhaps I can use the excuse of my birthday."

Surprise lit his gaze. "It's your birthday today?"

"Yes, for the next few minutes. Though I had forgotten about it." Her head fell back to the carriage pillow. "I didn't even have a slice of cake. Is it not funny how the little things matter when you least expect it?" She did get a kiss, however, so she wasn't too unhappy.

"I'm sorry I cannot retrieve a slice for you, but I do wish you a happy birthday."

Her eyes met his. "Thank you, but it doesn't matter. I don't celebrate my birthday, and I usually bake my own cake just for fun."

"You make your own birthday cake? In the kitchen?" A slight lift in his brow. "Is that not celebrating?"

"So many questions, but yes, Mr. Duke, where else would I bake a cake other than a kitchen? It's just something I like to do for myself. I like to spend that time alone." Though on reflection, her arriving at the Havendish party and then leaving on her birthday might cause her father to be more suspicious than normal. Well, there was nothing she could do about it now.

"I just never considered you would be the sort of lady who would bake cakes, but in hindsight, thinking back, I shouldn't be all that surprised."

Hah! "I'll have you know I do make delicious cakes."

"Then I shall love to have a taste of it someday—if you allow me the privilege," he added, his voice dropping low.

Taste . . .

Her gaze slid down to his lips.

She might not have a bite of cake, but could she have a bite of something else?

What are you even saying, now, Louisa?

"We shall see," she murmured, distracted.

"Of course," he responded. "Since I cannot give you cake, is there something else you would like for your birthday?"

What a breathlessly dangerous question. "And if there is, you shall give it to me, no matter what?"

"If it's within my power, yes."

Power . . . mmm. She felt the slight shift of it . . . straight onto her lap. "Really? Since there are only a few minutes left of my birthday, what do you imagine you can give me?"

"Indeed." A small line appeared between his brows. "I only have coins on me."

"Coins? I have enough of those myself."

His gaze bore into hers. "Then, if you don't mind if it's a day or so late, I shall give you something else."

"Why give me anything at all?" she shot back.

He paused. "It seems like the right thing to do."

The right thing to do . . . The idea startled her. Why give her anything at all and why ask for anything? But Louisa could not deny she'd become exceedingly curious about the man. What would he think she should have for her birthday?

"I wouldn't say that we've been doing much of the right thing lately." She smiled, averting her gaze. "Not in the eyes of the very society we hail from, at any rate."

"There is more to life than where we hail from."

She glanced back at him. "Is that why you are acting as though you're employed by Bow Street?"

A faint smile. "Something like that."

From all the rumors she'd heard, and from all the glimpses she'd caught of the man over time, she still couldn't help but be captivated by even the slightest of smiles. She felt . . . if she could . . . *Louisa* . . . just reach out to touch . . .

"What are you doing?" a low voice breathed.

She blinked, snatching her hand back, only then becoming aware she'd actually traced her thumb across her lower lip, where his had pressed earlier.

The tip of her thumb tingled. She rubbed it against her skirts, her gaze drawing to her dress. Black. Like night. Like sin.

No.

A *bit* of sin.

"There is something I want," Louisa suddenly said, inhaling deeply. "Something within your *power to* give me before my birthday ends."

A brow arched, and one crinkle appeared between the two. "What is it?"

Should she say it?

Could she say it?

It's your birthday, Louisa.

She could enjoy it, even if just for one moment.

A hundred objections entered her mind. She'd never cared for powerful men, and then there was the family feud, though she didn't waste much thought on that. But for all the objections, and the fact that it may seem rather shallow, they had accomplished a mission, and she had a handsome man before her, and she was tempted . . .

She pushed back from her seat and half-rose, leaning toward him, placing her hands on each side of his face, locking him in.

"Louisa."

"You saying my name like that isn't helping. Indeed, it seems rather thrilling, even forbidden—my name on your lips."

"What are you doing?" he asked hoarsely.

"You keep asking me that."

His eyes burned. "You keep confusing me."

"A confused Duke of Mortimer. That will not go well in your investigation, it seems like."

"No, it won't."

Her heart pounded, louder than any time before. "And yet you are not pushing me away."

"I do not push ladies."

She grinned at him, his firm, dead serious answer. "That's good, because I know what I want for my birthday."

"I feel I shouldn't ask anymore."

He sounded so helpless, she laughed. "A kiss," Louisa stated boldly. "I would very much like a kiss."

A . . . kiss.

Oliver's mind shut down. Before, she had punched him to show her shock and perhaps even ire, now she wanted him to kiss her again. As a birthday *gift*? Surely, no kiss from him could be considered a gift. He'd only done it in the first place to block her from the sight of the passersby, as well as cutting off his name being spoken, but that didn't mean the moment his lips landed on hers it hadn't sent a punch of its own straight to his gut.

The impact had been breathtaking.

Startling.

Deuced discomforting.

He didn't need to think about her request. There could be only one answer. "No."

"*No?* Why not?"

Many reasons. The mere idea of kissing her again sent a new storm tearing through him, warring with his better judgment, which should be his *only* judgement. The willpower it had taken back in the garden to keep his lips unmoving against hers had nearly brought him to his knees.

"Your request is not within my power."

Her disbelieving gaze narrowed on him, accusing. "It feels like it is very much in your power."

And yet it wasn't because he knew the truth—his power would be lost the moment his lips touched hers again.

This angel . . .

The faint glow from the carriage lamps outside provided just enough light to outline the interior, casting dancing shadows across her breathtaking features. Her eyes held his steadily, and her breathing seemed to remain steady, too. However, Oliver could glimpse the tension in her posture, the way she held herself completely still.

She was close, so damn close.

"I believe you overestimate my strength of will, Louisa."

Her shoulders softened fractionally, a seemingly unnoticeable action that a man like him would never miss. She had come to some sort of decision. And whatever that decision, it would be deuced tempting and damn hard to resist.

He wasn't wrong.

Oliver pressed back against the seat, but there was no escaping her as her hands moved from where they hemmed him in and settled on each side of her face.

"Louisa."

"As I told you, saying my name like that doesn't help," she said with a smile. "It's my birthday, Oliver. Will you really deny this request of mine?"

Oh, he very much could, but his body couldn't seem to move as she lowered her head to his, her eyes lighting up with each inch gained.

He was mesmerized by that look.

And then her lips brushed across his. So softly, he thought he might be imagining it. Certainly not like the press, or rather peck, he had given her earlier, but a simple, word-defying *brush*.

Oliver gripped the seats—hard—his muscles straining to keep from pulling her closer. She lifted away from him slightly, barely, only to lower her head again and brush her lips over his again, tempting him, *daring* him not to respond. Her tongue grazed at the seam where they joined.

He heard a snap in his mind.

He felt it in his body.

This had been unfolding since the first moment they met at her house after he broke in. Every encounter, every word spoken, chipped away at something inside him no matter how profession-al he had tried to keep their encounters. But now? Now she had successfully pushed him to the brink of every limit he had set for himself.

Oliver lost the battle with his mind.

His hands circled her waist, hauling her up against him as his tongue darted out, claiming those mischievous lips. He did not relent until she yielded, granting him access to her warmth, her taste.

It wasn't a gentle kiss.

Nor was it rough.

It was the kiss of a man who had reached his limits and a woman who had driven him there, but who matched him at every step. He groaned as the scent of sweetness wrapped around him, clinging to him like an embrace he couldn't escape.

And he couldn't.

He didn't even try.

She shifted, settling onto his lap, her arms winding around his shoulders. He hugged her closer still, until his chest pressed up against hers, leaving no space, no part of them truly separate.

She stole his breath.

He couldn't even rear back to gasp for more, his head trapped between her and the velvet-lined seat.

God above.

Fortunately, she seemed to require breath as badly as he did, for she pulled back, her breathing just as rushed, just as bothered as his.

He dragged in several deep breaths.

Christ, she was beautiful. Even in this moment with the dampened light shimmering across her skin. Especially in this moment. The lower half of his body tightened.

No.

Dangerous.

He gripped her waist and in one smooth motion deposited her back onto her seat, taking a moment for his lungs to reclaim their normal rhythm.

"That was dangerous, Louisa," he warned, his tone serious.

She laughed, bright eyes shining with stars. "But it was a marvelous birthday gift."

A curse flew through his head. "Only you would see a kiss as a marvelous birthday gift."

"Well, since you stole my first kiss in the Havendish garden, you might as well claim it thoroughly."

Oliver didn't rightly know what to say to that. Did all women distinguish between pecks and kisses the way Louisa did? Did they all hold their first kiss as sacred? Don't be a damn fool, Oliver. Of course they do. As for the first point, peck versus kiss, he couldn't say. But he wondered what she would think if she ever remembered that she had also pecked him once on the cheek ten years ago. Not that it had any bearing on what had happened here tonight, but he had never been quite able to shake the memory.

He hoped she didn't remember—never remembered.

For with that memory, would come others.

"I never meant to steal your first kiss. My apologies."

"Oh, lord, please don't apologize for kissing me on my birthday. That will only make me feel wretched."

Oliver forced the tension from his body, settling back into the seat. "And we can't have you feel wretched on the last second of your birthday." He pulled out his pocket watch, only to catch the hand tick past midnight. "It's officially over."

She chuckled. "You know, fleeting as the moment was, this might be the best birthday I have spent in ten years."

Oliver glanced at her. "Surely not."

A bittersweet smile formed on her lips. "No, it's true. Not many people know this, but ten years ago today, or I should say yesterday, I was taken and held captive, spending my birthday in darkness. Ever since then, I have spent it alone. Even my family knows to leave me be on this day. This is the first year I not only went on a bit of an adventure, but I retrieved an important book, and I also claimed my first kiss."

All the tension rushed back to his body. He was aware it had been ten years, but he hadn't realized it had fallen on this very night. Her *birthday*.

He cursed his father all over again.

Ah, Louisa, Louisa.

You did well today.

"Well," he answered softly, hoping to provide some form of comfort even though it might fall short. "In that case, may all your birthdays from now on be as eventful and filled with all you wish and desire."

"Most people would gasp in horror at my story of being kidnapped."

He nodded slowly, attempting to mirror the curve of her lips but failing. "That is horrifying, Louisa."

"You didn't gasp, though," she teased.

"I inwardly gasped."

"Lord, you are such an arrogant rogue, you know that?"

Perhaps arrogant, but rogue? A newly minted one, perhaps. Otherwise, would he ever have kissed her? And yet, he couldn't help but be glad that he had. The twist of contradiction lashed at him. "I am extremely grateful you are here alive and well."

The quirk of her lips never faltered. "You are right. That is the best gift, is it not? That I can be here, alive and well on my birthday. It could have been worse, correct?"

"I've found that it's better not to dwell on those it could-have-been sorts of questions," Oliver said steadily. He had no desire to revisit the past, nor could he imagine she did either. Yet, she seemed far stronger than he, confronting the recollections, the remembrance, with a calmness, even some humor, that he could not fathom.

A small chuckle. "Right again."

Silence settled between them.

The clatter of the carriage wheels on the uneven road, accompanied by the occasional jolt as they hit a particularly deep rut, slowly soothed the discomfort that had settled deep in his limbs. But it couldn't erase it all.

Yes, I'm glad you are here alive and well.

Chapter Thirteen

A KISS BY any other name would still be a kiss.

Whether it be a peck, a brush of lips, or a scorching kiss as Oliver, the Duke of Mortimer had delivered. The beat of her heart had yet to settle, and the echo of his lips remained. Her fingers itched to press against them and calm the prickles that still lingered. Even the tremor of the touch of his hands on her had yet to fade. And she couldn't seem to shake the scent of sandalwood that clung in her nose.

The kiss had left a mark.

An indelible one.

Lord, oh, Lord! I want another.

But one look at the man and she could tell that any control that was going to snap tonight had already snapped. There would be no more snapping.

A pity.

She rather liked the duke.

She certainly couldn't understand why her father loathed the Cavanagh family so. If it had to do with Oliver's father, she could understand he might have his reasons. But why carry those reasons over onto the son?

The image of a boy, perhaps a young man, flashed in her mind, causing her chest to contract with uneasiness. A face, or rather the suggestion of one, hovered at the edges of her memory, blurred and unformed. Try as she might, she could make out his features. A whisper of soft, cooing words. A distant stirring of pain. A shadowy canvas that disappeared the moment she blinked.

She exhaled, pressing her hand to her temple. What was that? The sliver of a memory? The shard of a dream?

"Is something wrong?"

Mortimer's voice snapped her back to the present. She glanced up to find his gaze on her, so unreadable and yet so perceptive.

"No." She forced a smile. "Just a passing thought."

He didn't look convinced, staring at her for a full minute before nodding. "Very well." His focus returned to the ledger.

To distract herself from the haunting chill of that brief flash, she bit her lip and braved his annoyance, sliding into the space beside him, her skirts brushing against his leg, heat bleeding through the layers of fabric. The reaction was instant. His hand faltered on the ledger, fingers pausing mid-turn, the air between them suddenly taut. Did he feel it too? Or was she simply losing her mind?

She cleared her throat. "I want to see as well." The light wasn't good in here, but the moonlight and carriage lamps provided enough for determined eyes.

The duke said nothing, merely calmly turned the page.

"Well, at least they aren't written in the form of wagers," she said after a moment.

"You went through the betting book."

"Of course. Who wouldn't? Though honestly, I only gave it a few peeks and then got bored trying to decipher all the scrawls and confusing abbreviations. This is much more detailed."

"That is to be expected. Here we have clear dates, details of contraband, routes, but also abbreviations of names."

How bothersome. "Something tells me *you* will enjoy deciphering these names."

"I do like puzzles."

"Of course you do, otherwise we wouldn't be here, would we?" She glanced from the ledger to his face. "So, will you copy the pages?"

"It would be the clever approach and should be enough to get a clear idea of who and what so that we can cross reference it with the betting book. That, with the betting book, should be enough evidence to dismantle the organization."

It made sense. "Do you think everyone involved has ledgers like these?"

"I'm not sure." He paused thoughtfully. "But the barman at my lodgings did say Talbot and your stepmother are visiting coastal towns."

Louisa pursed her lips. "They are visiting friends, mostly friends of the duchess, so it could be—and I'm only speculating—that she might be visiting her criminal partners. Any friend of the duchess could be part of this club of hers. All hyenas, I tell you. However, my interest in their schedule doesn't go beyond knowing they've left the house and provided me a bit of peace, so I'm not sure."

"Because of the duchess." He paused. "You really do not like that woman."

"And understatement," Louisa said. Camilla did nothing overtly cruel, spoke no words of open hostility, yet the malice simmered beneath her surface like an undetected poison. "I get shivers whenever I am in her presence. And not the good kind, I might add." *Not the kind of shivers like when you kissed me.*

Oh, Lord! What was she thinking?

A sudden thought burst into her head like a bright light. "If Lady Havendish has such a ledger, wouldn't the duchess have one as well?"

Hot eyes locked with hers, their depths lighting up too. "It is very plausible."

She read the question he didn't ask: *Would you help me retrieve this ledger if it existed?* "Well, then it seems that we shall have to make haste to copy this ledger, trade it for the betting book, and return to Ashford before Lady Havendish discovers her ledger gone and connects all the crumbs that point back to me."

He nodded, his lips twitching. "You are right."

"There is also that Reaper fellow. He won't be happy to find we have set off without him." But she could imagine his face, and it brought a heap of satisfaction to her heart. As reckonings went, it wasn't much, but it was still a sweet treat.

"It can't be helped," the duke said lightly. "He wasn't there when we retrieved the ledger, and we couldn't wait for him. As long as we still honor the deal, let him bark."

"He's going to bark that we took a different route back."

"More's the fun."

Louisa chuckled. "Don't like him that much?"

"I don't like him lingering about us."

"I can't say I disagree. Those brothers . . . they are dangerous. Not men to be trifled with, and the words that roll off their tongues are particularly infuriating."

"Agreed."

She hoped her brother was doing all right. She would never forgive herself if she had put him in any sort of harm's way. But she trusted Mortimer, and so she trusted that Mr. Helgate would look after Leo. He had also seemed rather fond of Leo.

Now all she had to do was look after herself and not pounce on the man beside her, who looked ever so delightful in uniform, and demand more kisses, especially when doing so could only complicate everything.

You only live once, Louisa, her inner voice whispered, then more loudly roared, *Complicate some matters!*

Urgh!

But she still had to choose carefully who she complicated matters with. She had vowed no powerful men. Yet, there was a lingering temptation to break her own rule. It was fine to be bold once in a while, wasn't it?

Her heart gave a flutter. Boldness was a dangerous thing when it came to men like him. But that made it all the more exciting. So, if she wanted to be bold, she couldn't wait forever. The duchess would be dealt with soon enough, but the fallout . . . what would it bring? She shuddered to think. The tide would shift, that much was certain. And her family . . . what it would mean for her family, she couldn't say.

Speaking of which, "You are aware that my father might hold you responsible if you take down his wife?"

A moment of silence. "The thought has occurred to me, yes."

"Are you not worried?"

"Worried . . . It's not as though I am doing it publicly. My aim is not his wife, but the organization itself. If he tries to blame me for her actions, that wouldn't make him much of a man, now would it?" He glanced at her. "Are you worried about me, Louisa?"

"You *are* helping me."

"And here I thought you were helping me."

"Let us just say we are helping each other, then. I've always had this feeling that Camilla was trying to sink her nails into my brother. You are helping me prevent that, and also revealing that woman's true character."

"Unlikely allies, you and me," he agreed.

"It's the unlikely allies that make for the best ones, if you ask me."

"I cannot agree on that score, only to say that you are the exception."

Louisa beamed at him. "I quite like that." Being his exception. She also quite liked being in this man's company. Sharing with him this adventure. Searching for clues with him. Traveling with him.

Oh lord, didn't she like him a bit too much?

They would soon be parting ways. And the leap in her pulse at that thought wasn't a good sign. She didn't want to part ways. And yet, they would have to. The thought lodged in her throat and sat there like a lump. She liked him too much. More than she should. More than was wise. She liked the way he looked at her, sharp and knowing. The way his voice curled around her name. The way, despite his title as enemy, she felt safe beside him in a way she had never known before.

Foolish, so foolish.

Theirs wasn't a story that would ever have a happy ending. Her father's hatred of the Cavanagh family ran too deep. They wouldn't even be able to be friends after this. Well, perhaps they could be secret friends. She would have to content herself with that.

So why did it feel as though her heart was crumbling?

OLIVER STARED AT Louisa's profile, her lashes fluttering gently as she slept, her head resting against his shoulder. The faintest hint of her scent—that subtle sweetness—embraced him once again without room for escape. Even just this side of her face, with the curve of her cheek and the soft line of her jaw, was beautiful. She had no idea how she affected him. No idea that she had blown into his life like a storm, disrupting everything.

There had always been a sharp divide between his world of business and the personal lives of others. Louisa, however, was different. She wasn't something he could file away neatly in one category.

She was somewhere beyond.

Somewhere he shouldn't be able to touch. And despite his better judgment, despite all his good intentions, his heart raced with each breath she took. This was a complication he didn't know how to manage. He had never been one to let his emotions rule him. His father had taught him that—even though that man, in Oliver's view, had made every single decision in his life based on emotion. Perhaps that's why Oliver avoided doing the same.

Her question hadn't been out of place either.

Talbot *would* blame him.

Perhaps the man would not fully blame him for his wife's actions, but he would blame Oliver for bringing it to light. He would believe that Oliver had targeted his family, doing it on purpose, which couldn't be farther from the truth. And if he ever learned of Louisa's involvement, not even to mention little Leo's, Talbot would aim all his pistols at Oliver.

And fire.

There would be no end to the chaos that would follow. Talbot wasn't the type of man who could be reasoned with.

God, family feuds were so tiring.

The carriage slowed, and Oliver peered through the window. They'd arrived at Helgate's. Not the property they had first met at, but another one belonging to his friend. A smaller property than the first, perfect for one or two people to lay low when things get a bit tough in their line of work.

The moment the vehicle rattled to a stop, he placed a hand beneath Louisa's jaw and gently lifted her from his shoulder and settled her head against the seat, moving to open the door and jumping down. He didn't know if Helgate had even made it. If not, then it meant he hadn't been able to shake his Fury detail.

Not that they had any real need to since Oliver had planned to honor their deal from the start, but he was not so kind as to allow those ruffians to call the shots and walk all over them with their demands just because he needed something they had. Shaking off those two, he was sending a message: The Furys didn't have them in their grasp as they might have thought.

The door of the cottage swung open and a tall figure emerged, striding over. "You returned faster than I imagined you would."

"We found the ledger sooner than I expected," Oliver said softly. He nodded at the house. "The boy?"

"Sleeping," Helgate confirmed, a wry smile curling his lips. "Entertaining fellow."

Oliver nodded, lips twitching. "The young heir is indeed quite the character, and if he continues on this path, he will make a great duke someday."

Helgate craned his neck at the carriage. "The lady?"

"Also asleep."

Helgate nodded. "I've prepared a room for her, though, I must warn you, there are only two bedchambers in this house, I'm afraid."

Oliver dismissed it with a wave. "Not an issue. Did you have any trouble with Fury?"

A flash of irritation crossed Helgate's face. "That man is a walking stormcloud. He didn't speak a word when he arrived. And not a word passed his lips right up until the moment he fell asleep after I laced his drink with a little something extra."

"He actually drank something you offered him?"

"Not something *I* offered." Helgate grinned. "Something little Leo gave him."

Ah, well, that boy did have a way to disarm a person. "Don't tell Lady Louisa."

Helgate glanced around, chuckling. "Yes, yes. I see you got rid of your tail as well."

"It was easier than what you faced."

Helgate lifted a brow.

"A simple order and that rough and tumble pup scampered off to town," Oliver clarified matter-of-factly.

"And you found the ledger before he arrived back."

Oliver shrugged. "I would have knocked him out and locked him in the stables if he had come back sooner."

"So what's the plan then now that you have the ledger and we shook off our chaperones?" Helgate asked. "Return to Brighton or to Ashford in the morning?"

Oliver considered their options. The sooner they returned to Ashford, the sooner they could search for the other possible ledger. However, "Send two men to the Havendish property to watch out for any movement from Lady Louisa's family. The moment any of the Talbots leave, I want a man chasing the sun to inform me. As for us, we wait one day and one night. If Maxen

Fury does not find us here in that time, we head back for Ashford."

"What about the betting book?"

"They'll still have the book in a few days."

"You do realize you might anger those brothers?"

Oliver gave a light scoff, imagining all the ways they already angered two of the Furys. "If they wish to play in my league, they best show up in their best form. Besides, the duchess might have a ledger as well, and Lady Ophelia might still have copies of the book."

"I see." Helgate's eyes sharpened. "And you think the ledger would be better for evidence?"

He handed the ledger over to Helgate. "Have a look and see for yourself."

"With pleasure."

Oliver glanced over his shoulder, back at the carriage. "I'll go retrieve Lady Louisa." He was rather surprised she hadn't woken up, given that she struggled to sleep at times.

She must be exhausted.

Helgate nodded, and Oliver strode back to the carriage and peered inside. Still sleeping. He didn't bother to attempt to wake her, simply hooked one arm beneath her legs and the other behind her back and carried her from the carriage. He stirred against him, her breath warm on his neck, but she didn't wake up.

Helgate shut the carriage door for him, murmuring to the driver, and then led the way back to the cottage. The door creaked on its hinges as it shut behind them.

"It's small, but it will do in a pinch," Helgate said quietly.

"No bother."

Helgate led him to a chamber he had prepared, and Oliver nodded his thanks. "Go get some rest."

"What about you?"

"I'll keep watch."

His friend raised a brow but didn't say anything more as he

nodded and disappeared into the chamber across from them.

Oliver trod over to the bed and carefully laid Louisa on the mattress. She still didn't wake, which impressed him and concerned him at the same time. Anyone would be able to carry her away at this point. She had no sense of awareness.

Or perhaps she was just that comfortable.

He couldn't fathom ever feeling that at ease, especially in the arms of someone who could be an enemy. And family feud or not, a man was an enemy to an innocent lady. He couldn't help the protectiveness that swelled inside him.

He sat on the edge of the bed, his gaze roaming over her face. What he wouldn't give to rest as peacefully as she did at the moment. Even if just for a minute. One minute to close his eyes.

Oliver carefully lowered down onto the mattress beside her, one of his feet still on the ground, unwilling to fully surrender to the temptation. He would rest his head just for a few heartbeats.

Just one minute.

Then he would rise, move to the drawing room, and keep watch for any sign of Reaper or one of his brothers, who were sure to be on their way. They might not know of Helgate's cottage, but given their resources, they should be able to locate it without much difficulty. If they didn't, that meant they were at an impasse, neither side willing to give an inch.

Oliver didn't mind.

He didn't need to give an inch.

Not yet.

He'd waited this long to claim to book, he could wait a few more days. His shoulders relaxed into the pillow. He closed his eyes. How many seconds left?

He should rise soon.

Just one more moment.

Chapter Fourteen

LOUISA WOKE UP with a hefty weight pressing down on her legs. Her eyes slowly fluttered open, unsure of what to make of this weight. She scrunched her brows, adjusting to the light filtering into the room. Seagulls chirped in the distance, along with the sound of waves crashing onto the shore. There was also a brisk breeze that made her want to snuggle deeper into the weight, since it was comfortingly warm.

Wait. No, Louisa.

This weight and this warmth were not normal.

She blinked a few times, her eyelids still heavy, wanting to speed up the dissipation of the grogginess of sleep. She was in a chamber. That she could tell. She could also instantly tell from the mattress that it wasn't the same chamber as the first one she'd slept in at Mr. Helgate's house. This one was a bit harder. They must have reached their destination then.

But how did she get from the carriage to here?

Priorities, Louisa!

Why was there a . . . weight . . . Her fingers brushed against something, no, *someone*, just as her gaze collided with a throat. A throat that trailed off into a chest.

You ninny!

Of course, a throat was attached to a chest! But this . . . this . . . just a *part* of this chest was showing, and yet her heart jolted, then began galloping inside her own chest.

Her gaze trailed up the chest, then the throat, to a familiar jawline, up to an exceedingly familiar arched set of lips, until it settled onto the complete face of a slumbering man with his eyes peacefully shut, as though sleeping in the same bed as her—no, having one leg thrown across her—wasn't the strangest thing on earth!

But that was not all.

She was on her side, and below her head was an arm, and thrown across her body was another arm.

Dear Lord in Heaven!

She was completely enveloped by the duke!

But that still wasn't all!

Her arm—lawks, *her* arm—circled around *his* waist. And one of her feet neatly tucked over his. She was embracing him back! They were enveloping each other!

Calm down, Louisa.

At this rate, her heart would climb out of her throat and explode all over the scene.

A throat cleared.

Her eyes dropped down and back up again. It wasn't his throat. And it most certainly wasn't hers. Her brows furrowed. She lifted her head to glance over Oliver's shoulder, only to meet the gaze of her brother. The boy's gaze bored into hers with interest, as though he had stumbled across a very intriguing thing.

He had.

So had she, for that matter, since she couldn't recall a thing.

"I see you are awake," Leo said, cocking his head. "So you can answer my question now."

"And what question would that be?" Louisa asked rather dumbly, her throat still raw from sleep. She cursed her addled brain.

"What exactly am I seeing, Louisa?"

She blinked, not quite sure how to answer that since she didn't know what she was seeing either. "You should know that better than me, shouldn't you? How long have you been standing there, staring at us?"

"I don't know, ten minutes, perhaps. I'm not sure if I'm still dreaming. If I'm not, it seems that I just found my sister in the bed of our gardener."

Well, how could she argue against that? Her mind also hadn't caught up to the situation. "To be fair, he is not our gardener."

"But you are in bed with him."

Well, yes. "Your eyesight is still as sharp as ever," Louisa muttered. Honestly, she was curious, too. Her gaze shifted to the duke, who remained oblivious as he continued to sleep, the rise and fall of his chest almost peaceful. He seemed younger this way. Not at all like a powerful man in the world. The entire scene felt strange.

"Does that mean . . ."

Louisa held her breath, not knowing what her brother might say, and not knowing why she was holding her breath because of it.

"Does that mean I can sleep in the same bed as Miss Hale?"

The words, when they finally came, echoed in her mind louder than they did in the room. Louisa shot upright at the same time a chuckle came from beside her. Her eyes whipped to the man in bed with her, locking with his deep amber ones. Her heart thumped at the amusement she found dancing in the depths of them.

Wait, no, priorities! She glared at her brother. "No, you may not!"

"Why not?" he asked. "You slept in the same bed as the gardener. You are even holding him."

Right, she was! Louisa snatched back her arm. Priorities, priorities, priorities. Which should be to extract herself from the duke first! She yanked her foot back as well. The duke, on the other hand, was much slower to retract himself.

She sent him a hot look.

He chuckled and slowly sat up, drawing his body to rest

against the wall at the head of the bed. "My apologies," he said, his voice still thick with sleep. "I meant to sleep in the drawing room."

"Then why didn't you?" Louisa bit out, trying hard not to notice just how devilishly handsome the Duke of Mortimer was with bed hair, several strands tumbling over his forehead. Normally, since he dressed so humbly, he didn't seem to care much about styling his hair. But this—this was another roguish level altogether.

It was unfair, truly. He had no business looking so effortlessly, dashingly disheveled.

"I merely rested my head on the pillow for a bit and must have fallen asleep."

Louisa scowled, hoping the heat rising to her cheeks wasn't visible but entirely internal. "You shouldn't have rested your head on the pillow at all!"

"I know." Dry humor flashed in the depth of his gaze. "It was too tempting to resist."

Louisa had no response to that, so she turned back to her brother, who simply stood staring at them curiously. "As you heard, this was a mere accident never to be repeated again. Don't bother the servants with ridiculous requests."

Leo gave a small pout. "Then you put a ridiculous request to our gardener and that's why he's here?"

"I am to blame this time," Mortimer told Leo. "When you are an adult, only then can you bother ladies with ridiculous requests."

Oh, lord. Change the subject. "I cannot believe I slept like a log last night. It's never happened before. At least not in the last ten years."

"Perhaps this will mark a change in your sleeping habits," Leo remarked, his tone still sour.

Louisa rubbed her eyes. "One can only hope. Where is Mr. Helgate?" she asked her brother.

"He had an errand to run, but he prepared water and a cloth

so you can wash yourself. I also brought your traveling bag with your clothes."

Bless Mr. Helgate. "How about you? You didn't get into any trouble, did you?"

Leo shook his head so fast it's a wonder it didn't fall off. "I did not! We caught two fish yesterday."

"Did you cook them?"

His brow scrunched. "No, he said they were too small and tossed them back into the sea."

Louisa smiled at his indignation until she met the duke's gaze. "What are you still doing in my bed?"

He chuckled with indulgence and rose. "I shall make us some tea. Will that help aid your forgiveness in my slip?"

Tea? It would take more than tea, though it did sound good. In fact, it sounded like just what she needed. "It shall certainly help."

Louisa watched him stride from the room, her brother trailing behind him, utterly at ease in their "gardener's" presence. The moment they were gone, she clutched her heart, falling back onto the bed as if the breath had been knocked from her lungs. What on earth had just happened? How had it happened? Why had it happened? It wasn't merely that he had been in her bed—that alone was enough to send her wits scattering—it was the ease with which he had occupied it, like he belonged there. A force that could upend her life with a whisper. Although he had explained himself, that didn't prevent her mind from racing along with her heartbeat.

He had looked rather harmless in those moments of sleep— not at all like a man who could bring entire rooms to silence with his mere presence—and she had to admit that for a reckless moment, she'd forgotten he was a duke, and a powerful one.

That seemed to happen a lot these days.

A bit of fun and boldness was one thing, but she could not— must not—forget that he was precisely the kind of man she had sworn never to lose her heart to.

And for good reason.

OLIVER STEPPED INTO the small kitchen to find Helgate busying himself with an array of jams, cheese, and bread, as well as boiling water for tea.

"I thought you had an errand to run?" Oliver asked, his voice still rough.

His friend snorted. "And I thought you were keeping watch."

Oliver scratched the top of his head. He had thought so as well. He hadn't meant to fall asleep. He also hadn't meant to wrap himself around Louisa like that damn octopus in Havendish's tank. But instead of feeling remorse, he had felt strangely at home when he'd heard her and her brother bickering, and his body had awakened along with his mind with her body so close to his.

That was the part that unsettled him. Not the moment itself, nor the heat of her against him, but the ease of it. As if his body had known something his head refused to acknowledge. Christ, his muscles tensed with the mere memory of the way her limbs wrapped with his. A man could lose himself in a woman like that. He could lose himself . . .

His friend grinned, motioning to the spread. "I returned ten minutes ago." He sent Oliver a look that spoke volumes. "The boy insisted on waking you."

Oliver looked to Leo, who pretended to be enthralled by a speck of dust on the wall. Just how long had this little brat stared at them sleeping? He thought Louisa had asked, but he couldn't recall the answer. It couldn't have been more than a few minutes. "Is there something you wish to ask me, young master?"

The boy's head whipped up to him, and he pursed his lips, brows furrowing, before asking, "Are you going to marry my sister?"

Oliver nearly choked on air. Of all the all the blasted questions . . . His gut tightened at the bluntness of it. He ignored

Helgate's snicker, and measured his words. "Will you marry Miss Hale if you sleep in the same bed as her?"

This time it was Helgate who choked.

The boy hesitated.

Oliver pressed more. "Why do you want to sleep in the same bed as Miss Hale?"

Leo didn't hesitate this time. "Because Louisa did it with you!"

"Oh? And why do wish to do what your sister does?"

The boy paused again, but not for long, "Because it's only fair."

These two . . . The siblings truly doted on one another. There was no other explanation for it. Even if it sometimes expressed itself in odd ways.

"Fair?" Oliver chuckled. "Then if she did it with me, as you say, shouldn't *she* be the one asking *me* to marry?"

The boy suddenly nodded his small head. "Yes, she should take responsibility for you."

"I doubt your father would agree."

Leo cocked his head. "Why?"

At the boy's innocent question, Oliver froze. Would Leo tell Talbot about the gardener—which Leo was fond of calling him despite knowing he was not—that Louisa had hired? That she had slept in the same bed as him? Whether Leo called him a gardener, footman, or Bow Street Runner, it was enough to get her into all sorts of trouble. Would this become a problem for her in the future? He hoped not.

"You should ask your sister about that."

"Ask me what?" Louisa asked, striding into the kitchen like a breath of fresh air. Her hair hung loose, and she wore a dress of soft lavender that made her seem too delicate for the world she willingly strode into. He had seen her weather storms, defy expectations, and yet she carried herself like a woman untouched by hardship. Her independence never seized to surprise him, seizing each day as it came, without the aid of anyone. Many women would already have lamented the lack of a maid.

She had paused in the doorway, one brow arched in humor, but there was something else there too. A flicker of curiosity? Suspicion? Had she overheard them? A flush burned his ears, but he still said, "Why your father wouldn't allow you to assume responsibility for spending the night with me."

Again, she surprised him by laughing. "That is because Papa does not like our gardener, footman, Bow Street man."

The boy sent them both wounded looks. "You are taking me for a fool."

Louisa reached out to pat his head affectionately. "I shall tell you more when we get back the book you handed over to ruffians. Or have you forgotten why we are here?"

The boy's cheeks flushed with embarrassment, and he hurried over to plop himself down into one of the chairs, arms folded stubbornly.

"Lady Louisa," Helgate greeted. "I'm glad to find you in good spirits."

"Yes, well, we accomplished our mission so there is little that can dampen the mood," Louisa said with a bright smile, settling herself beside her brother.

Oliver swallowed his smile as he watched her. Louisa was a force of nature, and he was only beginning to understand how she moved through life without fear. He found her distressingly admirable.

Helgate nodded. "Please, take a seat and help yourself. The water should be ready soon for tea."

"I thank you," Louisa said.

Helgate continued, "Miles sent word that your friends from Brighton are scattering to find you."

"Speaking of which," Louisa started, "just where are we?"

Helgate chuckled. "Still on the outskirts of Brighton but on the other side."

"That seems rather devious," Louisa said, then she laughed. "Oh, those Furys must be positively furious."

"Well, even if they do rule the seedy parts of Brighton, they still need to be taught that we don't all bow to them," Helgate mimicked Oliver's thoughts. "Besides, they are nothing but tiny little jackals nipping at the heels of those above them."

"A tall statement," Louisa mused.

Oliver took a seat across from her, casually resting his hands on the table. "Tall but entertaining."

She laughed again, her eyes sparkling. "That is true, and though they may nip at heels, they do seem like the sort to bide their time and bite when you remove your boots, and even the tiniest creatures can have a painful bite."

Helgate filled a big pot with tea. "Then I shall just have to remove their teeth."

"What a vivid image," Louisa murmured.

Leo nodded. "Very vivid."

"So what do we do now?" Lousia asked. "Wait for them to find us?"

"Exactly." Oliver filled her cup with tea and pushed it towards her, then did the same for the boy. "We have what they want, so they can come find us now."

"I shall never understand the machinations of men."

"It is not for you to understand, sister," Leo intoned in his wisest voice.

Oliver chuckled as Louisa shot a glare at her brother and pinched his cheeks. "It's not for boys to understand either."

"But it is for them to learn," Helgate offered slyly.

"Do not put such thoughts in his head!" Louisa redirected her glare to their host.

Helgate gave an innocent shrug. "I believe it might be instinctual to us."

"Stop talking nonsense," Oliver said to his friend before the lady across from him leaped up to box some ears. "It all depends on the man."

"That is true as well," Helgate relented, placing the spread on the table before taking a seat, and the kitchen fell into a pleasant silence as they busied themselves filling their stomachs.

After a moment, Leo asked, "Shall we go fishing again to-day?"

"Sure, why not?" Helgate said. "It's not as though we are hiding." He looked to Oliver. "What about you? Will you and the lady be joining us?"

Oliver glanced at Lady Louisa, who shook her head. "Me, fishing? I do not torture myself in such a manner. Besides, I'm not sure I need to be here waiting alongside you for those rough fellows to return."

Oliver frowned. "You wish to return to Ashford?"

"No!" Leo exclaimed. "I wish to go fishing."

Louisa exhaled, reaching for her tea. "You can go fishing, I shall not stop you. That is," she glanced at Helgate, "if Mr. Helgate doesn't mind your continued presence in his home. Otherwise, you can go fishing in the pond at home."

The boy pouted, sending a pleading look at Helgate. "Of course, you are welcome to stay as long as you want, Little Leo."

The boy beamed at his sister.

Oliver almost felt sorry for his friend, but he felt certainly sorry for himself. If Louisa insisted on returning home, there was no way he would allow her to do so alone. Those brothers were looking for them, and while they might have a bit of the upper hand now, if the Furys found her and decided to take her as leverage—*kidnap* her for leverage—Oliver didn't know what he would do.

There would be hell to pay.

Chapter Fifteen

LOUISA RECLINED AGAINST the seat of the carriage, the provocative scent of sandalwood playing with her senses once more. Not just her sense of smell—she could almost see its tendrils unfurl and cling to her skin, coaxing her lips apart to coat her tongue, and whispering against her ears, as though this scent had embedded itself into her whole person.

Was this what they called being utterly aware of another human being?

She had never experienced it on such a supremely deep level before. It would have been much better, and less distracting, if he had let her return home alone.

She snuck a peek at him before averting her gaze. "You didn't have to accompany me, Duke."

"Duke? What happened to Oliver?"

"*He* was found in my bed this morning and needs to be punished," she snapped without thinking about what she was even saying. Louisa's cheeks heated. "It's called distancing oneself a bit."

"Well, I couldn't let you return by yourself either."

She scoffed. He very well could, and he knew it! "Why not?"

"Because we are partners."

Her head whipped back to him. Well, if that didn't set a woman's heart aflame . . .

He cocked his head, smiling at her.

Heh. She must look like a complete ninny to him, acting like a child after waking up in his arms. Why was she even still reacting like this?

"Wasn't it you who said that we make a great alliance?" he asked.

"I believe my words were that unlikely pairs seemed to make the best alliances." Or something to that effect.

He nodded. "Then we should capitalize on us being an unlikely pair and keep our alliance in full force for the time being."

"Meaning you cannot stand me searching for a ledger without your hawkish eyes present."

"That too."

"Not even hiding your true intentions, I see."

"You misjudge me," he murmured. "My true intention is to stay by your side while we see this through."

Words that made some sense, unlike the duke's sleeping posture. *Lawks, don't think about it, Louisa.* That would just make her heart jump about her chest. Honestly, she hadn't hated the feeling of their closeness. She had quite enjoyed his warmth. But how on earth was she supposed to forget about it now that it was seared into her consciousness?

Gah!

It was much too early—barely noon!—to be thinking about such things.

"Does it bother you—my staying close?" he suddenly asked, the question catching her off guard.

Her brows knit together. "I . . ." Did it bother her? Well, certainly, but not in the way he might imagine. He must believe she was flustered in a horrified sort of way instead of flustered beyond breath in an *I liked it* sort of way. "I am not bothered."

"Are you sure?" His voice filled with skepticism. "You've scarcely looked at me since we departed a quarter of an hour ago."

"What are you saying? I scarcely ever look at you." Liar, liar.

"Ah, yes, you are quite right. That does seem to be the case."

She snuck another peek at him, only to catch him arching a brow. The flush of warmth traveled down to her collarbone. "Now you are just teasing me."

He lifted his hands in surrender. "You caught me."

"I must admit that the Duke of Mortimer teasing a woman—I could never have imagined such a thing if I had not experienced it myself."

"Who is teasing whom now?"

Well . . . she had to admit she did rather enjoy this, too. "You are not as I imagined, Oliver."

"And how did you imagine me?" He scratched his chin, the action drawing her gaze down to his lips. She quickly flicked her eyes up again.

"Cold. Rigid."

"I am that," he agreed. "Also not."

Was he teasing her again? Well, she could attest to that *also not*. She had experienced both the heat and the ice, and she had enjoyed the latter more than she ought.

"You are certainly more than just cold."

"You are going to agree just like that?"

"There is nothing to disagree on." She considered him. "Well, perhaps toss indifference into the mix of hot and cold. Tell me, is that indifference a mask?"

His brow furrowed. "I shall not claim it to be a mask." He paused for a moment. "Perhaps more of a shield, if I were to put a word to it."

"A shield?"

"An impenetrable barrier. Erected to ward off and defend against expectations, even judgments people might place upon me if any crack showed. It's become, I suppose, a way of life."

She had never expected him to say anything like that. Her heart suddenly ached for this duke. He was the way he was because he *had* to be. He had grown up shielding himself from whatever he thought might bring him harm.

Just like her.

Perhaps they were more alike than they seemed.

"Ah."

He arched a brow in question. To be fair, it was a very brief response to his honest answer.

"Well," she ventured in reply to his look, "I suppose it makes sense that you cannot possess power without possessing a shield."

"Wise words."

She smiled at him. "I do declare my brilliance."

A rare snort came from him. Louisa was about to tease him further when the driver called out, and the carriage started to slow. More shouts filled the air.

"Dear Lord, what is going on?" Louisa peered out of the window to try to catch a glimpse. She suddenly recalled Theodosia mentioning being robbed by highwaymen and gasped.

"What is it?" His face joined hers, and she swore the small hairs on their cheeks touched.

"I think it's highwaymen."

She felt him stiffen, and he suddenly pulled her away from the window, dragging her up against him, which meant she was practically sitting on his lap again! But this time she wasn't distracted by a kiss. *She felt everything.*

His arms encircled her like a vise.

"Devil take it."

Louisa still hadn't shaken off her shock of their sudden close proximity. His body had turned as hard as steel, the exact opposite of how it had felt this morning.

His breath tickled her ear right before his words followed, "Stay inside. I'll handle them."

"I'm on your lap!"

He stilled before swiftly depositing her next to him. "My apologies, I reacted out of instinct."

She shook off her daze. "They shall be armed. How will you handle them? You are not made of marble, you know."

His lips twitched, but only for a swift second. "I know, but I shall be fine." Two fingers caught her chin as deep eyes bore into hers. "Give me your word that you will stay here."

"I cannot do that."

"Damn it, Louisa. This is a dangerous situation. I need your word."

She placed her hand over his mouth. "What if I get dragged out of the carriage or they threaten to kill you if I don't step out?" She held his gaze. "I cannot make this promise."

"Then at least give me a few minutes."

"Fine." She could do that.

He placed his hand on the door, shooting her a last glance. "Are you ready?"

Louisa didn't know what he planned to do, but she gave one curt nod. "As I'll ever be."

Oliver flung open the carriage door to come face to face with . . . Louisa's eyes widened as a man came up to the door and filled her view—a bloody, bedraggled Helgate.

"What happened?" Oliver demanded.

"Those damn Furys."

Louisa swallowed at the sight of his bruised face. Her gaze darted beyond him, her heart sinking to her shoes. "Where is my brother? Where is Leo?"

"They took him."

"What?" Louisa's breathed. Her world plunged into the deep, vast ocean. Taken? That one word was an anchor dragging her to the bottom of the ocean floor.

Her mind turned blank as a sheet of paper. What did he mean they took him? Was Leo not here? Certainly . . . certainly . . . he must be here!

She grasped onto the duke's voice when he asked in a low voice, "When?"

"Right after you left. There were two of them. Snatched the lad from the beach while one distracted me."

"You mean beat you."

Helgate cursed. "You should see the other man. They took

Leo, I couldn't stop it, but I still have the one who planted the bruises."

"That's good."

Good? How was that good? Louisa's mind spun, and she sought for calm. Spiraling would not do her brother any good. She inhaled slowly and exhaled even slower. And repeated.

"Those tiny jackals do know how to bite," Helgate growled. "And they did wait for the boots to come off. The moment you cleared, they struck."

Those blasted Furys! This was to prove a point, wasn't it? A move of power. A show of . . . well she didn't know, but it certainly wasn't a show of strength!

Drat, drat, drat.

Why had she ever thought she should leave her brother behind?

"Louisa?" a soft voice probed. "Just breathe."

She swallowed, took another deep breath, and managed, "I cannot believe they kidnapped my brother. They will be at The Raging Stag, won't they? Well, they shall have my rage today!"

The duke cursed. "He will be all right, Louisa."

Her gaze lifted to meet Oliver's. "Are you sure? How do you know that?"

"They won't hurt him," he said reassuringly.

Perhaps not physically, but that was an impossible claim to make. Her kidnappers hadn't injured her either, but that didn't mean she hadn't been hurt.

Oh, dear God.

Leo.

She clutched at her chest and dry heaved, struggling to once more catch her breath.

"Louisa!"

Strong arms enveloped her, but she couldn't seem to grasp at their hold as memories of her own kidnapping ten years ago rushed in. Several men. Thick puffs of smoke. Water dripping through the roof. The mocking laughter of men. Coldness.

Darkness.

Then . . .

A low, male voice whispering through the abyss in reassurance. *You shall be all right.* Louisa's breath hitched as the frame of a tall youth flashed across her mind. No, it should be that of a young man, not youth, but she could not be sure. In her memory, she could only see his mouth move, whispering those words of reassurance over and over again. Nothing else.

How . . .

Who . . .

Wasn't it just a dream? Who was that young man? Why had he shown up in her head at this very moment?

"Louisa."

A palm cupped her cheek and turned her head. Her gaze met Oliver's. "I will get him back. I promise."

I promise.

Hadn't that young man whispered the same thing?

"I do not make promises lightly," Oliver went on. "I've only made one other promise before in my life. This is the second. I will not fail him. Or you."

RAGE GRIPPED HIM in a tight vise.

Anger coursed through his blood, sank deep into his bones, and lit multiple sparks there. He dragged his free hand through his hair to calm himself while keeping the other on Louisa. Of course she would not be taking this well, given her history. Worse still, her brother was the same age she'd been when she was kidnapped all those years ago. And those bloody brothers had just dredged up whatever horrible memories that still clung to her mind.

He wanted to throttle Maxen Fury.

But rage would not help him, Louisa, or Leo in this situation. It would just cause him to make mistakes. He gently rubbed

Louisa's back in comfort, not sure if he was doing it right, but she wasn't pushing him away.

"Get in," Oliver said to Helgate. "We're heading back to Brighton."

Helgate nodded and quickly secured the reigns of his horse to the carriage, instructing the driver, "There's a crossroads up ahead where you can turn around." He entered the carriage and shut the door, his gaze flicking between Oliver and Louisa. "My apologies that I must bring you this wretched news."

"What's done is done." They could not have known the Furys would retaliate in such a swift way. "I underestimated them."

"They bloody underestimated us!" Helgate spit out. "They have just carved out a spot at the top of my black books."

Beside him, Lady Louisa inhaled deeply and straightened, a cool mask of calm settling on her features. "Are you all right?" Oliver asked even while knowing she was absolutely not. The best he could do for her now was to treat her as though she were and as though they had everything under control. He reluctantly pulled his arm back.

She nodded. "They must be the first scoundrels I've met who are unafraid of your ducal title. And my father's, for that matter."

"It could be because their half-brother is the current Duke of Crane," Helgate suggested.

No, it was more than that. "Or they know they are untouchable."

"No one is untouchable," Helgate growled. "Have they not considered our retaliation? *My* retaliation for taking a boy from my care? They will learn I hold grudges for a lifetime. It makes me happy."

"No, it's not just that," Louisa said. "Our situation is unique. They must know that the two ducal families are enemies and that we have much to lose by exposing"—she motioned between her and Oliver—"our alliance."

"So what? You shall get a scolding from your father," Helgate said. "That is hardly enough to make them think they could kidnap a young boy with impunity."

"Louisa is right," Oliver said. The Fury brothers knew he and Talbot weren't on good terms. Reaper Fury had even commented on it back in the Havendish stables. But they wouldn't trouble themselves with simply carrying tales to Talbot. Their style was more blunt.

But even so, they would know—or at least have guessed—that Oliver wouldn't want Talbot to find out about their bond, alliance—call it what you will—they had formed, that they had leverage on that front. And they should have also estimated that he wouldn't allow anything to happen to that boy while he was under Oliver's protection.

And they were right.

The boy's kidnapping was an invitation.

A vicious one.

He could call their bluff, but he'd rather not underestimate them again. If they did inform Talbot in some equally vicious way, Talbot would most assuredly retaliate. Against them. Against him. Talbot would certainly reveal the details to Louisa about her kidnapping in an attempt to break the every and all connection between them, and would probably, if he were smart, lump him in with the likes of the Furys to help seal it.

He cursed.

She would turn against him. Hate him.

Oliver didn't want that.

God, he didn't want that at all.

"We have more at stake than they do," Oliver finished.

"So, they've got us by the jugular?" Helgate said with a deep scowl.

"No, we still have the ledger."

"They must want it badly," Louisa murmured. "We haven't even had time to copy its pages."

"Oh, I copied it last night," Helgate announced, his brows smoothing to make way for a grin.

"You did?" Louisa exclaimed. "When? How?"

Oliver arched a brow at his friend.

Helgate shrugged. "Your brother has atrocious sleeping habits, and rather than spend the night being kicked in places I'd rather not, I copied the pages. It's rough, but it's there."

Some of the tension left Oliver when he glimpsed the smile Helgate's news brought to Louisa's face. He could hug his friend. He glanced back at Helgate. "Why didn't you tell us?"

"Honestly, it slipped my mind."

He stared at his friend blankly. It slipped his *mind*? Do things with such importance as this slip people's minds? A certain betting book and a woman in a white night rail suddenly came to mind. Very well, such things could happen, but they shouldn't happen to a man such as Helgate.

"What?" Helgate muttered sheepishly. "You didn't seem to worry much about the ledger, which is why it must have buried itself beneath other matters."

"Well, they seem to be worrying about it," Louisa said flatly. "I have half a mind to swap it out with a fake one and hand them that."

Oliver thought about that. "As much as I adore that idea, the risk is too high."

"A pity," Louisa murmured.

Oliver nodded. "Unfortunately."

"It's rather interesting that they know about this ledger in the first place," Helgate said, his head falling back against the seat. "The Fury network runs deep, it seems. My fingers are itching to untangle it."

"It might not be as deep as you imagine," Louisa said. "You weren't there at the Havendish masked ball. They are extravagant people. I wouldn't be surprised if they let slip about their dealings to others."

"I agree." Oliver thought about the octopus. "They aren't the most subtle."

"You mean to say the organization is ripe for the picking,"

Helgate murmured thoughtfully.

Oliver nodded.

"What do you mean?" Louisa looked at him.

Oliver got caught in her vivid eyes for a moment before he answered, "Overconfidence is the number one reason criminals get caught."

"Ah, so they believe they have become untouchable," she murmured. "The Furys believe they are untouchable, too."

"Hah!" Helgate barked. "A symphony to my ears."

Oliver ignored him, and met Louisa's gaze. "Yes, but there is an important difference between them and the organization the women run. The Furys' confidence is steeped in calculation and caution."

She nodded thoughtfully.

Helgate rubbed a bruise on his face. "The women's hold on power started slipping when they started their antics in London. Turkish trousers come to mind." He leaned forward to grasp Louisa's hands. "That aside, your brother will not be harmed. Those bastards might be tough, but they are smart. Safe and well, your brother is of use to them. The moment they harm him they start a war—and they know that."

Oliver scowled at Helgate, then at the man's hands. "What are you doing?"

Helgate flicked a glance at him. "Comforting a lady."

He yanked his friend's hands away. "Well, stop it."

"Are you telling me to stop comforting a lady? What a cold rogue you are."

Curse Helgate. Oliver clasped one of Louisa's hands in his. "Ladies don't touch strangers carelessly."

"What?" Helgate said affronted. "I am no stranger!"

"You are more a stranger than I am," Oliver pointed out. "If the lady needs comforting, I shall comfort."

"Enemies over strangers, I get it."

"Have you ever comforted anything in your entire life before?" The man might appear friendly and accommodating, but

Oliver knew better. Helgate was as cold and brutal as they came.

His friend grinned. "Does comforting myself count? I've nursed a few wounds in my life."

"Settle. Back."

Helgate suddenly laughed, lifting his hands in surrender. "Very well, very well. But since the lady didn't protest, I still claim no harm was done."

"I . . ." Louisa started before her voice trailed off. She cast a curious, hopeless glance at Oliver, who squeezed her fingers.

"No need to respond to him. No need to respond at all. And you can retrieve your hand from me the moment you don't require comfort."

"Uh, thank you, then," she murmured, and suddenly smiled, such a warm smile that it set his heart to racing. "For the comfort."

His body went hard as stone. And hot. It seemed as though a fire had lit at the center and now gushed out to every one of his limbs. Heat spread everywhere. He cleared his throat. "It's a pleasure."

Oliver cursed at his friend's low laughter.

He wanted to send the man a warning look but also didn't want to lock eyes. He didn't bloody need a reminder of how strange his actions were. How out of place. He knew. But he couldn't stomach the sight of her hands clasped in Helgate's.

Which was deuced ridiculous.

God help him.

Chapter Sixteen

L OUISA STARED AT the big hand that encased both of hers. She'd retracted it earlier from his grasp, determined to keep her composure, but after she started nibbling the tips of her fingers, they had both been caught again, trapped in the warmth of his steady grip.

She ought to pull away.

However, no matter how much she debated the issue with herself in her head, her fingers remained nestled in his.

In truth, the duke's comfort certainly distracted her from the real matter at hand—retrieving her brother. It was a touch embarrassing with Mr. Helgate's sharp eyes on them, though God bless the man, he looked everywhere but their hands. Looking at him now, pity rose in her breast—his face was turning bluer with each passing minute.

"We're here." Helgate peered through the window, letting go of the curtain as the carriage drew to a halt. "Time to beat some Furys."

"No," Oliver said, finally withdrawing his hold on her hands, her fingers twitching at the loss. "No violence. Where is the brother you caught?"

"He should be with my man in another carriage, waiting."

"Is he conscious?" Oliver asked.

"That we shall have to see," Helgate said with a cold grin.

Louisa hoped the one they caught sported more bruises than Mr. Helgate! "Let us go." She caught Oliver's eye. "You have the ledger?"

He glanced at Helgate.

The man patted his chest. "Right here."

She let out a shaky breath. "Then let us make the exchange." They exited the carriage one by one, Oliver offering a hand when it was her turn. She accepted it, not questioning how he only withdrew his hold after they entered The Raging Stag where they'd all first met.

She had hoped never to return here.

However, now that she was here, she steeled herself, and the first thing she saw was the man called Maxen Fury seated at the bar on a stool. Another man, similar in looks, stood behind the counter, leaning over and conversing with the lone occupant. The same smoky scent filled the dusky space, even though not a single cheroot was lit.

Her gaze flicked over the empty tables, landing on a small boy who had looked up when they entered. His eyes lit up when they met hers across the room.

Leo leaped to his feet and rushed over. "Sister!"

All her anxiety melted away with that one exclamation.

The men didn't stop him, and soon she hugged her brother tightly, not forgetting to shoot a nasty glare at the two men who watched with infuriating indifference.

She grabbed Leo's cheeks and inspected him. "Are you all right? They didn't hurt you, did they?"

Leo shook his head furiously. "I'm not hurt."

What a relief. "Were you very afraid?" Louisa asked her brother, searching his gaze for any sign of terror masked as bravery.

He shook his head again.

Her brows furrowed. "You weren't?" She stared at him more intently. Dare she believe him? They hadn't locked him up, and though she hated to admit it, they seemed to have given him most of his freedom.

"No! I knew you and your gardeners would come for me!"

"Honestly, you are hopeless." She straightened, not forgetting to shoot another glare at the men at the bar for good measure. "This is why I don't like powerful men, fortune hunters, and *criminals.*"

"Can I resent a part of that statement?" Oliver remarked in a low voice from the side.

Louisa, feeling much better now that her brother was back at her side, murmured back, "You're a duke, aren't you?"

"And yet I have felt powerless ever since the moment you jabbed a knife at me."

Helgate cleared his throat. "Is this the time for this?"

Louisa averted her gaze. Probably not.

"You've reunited with your brother," Maxen said in a low drawl. "Are you not going to allow us to reunite with ours?"

Mr. Helgate turned back to the door and to a man who stood there. Louisa hadn't even noticed him until now. She hadn't given much thought to the Fury that Mr. Helgate had apprehended, but now, grim satisfaction curled in her breast. That's right—they had the ledger *and* a brother. However, the feeling didn't last long. Indulging that sort of satisfaction felt very much like she was engaging in the very thing she loathed in powerful people.

She nipped it right in the bud.

A short moment later, he reentered with a lump of man on his shoulder, striding over and unceremoniously dumping the unconscious figure at the feet of his brother.

Dear God, was that Reaper?

The outspoken ruffian had turned into quite a pitiful sight.

Maxen Fury stared at his brother before lifting his hard gaze back at them. "Was this truly necessary?"

"Was it necessary to snatch a young boy from the beach?" Louisa snapped, unable to hold herself back upon hearing that vexing question in that equally vexing tone.

"We treated your brother like royalty," the man said calmly.

Louisa's fingers twitched. "Is *this* your castle, then?" she challenged. "You are the ones in the wrong."

"And what about you, my lady?" Maxen asked. "You and your friends gave both my brothers the slip, and then he got beaten to this degree."

Honestly! "Who told you to send them to keep an eye on us?"

"If we hadn't, would you have brought us the ledger?" The man behind the bar cocked his head. "Seems to me the answer is no."

Maxen smiled, and not sweetly. "That's not it. They were forcing us to come to them."

Smart man.

"And you did," Oliver said dryly. "Though your methods leave something to be desired. You must want this ledger badly."

"I do."

"The book?" Oliver sent simply.

The brother behind the bar reached down and placed it on the counter. "The ledger?"

Louisa watched and Helgate removed it from the inner pocket of his jacket and tossed it to Oliver. She almost thought the duke would flick it onto the floor beside the crumpled Reaper—she almost wished he would—but he surprised her by striding up to the bar and placing it right next to the betting book.

Both men then pulled their desired book toward themselves. *That's right.*

A man such as Oliver wouldn't lower himself by doing anything else. His actions showed courtesy and respect. Not for the men, Louisa thought, but for their treatment of her brother.

There was something breathtaking about that.

He retreated from the bar, walking backward until he was beside her, never once showing his back to the men.

He didn't trust them.

Good. He shouldn't.

They shouldn't.

Louisa glanced at Oliver's face. Not an ounce of emotion was visible to the eye. His mask—no, his shield—was firmly in place. Her gaze drifted back to the Fury men. They too, had their shields in place.

Urgh.

How tiring.

She didn't know how they did it or how they kept it up. She certainly wouldn't be able to. Her emotions tended to explode out for the world to see.

"Our business is done here," Oliver announced. If there had been no emotion on his face, there was even less in his tone. He could have been speaking to an ant, for all the feeling those words conveyed. It did, however, carry a note of finality.

Maxen inclined his head.

"Hah!" Mr. Helgate suddenly exclaimed. "*Your* business with him is done. Mine business with him has just begun."

Louisa's shocked face turned to Mr. Helgate.

"And what business is that?" The brother behind the bar asked.

Mr. Helgate's smiled rather fox-like. No, utterly fox-like.

He rubbed his jaw as he stared the man down. "You have my attention now. That's not a good thing to have."

Silence followed his statement. Not a comfortable one, but one filled with unspoken calculation.

She'd been so concerned about her own feelings that she'd never truly, deeply considered how Mr. Helgate must have felt that a charge had been snatched on his watch. Given the bloody state of the man on the ground, she could just believe that his attention was not the sort you wanted on you.

Best to leave.

"Let's go," she said to Oliver. The sooner they left, the sooner her heart would settle. She wanted to take a day to rest. Then, tomorrow, they would leave for Ashford again. Even though all she wanted to do was fall onto her bed with lavender pillows and forget this disaster, she couldn't imagine being enclosed for hours upon hours in a carriage today.

A hand settled on her back and guided her and Leo from the tavern, Oliver and Mr. Helgate following closely behind. No words were spoken between the two parties as they left.

What she needed was the view of the beach from Mr. Helgate's cottage. The smell of the ocean breeze blowing away the unease of those memories of her own kidnapping. And then there were those brief flashes . . .

Who was that young man from her memories?

Would she ever remember?

Did he even exist?

⟫✦⟪

OLIVER'S BOOTS SANK into the sand as he made his way down the beach, a blanket draped over his shoulder, toward Louisa, who wandered along the shore. She'd once again surprised him when she'd asked Helgate if they could spend another night at the cottage. He'd thought she might insist on returning directly home after the fright they'd had, but she'd wanted to breathe in the ocean air, she had claimed.

He was happy she'd made that choice.

She deserved a moment to catch her breath, and he was glad to help provide that moment.

He'd told her the truth earlier in the tavern. Ever since the moment she'd jabbed a knife at him, she had claimed all the power between them. No, perhaps even before that. Ten years ago, when he'd discovered his father had abducted a little girl and held her in the run-down cottage where he had always before found his escape, ruining his once sacred sanctuary with that one act.

He lifted his chin and inhaled deeply, dragging the smell of salt and seaweed into his lungs.

Ah, yes, this was why she wanted to stay another night.

The distance between him and the angel closed. She moved with a grace that seemed to match the flow of the waves lapping at the sand. Her hair tumbled over her shoulders in loose curls that danced with every step she took, shimmering in the evening sun. Her curves were gracefully sculpted by the soft folds of her dress, moving with each step.

Truly angelic. Utterly beautiful.

Oliver's heart pounded, a fusion of emotions too profound to name exploding into his chest. She had stirred something within him during their time together. Something he couldn't quite yet grasp with his two hands. Yet neither did he want to let it go.

"Louisa," he said when he was a few feet away.

She glanced back and smiled when their eyes met. "Did you find yourself in the mood for a stroll as well?"

"Something to that effect." He saw the gooseflesh on her arms. "You must be cold." He pulled the blanket from his shoulder, shook it out, and draped it over her shoulders, his finger brushing the pale skin of her collarbone.

Oliver swallowed and withdrew his hands.

"On the contrary, the breeze is quite refreshing," she said but clutched the blanket tightly.

She started walking again, and he fell into step beside her. "What are you thinking about, roaming the coastline all alone?" Oliver asked.

"Would you believe me if I said I wasn't thinking about any-thing?"

Oliver smiled. "No."

She chuckled. "You'd be right." She bent down to pick up a smooth pebble, rubbing it between her fingers. "I was wondering what life would look like if the duchess were no longer in our lives."

"You mean Leo's life."

"It must sound rather strange, but the way she speaks to him . . . I cannot explain it. It is too sweet, too false."

"No, I understand," Oliver said. In fact, he applauded Louisa for picking up on the nuances. Not many people would. "These women use their husbands and sons to manage the tasks they cannot, as you see with the betting book. And that control has to start somewhere."

"It's quite clever," Louisa murmured, shaking her head. "It makes them share responsibility. Shall we sit and watch the sunset?" She lowered onto the sand, patting the spot next to her.

"Clever, indeed."

Oliver followed suit, glancing toward the horizon. The sky, once a soft blue, had shifted to a brilliant tapestry of golds, pinks, and purples, each color blending seamlessly into the next.

Almost as radiant as the woman next to him.

This might be the first time he'd ever taken the time to enjoy the sunset.

"Lawks," the angel suddenly spoke. "It gives me the shivers just thinking about it. At least I haven't been wrong to feel off about Camilla's treatment of my brother. She probably wanted to groom him for use while winning him over to her side. Conniving woman!"

"You don't have to worry about that, Louisa," Oliver said softly. "I won't let that happen."

She folded her arms atop her knees and lowered her chin to rest upon them, turning her head to stare at him.

Oliver felt his ears heat at her regard.

"No?" she murmured. "Even though Leo is a Talbot?"

"Your brother is innocent. He deserves to stay that way as long as possible." When Oliver was the boy's age, if he wasn't at school, his father had him sit in on all his meetings, good or bad. He'd lost his own innocence too early as a result. But it was also this habit that had allowed him to learn about what his father had done to the young Lady Louisa.

"Words sweeter than romance."

He chuckled at that, arching a brow. "Have you ever experienced the romance of courtship?"

"I can't say that I've had a determined enough suitor." Her smile widened. A spark of mischief lit her gaze. "But I have had a *peck* and a kiss, and they were still a lot sweeter than any courtship as far as I can tell."

Oliver inhaled deeply, the cool ocean air pouring into his body, a striking opposition to the heat rushing through his blood. Here, with the sound of the waves and Louisa at his side, he felt a remarkable sense of peace. But it was a peace shadowed with a growing desire that gnawed at him.

"Speechless?" she teased, then chuckled.

"You've quite robbed me of my breath," he admitted, unable to tear his gaze away from her. Unable to break the connection. The spell she cast with her bright eyes, winding around him. He wasn't sure he wanted to break it. He certainly didn't want to think about anything else, anything that might shatter the enchantment.

After all that had happened, he needed a moment to catch his breath, too.

She was that moment.

"Then shall I give it back to you?" She flashed her teeth. "Your tongue."

God, Louisa.

The wind picked up, carrying a bite that prickled his skin, which he welcomed. However, he didn't want the angel to be even the slightest bit cold, so he moved closer to her, wanting to serve as a shield and warmer, but also—and this might be the real damn reason—he wanted to be closer. As close as she would let him be.

What the devil was wrong with him?

You are in trouble, Oliver. The thought echoed over and over as she leaned closer, craning her neck at him, one finger tapping her lower lip. Her eyes laughed at him. "Are you moving so close for the return?"

God, she drove him mad.

And yet, his head lowered to brush her lips. How could he stop himself? How could he deny her? He'd have to be made of damn stone to resist. Cold, unfeeling, a marble statue, as most considered him to be. But hot blood pulsed his veins, and at this moment, it burned.

Her fingers tangled in his jacket, pulling him down with her as she fell back onto the beach.

Her tongue met his in an urgency he praised, her lips answering his desperation in kind. She tasted like sherry—sweet, seductive, and utterly intoxicating. Christ, it wasn't enough. He chased that flavor, sought it out with a hunger that bordered on madness.

Fire coiled low in his gut.

Her hands looped around his neck, her fingers pushing up his hair. The action was so exquisite, Oliver's whole body broke out in shivers. He cupped her cheek, the other hand digging into the sand, clenching a fistful, trying hard to prevent it from roaming in places that might get him into serious trouble.

"Oliver," she breathed against his lips.

Another wave of shivers rushed over his body. Hell and damnation, what was he doing? He lifted onto one arm. "We should stop."

"No."

He stilled, eyes meeting hers. "I beg your pardon?" he said in confusion. No?

"We should continue back in our chamber."

Our chamber.

"We don't have a chamber," Oliver said slowly, and too damn raspy for his own liking.

Her eyes sparked like blue jewels. Naughty jewels. "Right, that was the other cottage," she murmured. There was a note of mischief in her voice. "But the one here is good, too. I was hoping you could wrap your limbs around me again tonight?"

Was she trying to kill him? "Last time was a mistake."

Her hands slid from his hair, dragging down to his chest, fingers digging into him like a silent, provocative demand. "I refuse to accept the word *mistake*. There is no such thing. There is only the moment, the opportunity."

"Louisa, do you even know what you are saying?"

She grinned. "Saying? I know what I am *doing*. I am seducing you."

Ah, yes, this angel was killing him. "Why would you do that?" he dared to ask.

"Because I might never have the chance again. And I am a lady who dares, Duke."

Oliver had been mistaken.

He was already in serious trouble. It had arrived long ago.

Chapter Seventeen

THE MOMENT THE carriage door shut behind them, their lips collided. Oliver had refused to return to a bedchamber to be seduced, but Louisa had been able to *seduce* him into being seduced in the carriage. Her hands plunged into his hair, fingers tangling in the thick strands. She loved its softness. Silky and wild beneath her touch.

Who knew the duke would let his guard down like this?

For *her*.

She understood that he was placing all the power into her hands by allowing her to take the lead. But while he might believe she was the one seducing him, in fact, she had been seduced by him with every touch, every word, and every look since he'd shown up that night in her house.

Her hands slipped from his hair, pushing him back into the seat with the firm pressure of her palms against his chest. With a daring shift of her hips, she straddled him, her pulse quickening at the heat of his body beneath hers. Honestly, she didn't quite know what she was doing, but this sense of being in charge drove her to act in whatever way felt right.

And this felt *so* right.

She had never felt more alive.

"Louisa . . ." His eyes flashed like amber flames, firm hands holding her waist.

"That is my name, yes," she murmured, and she brushed a finger over one of his flushed cheeks. "This is the first time I've seen such an expression on your face before. I quite like it."

"I haven't seen it myself," his voice turned gruff, "but yours is to my liking as well." A hard object pressed against her from below.

Her entire body blazed with consuming fascination.

Louisa regained her breath. "Then, do you follow all the ladies who are to your liking into empty carriages?"

His lips upturned into the widest grin she'd glimpsed on his face so far. Lord, it made her heart skip not one, not two, not three but several more beats all at once!

"You are the only lady I've ever followed into an empty carriage apart from my mother," he said in a low, suggestive way.

"That is strangely lovely to hear." Louisa beamed.

He chuckled, squeezing the flesh of her waist. "And this is from the lady who gasped at catching two servants kissing."

She lowered her head to his, a breath away from touching. "Perhaps they opened a whole new world for me."

"So we are not debating innocence from this moment forth?"

"I stopped questioning my innocence the moment our lips first met after our ledger appropriation in Worthing."

"Oh? Then what are you debating now? Dare I ask?"

Her nose touched the tip of his. "This is quite clear, is it not?"

His eyes sparked into hers. "I won't ask you if you will regret this choice."

"And you shouldn't. My regrets are mine; your regrets are yours. But this, just so that you know, servant of mine, I will never regret."

"Christ, Louisa." He nipped at her chin. "Then . . ."

She looped her arms around his neck and kissed him in answer. Her sentiments on the beach had been real—they might never have this moment again. After they confirmed whether or not the duchess also possessed a secret ledger, they would part ways. And if they were going to part, let them also share what they might never share again.

Let them part in an earth-shattering way.

Her fingers traced up the line of his jaw, his stubble tickling the palm of her hand. He had tiny, barely-visible freckles scattered across his cheeks, with that one notable freckle claiming its bold spot beneath his left eye.

She pressed back into his hardness and was rewarded with a groan whispering along her neckline. Lawks, she loved that sound.

She arched into him again.

He cursed. "Christ, woman, you are driving me mad."

Her hands seized his to guide them to her ankles before she dragged them back up her legs, and her skirt along with them. "Then we should do something about it, do you not think?" She let go of his hands to fumble with the buttons of his trousers.

Another curse. "Aren't we moving too fast?" he asked even as he bucked beneath into her.

She paused only long enough to answer, "This is not a moment for going slow, Oliver!"

He chuckled before catching her lips again. Her fingers continued their ministrations, pausing only once they had completed their task. She started when he suddenly lifted off the seat, not breaking their kiss as he shoved his trousers down. His manhood sprang forth, and a thrill of excitement shot through her like a cannonball.

His mouth broke away from hers. "Touch me," he breathed with a near groan, steering one of her hands to his member.

Dear Lord, how could she resist?

She encircled him with the palm of her hand, a thrill of excitement shooting up her spine when he guided her movements up and down at a slow pace. "Just keep pumping like that."

He was so hard. And yet, his flesh was silky smooth in her palm. One of his hands rested on her hip and the other snaked beneath her skirts to pull down her drawers. She lifted, knees pressed into the cushions, allowing him to make swift work of the garment before his hand finally, *finally* ventured to her woman-hood and *touched* her.

And Lord, that touch.

Her gasp coincided with his sharp inhale as the hand on his member tightened. A finger slipped inside her. The invasion felt strange and foreign, but also thrilling and fascinating. Louisa lost all reason—no, she only lost what little she had left.

She wanted this man.

She wanted the duke.

It was in this moment, as they touched each other's most intimate places on their bodies, that she could finally admit how much she wanted him. She *liked* him. Perhaps she had even fallen a little bit in love. Dear Lord in Heaven! In lo—

Another finger entered her, and she could no longer focus on anything, not even her own hand which lost its rhythm on his member. Instead, she gripped his shoulders. Tightly.

He arched his face into her neck, breathing in deeply. "How does it feel?"

"*Sensational.*"

His tongue darted out, grazing over her skin, tasting her. "Louisa, this position . . ."

"Might hurt?" She didn't care. She lifted her body so that she could guide him to her entrance. "I want this. I want myself atop you."

"You want power over me?" He guided her hand to his chest, where she could feel the wild beat of his heart. "You have it all."

By all that was holy, how could a man be so breathtaking? And Lord, he looked beautiful. His cheeks were flushed, just as she imagined hers to be. She leaned over to kiss the freckle under his eye.

She loved that little mark.

He guided her hips to his hardness.

Louisa's head fell back as he pressed into her, his mouth dragging down to her bosom. He scraped the bud of her breast with his teeth through her dress. And then he was inside her, breaching her last bit of resistance in one swift thrust. The pinch of pain, the fullness, the sheer arousal of becoming one with him stole her breath.

His whole body froze in place. "Do I need to stop?"

Her eyes opened to meet his, her lips quirking. "Why?"

He cursed and suddenly cupped her cheeks and kissed her like a man desperate for this very moment. His hips drove into her, and this time, he no longer hesitated. Louisa curved into each of his thrusts, her body more alive than ever, consumed by every sensation that set her aflame. One arm cradled her back, hugging her tight, and the other was down *there*, rubbing against the place where they almost connected. The fullness that threatened to retreat and then suddenly pushed back again.

She didn't want to miss anything.

They weren't beneath the stars anymore, but for the first time, Louisa learned that stars didn't need to explode in the sky, for her body scattered into a million of them as the heat that started to spark where his body joined hers, the region the palm of his hand claimed and pressed, exploded from below and traveled up her limbs with the speed of lightning.

Would she ever be able to collect those million pieces of herself again?

OLIVER'S HEAD FELL against Louisa's shoulder. He was still inside her, and his heart pulsed like a raging thunderous storm that had no intention of ending. Her sweet scent tightly cloaked him, fusing with the low undertones of his own.

He could breathe in this essence for eternity.

In fact, he could also simply remain here, in this moment, forever. Moving meant returning to the world outside, and he wasn't ready to return to a world where, ledgers and secret organizations aside, they were family foes.

He hugged her tighter against him while his breathing slowly returned to normal. Her arms had looped around his neck, and her fingers were once more playing with his hair. She seemed to love doing that. He loved *her* doing that. Ripples of gooseflesh traced over his skin each time she swirled a tendril between her fingers.

Never before had he done . . .

God, what class of behavior did this even fit into?

"You are overthinking. Stop it," her voice came from his shoulder.

He nuzzled his head against hers, his lips twisting into half a smile. "Oh? And how do you know this is what I am doing?"

She pulled away from him just enough to meet his gaze. "Your shoulders tensed for a second."

"That could mean so many things." And each and every single one of them were things he didn't want to think about.

"Or it means reality has found its way into the carriage."

Clever angel. He smiled, his fingers following the line of her jaw before tucking a wayward strand of hair sticking to the side of her face behind her ear. "I'm trying to keep it at bay."

She suddenly traced a finger over his mouth. "Another first, seeing this sort of smile on your lips."

"And what sort is it?" Oliver asked, his voice still a bit gruff. He nipped at that playful finger.

"A smile of contentment."

Contentment had surely settled into his bones. Laziness, too. Though for how long those feelings would remain, he couldn't say. If he were lucky, the whole night. If not . . . he'd best enjoy every stolen second of them in this moment, since there was no other moment like it. "As much as I want to, we can't stay here for much longer."

"I know." A small sigh. "The world awaits, does it not? What a shame that the line between dreams and life is as thin as a whisper." She lifted herself away from him, and the loss was palpable, its emptiness reaching the depth of his soul.

"Oh, dear," she muttered, glancing down at the disarray they'd created. "We've made quite a mess of things."

Oliver removed a handkerchief from his pocket and handed it over. He liked the mess. He liked everything they made.

"What about you?" she asked, her gaze lighting up on a certain member of his body, which had since calmed down.

A flush spread from his neck up to his ears. "I'll be fine." In times of need, one had to work with what one could. They quickly cleaned themselves and rearranged their clothing. Well, as much as they could. His mind shifted briefly to the looming complications of their situation. "Your brother is rather astute, so we must be careful."

She laughed. "That little brat does have the eyes of a hawk, does he not?"

Oliver hooked the last button into place, his gaze never wandering away from Louisa for long. Her cheeks were still flushed, and her hair a bit disheveled, but they could blame the Brighton breeze for that. He filed her angelic, tousled appeared in his memory, deep where it could never be shaken. Where time couldn't touch it.

"Come to think about it," she continued, "he won't allow you to sleep anywhere else but his bed, you know that don't you?"

Oliver nodded. Knowing Leo, that was likely true.

"A pity," she said on a sigh. "I had wished for certain limbs to wrap around me all night."

"*Louisa.*"

How was she supposed to keep a straight face if she continued to bewitch him with that bewitching tongue?

She laughed. "Very well, I shall stop lamenting my loss."

Oliver shook his head at her teasing. The once drowsy contentment was already starting to wear away as their appearance returned to their original state. Louisa had been right. A mere whisper separated dreams from real life. It was foolish to think he could grasp onto this dreamlike moment and hold on forever. Dreams and reality, the one couldn't exist without the other, but they also couldn't exist at the same time.

"How are you feeling?" Oliver asked, watching as she tilted her head to the side and combed her fingers through her hair.

She smiled at him. "That long hair and sea breezes don't work well together." The curve of her lips itched upward. "And that I'm still rather breathless, and I feel marvelous."

"I mean your body."

She let out a soft chuckle. "It feels a bit sensitive, that is all. Do not fret. I shall not expire because I seduced you. And you are also not allowed to feel remorse of any kind. I shall seduce you again if you do."

This woman . . . she always managed to surprise him. Undo him. "Very well, but allow me to offer one thing to you."

"Oh? Pray tell?"

He almost cursed at that intrigued tone. "A key to my door."

She pursed her lips in humor. "What door? The door to your house? Oliver Cavanagh, just what exactly are you suggesting?"

Ah, hell. He grimaced at his own words. "I mean, it's a proverbial key. An offer that you may always come to me and demand whatever you wish, and not only . . . this."

She cocked her head, studying him. "Why would you make such an offer to me?"

"It's hard to predict the consequences of this momentary dream, but more difficult to anticipate the results of everything we've done up to this moment."

"Do you mean the possibility of my father discovering that Leo and I traveled with you and that Leo was kidnapped for a few hours and so forth?"

Oliver nodded. "Precisely."

A moment of silence fell between them before she suddenly laughed. "Lawks, when reality returns, it truly *returns*."

He mirrored her sentiment. "Indeed."

"Thank you for your offer," she said lightly, tossing her hair over her shoulder. "I shall take your proverbial key and keep it safe."

He let out a low breath, relieved. "That is all I ask." All he *could* ask. He could offer her no more, other than his sincerity that he would not abandon her completely once they parted ways. If only their societal connection wasn't so complicated. But he couldn't ignore the fact that she was Talbot's daughter, and neither could she ignore that her father would never allow even the slightest of friendships.

Then there was the secret that hung between them. A secret that she didn't know even existed, and it certainly was not his place to reveal it.

Wasn't it?

No, it couldn't be. Even though he had been the one to go against his father's wishes and help her escape, if Talbot hadn't seen fit to inform his daughter of the details of her return home, there must be a reason for it, and he suspected it had to do with the trouble she had sleeping.

He might make it worse.

"The night . . ." Oliver trailed off, not certain whether he should ask or not.

Louisa arched a brow. "The night . . .? Do you have some-thing to ask? Now is the time. The moment we enter the house, you shall not have another."

Also so direct. Always so keenly aware of the shifting sands between them. "The night I fell asleep beside you in the second cottage—"

"Oh, *that* night." Her eye glinted with sudden mischief.

His pulse did something odd with that look. "Yes, that night. It didn't seem like you had trouble sleeping."

"Is that a question?"

He exhaled, rolling his shoulders to rid himself of whatever had compelled him to bring it up in the first place. "Not exactly. I suppose I was just curious about it."

"About you perhaps being the cure to my sleeping prob-lems?"

God. His stomach twisted. "I never said that."

She laughed, the sound light and airy, yet a shadow crossed her features. "Most nights, I struggle, yes, but there are nights that I am so exhausted that sleep claims me without effort. They are rare, but they exist."

He nodded, but the answer did nothing to quell the unwelcome pit forming dead center in his chest. "I hope that changes in the future."

Her smile turned sweet. "Thank you."

"Shall we go?" He still didn't know why he wanted to know. Had to know. Perhaps because that night had lingered with him far longer than it should have. Perhaps because he wasn't accustomed to being needed, even in the most unspoken ways.

"Yes, I must admit, I am famished."

"Miles cooked a pot of stew."

Her eyes lit with intrigue. "This Miles, why have I never seen him before? He is like a phantom."

"He doesn't like to be seen." Oliver opened the door and jumped from the carriage, landing with effortless grace before turning to offer his hand. She placed her palm in his and stepped out, only to gasp.

Oliver followed her gaze skyward.

Thousands of stars sparkled above them, stretching across the vast, endless night, not one cloud obstructing their shine. His gaze drifted back to her, and Oliver swore he saw those very stars reflected in her eyes.

The stars had caught her breath.

And she had caught his.

Chapter Eighteen

Two days later

EXHAUSTION TUGGED AT Louisa's eyes as she plopped onto her stepmother's bed. They had been traveling hard to Ashford these past days, or perhaps it just *felt* hard because she hadn't been able to sleep a wink since their evening in the carriage.

The very carriage they had traveled back in.

It was only natural for her to get distracted by the memories of their carnal night.

And imagine carnal days.

Nevertheless, she did drift off some of the time, but it could hardly be considered deep sleep. At best, she simply rested the heaviness of her eyelids. However, Oliver, the unescapable scent of sandalwood, the *carriage*—her awareness of these things never abated. The moments she drifted off, she only floated between their dreamlike night and the present that would surface with the drone of Leo's voice as he peppered the duke with questions and opinions.

Fortunately, that particular torture was over.

The mattress of the bed sank deeper, and Louisa glanced at Oliver, who lowered down beside her. His thumb traced beneath her eye. "You look tired."

"Tired? My body is practically begging for my lavender-scented pillows. Though sadly, my best ones are in London."

"Do they help you sleep?"

Louisa nodded. "But they will have to wait. First, we must try and find that ledger." Her gaze swept the chamber that she purposely never entered. She'd imagined wallpaper and bedding would be blood red or charcoal black. But the room seemed entirely normal. Entirely *unlike* Camilla.

"Then where do you suppose we search first?"

Louisa pursed her lips in thought, her gaze falling on her stepmother's writing desk. "I suppose it would be much too easy if she were to hide it in the same spot as Lady Havendish." She rose and strode over, bending over to search for any hidden compartment. "But perhaps we will be lucky. You look under the bed and mattress."

A few minutes later, they both had come up short.

Louisa strode over to the curtains and inspected them, then made her way over to the duchess's dressing room and started to rifle through her clothing items. How could one woman have so many red items? Though, was she really all that surprised? Camilla might secretly be the devil's bride. "It must be here somewhere."

"Unless she took it with her."

Louisa paused. Yes, that could very well be the case, but it would be an extreme loss. Unless they were to travel back to Worthing and hunt for that ledger. However, that would be a catastrophic blunder if Lady Havendish's ledger had already been missed. But, then again, would her stepmother really trust her friends enough to take her ledger with her? Somehow Louisa didn't think so. That woman was too shrewd to trust anyone blindly.

Also, many things could happen while traveling. Why, Theodosia had been robbed by highwaymen, who had absconded with the betting book. Her friend had been forced to chase them down and steal it back. Camilla wouldn't be quick to risk that either.

No, it was here somewhere. Louisa was sure of it. It was just a matter of trying to step into her stepmother's shoes.

If I were Camilla, where would I hide a ledger with detailed ac-

counts of my criminal enterprise?

Her gaze fell on a stack of books on the bedside. She padded over and picked them up one by one, tossing the ones with titles and printed pages onto the bed, until the only two brown, leather bound journals were left. Or were they?

"I wonder." Could it honestly be this simple? Would Camilla be this confident?

Oliver came up behind her, peering over her shoulder.

Louisa didn't leave him in suspense. She opened one of the books to a random spot, revealing neat penmanship.

April 7: Today the scab on my leg . . .

Dear Lord, no. Louisa flung the journal onto the bed. She didn't want to know about any scab on that woman's body. Oliver chuckled but didn't say anything. She inhaled a deep breath, opening the second journal, this one exposing an array of meticulously organized entries. Each page was filled with rows of dates, item descriptions, quantities, prices, and a column for Camilla's notes.

Louisa's eyes widened as she scanned the contents. The first entry read:

January 5: Silk bolts (imported from China): 20

Smuggled through Dover: 50 guineas

> *Notes: Silk received in excellent condition. Paid the customs officer to look the other way.*

Farther down the page, another entry caught her attention:

February 12: Brandy barrels (French): 10

Delivered to Worthing: 30 guineas

> *Notes: Sold to Lord Hamilton's estate. Extra payment for discretion.*

As she flipped through the ledger, the entries revealed a wide range of illegal activities: smuggling of luxury goods, bribery of officials, and illicit sales. One particularly disturbing note read:

March 3: Opium (Bengal): 5 crates

Distributed to local apothecaries: 100 guineas

> *Notes: Demand increasing. Secured higher price due to risk. Need to reinforce security.*

Louisa's jaw tightened as she took in the scope of Camilla's dealings. She had understood her stepmother was busy with illegal things, but reading about them in such plain language made her heart burn with anger.

Louisa turned another page, her blood suddenly chilling as one particular entry caught her eye:

May 15: Kidnapped (for ransom): daughter of CHL.

Ransom demanded: Open port for opium distribution

> *Notes: Transaction went smoothly.*

Kidnapping . . .
Transaction . . .
The book slipped from her fingers, and a dark, heavy fog settled in her chest. Memories she'd long buried tried to push to the surface.
No, not now.
She clutched at her breast, feeling as though the walls of Camilla's chamber were bearing down on her. She tried to inhale deeply, but her breath came out too quickly, and in too shallow, too frantic.
Then Oliver was there, hand on the back of her shoulders, rubbing in slow soothing circles. "Breathe, Louisa. Just breathe."
She followed the instruction of his voice, breathing and exhaling at his command until she could draw a breath without the threat of choking on air. Though honestly, the air in this chamber should be considered tainted.

"That woman is horrible," she bit out.

Oliver's hand lowered to the small of her back as he bent to retrieve the book. "I'm sorry."

"Don't apologize. That woman . . ." She looked at Oliver, jaw clenched. "This is enough to send her to the bowels of hell, isn't it?"

He squeezed her waist. "Yes, and I shall be able to cross reference the dates with the betting book to expose all who have been involved in some way."

"That is good." She paused a moment. "I . . . words fail me. How could she do such things? How could she see kidnapping as a mere transaction? Well, you did say confidence was the downfall of all criminals. She must be stopped at all costs."

"I agree," he murmured softly. "And we shall do just that." He suddenly shook his head. "Your stepmother is a confident woman, leaving such damning evidence on her bedside table. I suspect no one enters this chamber except for her and her trusted servants."

"But she is not here."

"Her servants, on the other hand, are. She must believe no one would ever think she'd hide the ledger in plain sight."

Well, it would certainly be her downfall. A reckoning would be heading Camilla's way soon, and Louisa couldn't wait. One thing did bother her, though. "My father . . ." Her gaze met Oliver's. "What if he is involved?"

"I don't believe he is."

"But you cannot be certain beyond any shadow of a doubt." He might very well be involved. And if that were the case, Louisa didn't know what she and Leo would do. The last thing she wanted was for her brother to be raised by a criminal, even if that criminal was a birth parent.

"Not beyond any shadow, no." His fingers squeezed hers in quiet promise of support.

Louisa swept an unforgiving gaze around the chamber. "We should probably leave. Leo must almost be done with his bath, then he will come looking for us. Will you stay to say goodbye to him? He will never forgive you if you don't."

She would not let him off, either.

An overwhelming sense of finality sank in. This was the end. Even if he lingered an hour or two, he would be leaving soon, and they would likely not meet again for a long time. And even when they did—*if* they did—there would always be an insurmountable distance between them.

"Oliver, I . . ." Louisa trailed off, uncertain what she even wanted to say. That she didn't want him to leave? That she wanted to sleep in his arms one more night? That she fancied him a touch more than she should?

"*What*, pray tell, is going on here?"

Both of them jerked.

Ah, a reckoning had come all right—a bit quicker than expected—and judging from the look of fury on the Duchess of Talbot's face, it seemed it was to be Louisa's.

⸎

OLIVER STARED AT the woman he had been after for a while now. Slippery as a snake, calculating as a fox, and ruthless as a tiger. Camilla Talbot had been a ghost in his world too long, always elusive and hard to see, always floating just out of reach. But at this moment, she was no ghost. At this moment, she stood before him, the very embodiment of cunning and pride.

Her gaze, sharp and cold, dropped to the ledger in his hand, her expression turning ugly. It was a look he had seen too many times from those who thought they were untouchable—those who had built criminal empires by grinding the world beneath their heel.

They got their comeuppance.

One way or the other.

Her lips twisted into a mock smile, but it was strained. Her eyes flicked to Louisa and back at him. "You shouldn't have come here, Mortimer."

"You are done, Camilla," Louisa snapped out. "We know everything, and this ledger will be your undoing. It's over."

"Camilla?" Another voice intervened, and a tall man came up behind her. The Duke of Talbot.

Oliver flinched. There would be hell to pay. Perhaps not today, though it was hard to say just yet. But this man, he would make sure Oliver never forgot this moment. This moment when their eyes met and Talbot's cheeks flushed several shades of red before his gaze fell on his daughter. One color surfaced above the others—vermillion.

He pushed past his wife and marched into the chamber. "What the devil is the meaning of this, and why the devil is your hand on my daughter?"

Oliver jerked, his hand still resting on Louisa's back, a touch meant for comfort, but now an infernal brand on his palm. One that would now cause a damnably rousing tempest. His fingers curled, then his hand fell to his side as Louisa stepped forward, taking up a defensive stance before him.

"What is going on here? That is what I would like to know!" She snatched the ledger from Oliver's hand. "Did you know your wife has been dealing in detestable, illegal schemes? That she is the head of a criminal organization of women?"

All the color drained from Talbot's face. His gaze darted to the ledger, then back to Louisa. His lips parted as if to speak, yet no words emerged.

Oliver clenched his fists, but he also caught the look of surprise on Talbot's wife's face.

"So you knew," Louisa said, her hands falling to her sides, the ledger still gripped in one hand. "Were you a part of this? Did you help her? Distributing opium? *Kidnapping children?*"

That brought Talbot to his senses. "Of course not! I would never do anything so despicable."

"Then what?" Louisa demanded, a tremor in her voice. "I am

dying to know."

The man dragged a hand through his hair. "Where is your brother?"

"Bathing."

Talbot nodded before his gaze passed over Oliver again. "You are investigating this matter?"

"I am," Oliver said stiffly. "And before you accuse me of anything else, I started my inquiry not knowing your wife was at the other end."

The duchess lifted her chin, her eyes chilling. "I have done nothing wrong."

Oliver gently took the book from Louisa's clenched fingers. "This ledger says otherwise."

The woman lifted her chin. "That is not mine."

"We found it in your chamber!" Louisa snapped with indignation.

"Then someone must have placed it there to frame me," the duchess argued.

Oliver wasn't about to let her off. "It's a simple matter of comparing your handwriting to another source, Your Grace."

"Hah! If you think—"

"Camilla," Talbot said in a warning voice, "it's over. I've suspected you were up to something for a while now, ever since Havendish got foxed and blabbered about some silk. He rambled on about his wife's intelligence and how the two of you made such a splendid pair. It didn't take long to find more clues, inconsistencies."

Oliver did not expect that.

"Then why didn't you do something about it?" Louisa demanded.

Oliver had to wonder the same thing.

"And what would you have me do?" Talbot countered. "I had to think of a way to deal with the matter without damaging our name, *your* name, your brother's name." A glare fell on Oliver. "That is not up for debate anymore, is it?"

"Do not look at him, Papa!" Louisa suddenly exclaimed. "*I* say that it is not up for debate anymore, and if you ask Leo, he will agree!"

"Your brother is only ten years old!"

"And yet he knows right from wrong better than you do!"

"James," the duchess started, "you must know I'm innocent of whatever they think—whatever *you* think—I've done. I have nothing to do with criminals or these crimes they've mentioned."

"We will talk about it later, Camilla."

The room fell into sudden silence after that last, darkly-uttered statement. All the occupants were in a strange, tense standoff. Oliver wanted to object, but he was in no position to drag the woman away. Her title, her position in society, made this an annoyingly delicate matter to navigate.

After a moment, Talbot inhaled a deep breath and directed at his daughter, "I did what I thought best at the time, which is a moot point at the moment. But what are you doing with Mortimer here?"

"Helping him find evidence against your wife."

"Louisa!" He swallowed whatever outburst might have followed, to say lowly, "And how did you know to help him find evidence? Did he approach you?" Talbot's dark gaze landed on him.

Oliver didn't dare interject and speak for Louisa. He would follow her direction. Unfortunately for them both, a little Leo darted into the room at that moment. "Papa!" His gaze fell on them. "Louisa? What are you and the gardener doing here?" His eyes widened. "I mean, I mean the Bow Street Runner!"

Oliver sighed. His explanation would be required after all, it seemed. "Would you believe me if I said I had no ill—"

"I will not!" Talbot interrupted, his glare turning wrathful. "This won't be the end of it. Now get the hell out of my house."

"What?" Louisa exclaimed and pointed at the duchess. "What about her? She is the real culprit here!"

"This is a family matter and will be treated as such."

"You cannot be serious!"

"I shall not forgive her for bringing shame to this family, Louisa. What would you have me do?"

"Have her arrested and account for what she's done!" Louisa didn't stop there but continued with a threat. "I shall never forgive you if you let her off, Papa!"

"And what about my forgiveness?" Talbot demanded. "My daughter is consorting with the enemy! I knew something was afoot when you arrived at the Havendish estate and the next day their house was turned inside out looking for a book, which just happened to coincide with your sudden disappearance. Then I return home to find you with a bloody Cavanagh?"

"I approached your daughter first, Talbot," Oliver said. "She is not in the wrong here."

"Why would you damn well approach her in the first place?"

"Because I had the betting book from White's which, along with the list of heiresses, also contains evidence of your wife's illicit transactions," Louisa exclaimed. "Would you have done any differently if you had been in his shoes?"

"Louisa?" Leo asked hesitantly before Talbot could say anything. "What is going on? Who is this man? Is he not a Bow Street Runner?"

Oliver cursed inwardly. "I am not a Runner, but I do help Bow Street on occasion."

"Do not poison my son's ears with your nonsense," Talbot snapped. "He is the Duke of Mortimer," he said to Leo, "our family's oldest enemy."

Leo's eyes widened even as Louisa's snort came from beside him. "Enemy? He might be the oldest rival, but the true enemy of our family is standing next to you, Papa!"

Oliver's grip tightened on the ledger. The duchess, who this whole mess was about, stood still as a delicate rose, with a look of pure innocence on her face. No wonder she had gotten away with so much. Even now, her husband was hesitant to take action. He finally understood what Louisa had meant by her stepmother putting on a face in front of the duke and dropping it the moment he was gone.

There would be no reasoning with the duke. The only reason the man had tolerated his presence up till this point was because he'd been rattled by events. But Oliver could sense that feeling was fading.

"I have what I came for," Oliver said to Talbot. He didn't want it to end like this, but what other choice did he have? He didn't dare look at Louisa, afraid he might give away too much in front of her father. "I shall take my leave. Bow Street will be in touch to discuss the proceedings with your wife."

"Are you delighted?" Talbot growled. "You finally get to ruin our family."

"I have ruined nothing."

"Nothing, you say?" Talbot suddenly laughed. "Your family started this damn feud with us! We might have come to some sort of accord with time, but that ended ten years ago."

Oliver froze.

No.

"The day you kidnapped my daughter."

A soft gasp filled his ears, and his heart plunged to his boots. He never wanted her to discover the truth. Never wanted her to loathe him.

"That's right, take a good look at the man you aided, for the blood in his veins is the reason you were afflicted beyond measure when you were but a little girl."

"Is this true?" Her soft voice stabbed at him.

How the hell had things turned from the duchess's atrocious dealings to his family? But he couldn't deny it. He had no right, for his family *had* done that to her. He glanced over to her, his gaze meeting hers.

"It's true.

Chapter Nineteen

LOUISA'S MIND DREW a complete blank.

Oliver had left only a few seconds ago after his admission. He'd strode from Camilla's chamber, his shoulders stiff but his steps firm. He hadn't looked back. Not even half a look. Not even a slight tilt.

The Duke of Mortimer . . . his family . . . they were behind the kidnapping all those years ago? The man who had kissed her, comforted her, *held* her . . . he was part of the nightmare that gripped her for the last ten years?

Her breath turned to ice in her lungs.

She might as well have been plunged beneath the surface of dark, freezing water. That darkness seeped into her mind, and she could hear the laughter, the droplets of rain dripping from cracks in a roof. Feel the hard mattress . . .

And a gripping fear that wouldn't let her go.

Her gaze shifted back to the spot he had occupied moments ago, denial pulsing from her heart.

No.

It couldn't be.

Surely . . . there must be some mistake.

"Louisa, you are forbidden to ever speak to that man again. Do I make myself clear?"

Louisa slowly turned to her father, meeting his furious gaze, the present moment coming again into sharp focus. Instant indignation rose at the command. "Then you are forbidden to ever speak to your wife again."

"James!" the duchess exclaimed, and Louisa thought she might cast up her accounts at the false display of grievance from that woman.

"That is not a reasonable request, Louisa," her father answered. "There are matters I need to deal with, and to deal with them I need to have a conversation with Camilla."

"What would be a reasonable request, then? What will you do when Bow Street arrives to hold your wife accountable for her actions? Did you know that two men with the surname Fury approached Leo to retrieve the betting book for them so they could have leverage over her?"

Her father's face paled. "What?"

Finally an appropriate reaction. "So you know about those burly fellows." Good. "Did you know they are at war with her as well? That your title does not scare them?"

"That's not true!" Camilla exclaimed. "I don't even know those blackguards. How can I be at war with them?"

"How indeed?" Louisa glared at the woman. "Then ask me where Havendish's ledger is right now."

The duchess's eyes widened, and a flicker of fear flashed across her features. "You gave it to them," she breathed, her words filled with horror.

"Oh!" Leo suddenly exclaimed. He'd been rather silent for a while, but this jolted him into verbal action. "That's why they kidnapped me—for that ledger!"

"They did what?" their father thundered, his face flushing a deep red once again.

"Yes," Louisa said flatly. "And the Duke of Mortimer helped rescue him." She didn't care if it was a bit of a rough summary of events, she wanted to ensure that her father understood the true enemy they were facing.

Her kidnapping . . . the Cavanaghs . . .

She couldn't dwell on that now. She had to make sure that their efforts to seek justice and stop criminal activity now were not in vain.

"Camilla is the reason for all of this," Louisa finished.

The duchess's face contorted in a supremely ugly fashion. "No matter what, you cannot let them arrest me. I am the Duchess of Talbot! The Talbot family name will be ruined if the truth is revealed!"

Louisa couldn't help herself—she laughed, bitter and sharp. Her stepmother finally seemed to be giving up any pretense of innocence. "So, Camilla, your true face is finally showing."

The woman's eyes narrowed, her lips curling into a sneer. "I will show you my true face, you just wait!"

"Camilla," her father growled, a low, dangerous warning. "I will deal with you later."

Leo suddenly grasped Louisa's hand in his. "Don't worry, sister, I am on your side."

A soft, relieved breath escaped her, and the throb in her chest eased a bit. "Thank you, brat."

Leo nodded solemnly, his young face set with determination, informing their father, "I don't know what is going on, but if Stepmother has done anything wicked, she should be punished."

"You are too young to understand, Leo," the older man said with a deep sigh. "There are many things to consider."

Leo stood taller, challenging the duke's authority without fear. "If you are talking about Louisa and myself, we shall be fine. It will say more about our character if we hold a family member accountable than allowing harrowing deeds to go unpunished."

Louisa stared at her brother, stunned by his words. She could hardly suppress the surge of pride swelling in her chest. Without thinking, she grabbed his cheek and squeezed it affectionately. "Little brat, when did you get so wise?"

"Have you forgotten?" Leo said with a grin. "I always follow you around."

Their father cursed under his breath. "Camilla, you are not to leave this chamber for the time being. In the meantime, pack your belongings."

Camilla's eyes widened in disbelief. "What do you mean by that?"

"My children have decided," her father replied, his tone clipped and resolute. "Honestly, I would have wanted nothing more than to deal with this matter silently, but your actions have not only brought a jackal into my house, it resulted in my children being placed in danger. I cannot tolerate that. I need to settle some matters here, then we will be returning to London."

Louisa blinked, the sudden shift catching her off guard. "We are?"

"Not you," her father said in a way that brooked no argument. "You shall remain here with your brother. Camilla and I will pay a visit to Bow Street."

"James!"

He ignored her. "I cannot predict the backlash, so I do not want the two of you near London."

Louisa wasn't daft. Her father also didn't want her near the Duke of Mortimer, who was probably already on his way back to London to hand over the evidence this very minute.

"Why didn't you demand the ledger from the duke?" Louisa asked, curious. It seemed rather out of character for him to let the duke go so easily.

Her father scowled. "What would be the point when he would just refuse to hand it over?"

Louisa understood. It was a matter of pride. Pride and power. Her father wouldn't ask for the book because he didn't want to lower himself to make the request and because he'd been confident—at that moment, at least—in his power to suppress it.

Louisa was suddenly tired.

She'd been exhausted before, but this . . . the life nearly drained from her body. She didn't want to think about the past, she didn't want to argue with her father, and she didn't want . . .

Oliver to have left like this.

She rubbed her temples, a low ache starting to form there. Her father had once again reminded her why she wished to avoid men like him. He wasn't a bad man. He cared for his children immensely. She believed he always did what he thought was right and honorable. But there was another side to him as well. A darker side.

We all have them.

But that didn't mean we all had to act upon that side. That didn't mean hatchets couldn't be buried. That didn't mean one couldn't look toward the future instead of the past.

Louisa sighed but lifted her head to stare straight at her step-mother. "Her servants are not to be trusted."

Her father nodded. "I'll handle them. Hire new ones while I am away."

"Will she return with you?" Louisa pressed. There were some things she would not tolerate any longer either. Such as Camilla's presence in her brother's life. "I won't accept her as family."

"This is ridiculous," Camilla said furiously. "No matter what happens, you cannot strip me of my title."

"I can if I press for a divorce."

Louisa's eyes widened. She'd never expected her father would ever consider such a thing. While not impossible, it was certainly frowned upon. And divorces were rarely granted, as they required an act of Parliament. However, it would make their stance on the matter clear if this matter became public. A clear divide.

In any event, this matter was between her father and his wife.

She had done what needed to be done. However, one point of interest still refused to be dismissed. A faint, stinging question lodged deep in her heart, unresolved, and she didn't quite know what to do with it.

Oliver . . .

His absence had left her cold.

She'd always known their adventure would end this way. Everything she had done, she'd done without regret. But coming to the moment, the moment when their paths split, she couldn't help but regret that the only thing she had left were memories of him—breathless, heart-stirring memories. And nothing else.

"The Duke of Mortimer . . ."

"He is not up for discussion, and his name shall never echo within the walls of our house. That is final."

Louisa stared at her father, but she didn't contradict him. There was no need to. Oliver had already left. And he wouldn't return. They had parted ways, as they were always meant to do.

Oliver couldn't move.

His mind still reeled from little Leo's announcement, Talbot's careless confession, and the horror on Louisa's face when he admitted the truth he had hoped for purely selfish reasons that she would never discover.

He stared at the steam rising from the untouched cup of tea before him. Around him, the light murmurs of conversation hummed, and in the corner, the barman laughed at something a customer said. He'd returned straight to the tavern below his Ashford lodgings after leaving Talbot's residence, which was far preferable to the unnerving silence in his room.

He should be happy.

He had gotten what he wanted and more. He would submit the evidence to Bow Street and expose the secret women's club, and they would dismantle it one member at a time.

So, why did he feel so deuced empty inside?

It couldn't be just because Talbot had revealed the truth to Louisa. It didn't make any sense. His hopes aside, she still deserved to know the truth.

And Bow Street wasn't likely to let the Duchess of Talbot off lightly. They might even be inclined to use her as an example for all the other members. They would also probably send someone to Brighton for the Havendish ledger once he reported its existence. Bloody Fury men. They deserved whatever trouble the law could bring to their little tavern.

But what weighed on him most was the way all of this would affect Louisa. He'd known, of course, that it would touch her in some way, but he'd never allowed himself to truly consider it. Never paused long enough to grasp the depth of what it would cost her. He hadn't dared. He wouldn't have been able to do his job if he had. He didn't want to do it now.

But he must.

Because once again, a Cavanagh would be responsible for causing the Talbots some form of distress. Oliver dragged a hand through his hair. But it hadn't been enough to stop him. Louisa wouldn't have wanted him to stop either, no matter the consequences to her.

"Well, well, well, what do we have here?"

Oliver's muscles tensed at the sound of the familiar voice. He slowly turned to catch Helgate's smiling face. He scowled, not in the mood to be pestered. For a moment, he thought of ignoring the man entirely, but that would only make the pestering worse. "What are you doing here?"

The man pulled up a seat and joined him at the bar. "Miles and I left for Ashford shortly after you. Thought I'd see if you were still around."

Oliver's glanced over his shoulder to sweep the tavern with a glance. "And where is Miles?"

"Retrieving things."

Oliver grunted. Nothing about Miles and Helgate surprised him anymore. The one was full of smiles, whereas the other was a true phantom, just like Louisa had said.

Helgate knocked on the countertop. "Why the sour face? Did Talbot's wife not have a ledger?"

"No, she did. We found it."

"Well, I'll be damned!" Helgate slapped him on the back. "Isn't that something to celebrate?"

"There is nothing to celebrate."

Helgate raised a brow, his smile faltering slightly. "Why not?"

Oliver let out a dry chuckle, though there was no humor in it. "She knows about the kidnapping—her kidnapping," he admitted, the words feeling heavy as they left his mouth. "She knows."

"I see." Helgate's voice dropped a notch. "So, that's why you look like you've been dragged through a field of nettles. She didn't take it well, then?"

"I didn't stay to find out." The look in her eyes had been enough. He hadn't been able to stand it. "Talbot returned with the duchess as well."

Helgate whistled low, the sound slicing through the tavern. "So that's how it is. Found you with his daughter, did he? Honestly, Mortimer, what did you expect? Your families are enemies. No matter what, the duke would never entertain you."

Oliver stared into the full cup of tea that had lost its steam. He had known. However, knowing and experiencing were bitterly different. "I didn't want it to end like this."

"A pint of ale, please," Helgate called to the barman before turning back to Oliver and asking, "How did you want it to end, then?"

He didn't know. Not like *this*. "I never thought about it beyond each moment."

Helgate smirked. "Well, there is your problem then."

Oliver narrowed his eyes. "Why is it a problem?"

Helgate's ale was placed in front of him, and the barman answered for him, "Because women love when men obsess about the future."

Oliver scowled at the man. "Not *this* woman."

The barman shrugged. "You should have just brought her a jewel, then you wouldn't be sitting here with female trouble again."

"Again?" Helgate's brow shot up, his whole face lighting up in intrigue. "Well, I'll be damned."

Oliver gritted his teeth. "What?"

Helgate's smile deepened. "You are in love with her."

Oliver jerked back, as if the words had physically struck him. "I am not."

Helgate chuckled, clearly enjoying his reaction. "Yes, you are. You're in love with Louisa Talbot."

Oliver stood abruptly, his chair scraping against the floor. "I assure you, I am not."

"I assure you, you are." He took of long sip of ale before saying, "You can tell yourself whatever you like, my friend, it doesn't change the truth."

"And just what would you know about love?" The man had never courted a woman in his life, neither had he been close to any woman in the fifteen years Oliver had known him.

Helgate shrugged. "I know it's not the simplest path to tread when there are more straightforward ones available."

"Hear, hear," the barman agreed, nodding at them before leaving to help another customer.

Oliver couldn't refute that bold claim either. For men like them, the simplest paths were business transactions, which was why they tended to also treat marriage as one. Gains and losses were weighed, decided upon, and put to paper.

Very straightforward.

Emotions, on the other hand, were messy.

And yet something about Louisa had wrapped itself around him, and no matter how hard he tried to resist, it refused to loosen its hold. But there was no path for him and Louisa to take. It had been cut off ten years ago. Probably even before that.

Oliver lowered back onto the chair stiffly.

"I see you are determined to clamp up," Helgate remarked. "Let me ask you this: Did you tell her that you were the one who saved her? Did you tell any of them?"

"Irrelevant."

Helgate leaned in, a hint of disbelief in his eyes. "How the devil is that irrelevant? It sets you apart from your father!"

"His blood still runs through my veins." As Talbot had pointed out.

Helgate scoffed, shaking his head. "Christ, you are so stubborn at times," he muttered. "Has it ever occurred to you that you might start mending this feud with Talbot if he knew you were the one who led his daughter back to his men?"

Oliver's lips curled in a bitter smile. "He wouldn't believe me."

"Does it matter what he believes?" Helgate didn't bother to hide his irritation. "You only want her to believe it anyway."

"Damn it, Helgate," Oliver snapped, slamming his fist on the bar. "I already walked away, now you want me to walk right back and mention this after the fact? I would look like a bloody fool."

"I hate to point this out, old chap, but you already do look a bit like one. A fool in love."

Oliver cursed the man. A fool in love? Wouldn't that be the jest of the season—a Cavanagh falling in love with a Talbot?

Christ.

But his chest *ached*.

So, he didn't feel nothing. He certainly felt something. But he wouldn't call it love either. They'd had a moment. Very well, they'd had a few moments. Breathtaking, irresistible, heart palpitating moments. But that's all they were, and that's why he felt rather discomposed by Talbot finally telling his daughter the truth about the Cavanaghs.

But Helgate also wasn't wrong. He *did* want her to believe it. If he ever told her about his part in it, that was.

Helgate sipped his ale. "In any event, if she deserves to know the truth, doesn't she deserve to know the *full* truth? Whether you pursue her or not, love her or not, at the very least, you ought to give her that. And you know it. Why else would I even have found you here still? You ought to have been on your way back to London, but here you still are. You couldn't bring yourself to leave, could you?"

No, he couldn't.

"What if she doesn't believe me?"

A hand patted his shoulder. "Whether she believes you are not is for her to decide. At least your conscience will be clear. Besides, the Lady Louisa I came to know these past few days is not to be underestimated. She possesses a capable mind of her own."

Oliver recalled the fury she had displayed when Talbot hadn't shown enough ire against his wife. Helgate was right. No matter what the outcome, whether he was hated or not, she deserved the full truth.

If nothing else, he could give her that.

Chapter Twenty

L OUISA SIGHED—AGAIN—DRAWING ANOTHER look from their cook.

"This can't go on, dearie," Cook said. "What ails you to darken my kitchen with all these sighs?"

Louisa sighed again. "Would you rather have me cry?" It was one or the other, and she wasn't in the mood to cry. If she started, she didn't think she would ever be able to stop, which she couldn't understand either.

She had no reason to cry. She ought to be happy. Everything had worked out in the end. It was over. No regrets. And she would never have to worry about Camilla again. That alone should have had her waltzing around the halls.

It must be the tiredness.

Or her father's shocking revelation about her kidnapping. She'd retired to her chamber immediately after everything that had transpired in the duchess's. She hadn't wanted to think about any of it. But she couldn't shut her eyes long enough to sleep. The moment she lowered her eyelids, flashes of ten years ago would return.

Laughter. Raindrops. A hard mattress.

Oliver's family had kidnapped her. Was he the one who had snatched her away from her family? Was he one of the reasons nightmares plagued her slumber? These were the thoughts that tortured her.

Not knowing the answer was so vexing!

"I'd rather you smile, dearie," Cook waved a spoon at her cup. "And drink your milk. You've been staring at it so long that it must have turned to ice."

Louisa would rather smile as well.

Her lips just . . . wouldn't.

That dreadful *"It's true"* kept ringing in her head.

"I should have asked him," she muttered to herself, but the duke had left so quickly in the wake of his admission. He hadn't even given her time to process!

And he had known the truth from the very start and said nothing. Had he perhaps presumed that she already knew but didn't care, or had he suspected she'd been left in the dark, and decided to keep her there?

This was what she loathed about the male species in general. They made up their minds entirely on their own about what was best for their female counterparts and what was not. It was so blasted infuriating.

She slammed her hand on the table. A maid who just entered the kitchen leaped nearly a foot in their air. "By Jove, that man will drive me to Bedlam."

Cook merely raised a brow. "Who are you speaking of, dearie?"

"Oh," Leo's voice came from behind the maid who had entered. "She fancies our previous gardener, turned footman, turned Bow Street officer, turned Duke of Mortimer, family enemy."

Louisa shot him a glare. "Thank you for the recounting, brat."

"Ah, I see," Cook said, wiping her hands on her apron.

"What do you see?" Louisa asked, pulling a face. "Because I can't see anything from where I am seated."

"That's because you chose the wrong seat," the older woman replied matter-of-factly.

Louisa folded her arms. "You know about the family feud?"

Cook turned back to her work with a sniff. "I know both heads of the two families were as stubborn as mules, and before they were enemies, they were the closest of friends."

Louisa sat up straighter. "Really? I cannot imagine it."

Leo dropped into a seat beside her, his expression skeptical. "Me neither."

Hah! What did this brat know? Still, she had to admit it was a pleasant change to see that his definition of "following her" had shifted from spying to simply . . . joining.

Cook rummaged on a rack and pulled out a large pot. "The two dukes fought over one woman—your mother."

"Our mother?' Leo asked with interest.

Louisa barely had time to process the revelation before an image took shape in her mind. "She chose my father."

Cook nodded. "Correct."

"Is *that* how the feud started?" Louisa asked, incredulous. Over a woman?

"Oh, there is a bit more to the story than that, dearie," Cook said, filling the pot with water. "Your mother was the other duke's betrothed. I believe your mother and father eloped back then."

Louisa's jaw slackened. *Oh.* "Oh, so the Duke of Mortimer was angered by them both . . ."

Leo scoffed. "This is why I have no time for women."

Louisa shot him a flat look. She sensed the influence of a particular male. "Just what did you and Mr. Helgate talk about?"

"Oh, many things," Leo said lightly.

"Not going to say, are you?"

He lifted his chin. "It was a conversation amongst men."

"Right." Why did she even ask?

Cook chuckled, shaking her head. "It good not to be interested in these things at young master Leo's age."

But Leo wasn't finished. He turned to Louisa, asking, "Are you going to defy father for your gardener?"

Her heart gave a traitorous lurch, so sudden and forceful that she almost pressed a hand to her chest. "Why would I do that?"

"Because you slept with him."

The simple answer knocked the breath from Louisa. She coughed, and she nearly choked on air almost at the same moment Cook dropped the spoon.

Leo! You and your tactless tongue!

Heat rushed up her neck, her gaze darting between the wide-eyed maid, the shocked Cook, and her infuriating brother. "What are you talking about?" Did he know what they had done in the carriage? Had he overheard something?

He looked at her funnily. "I saw you—in the morning at Mr. Helgate's cottage. Don't you remember?"

"Oh, *that*." Relief came swiftly, as did a fresh wave of mortification. She waved her hands at him, Cook, and the maid, who still looked as if she'd been struck by lightning. "He fell asleep beside me. It's not what it sounds like." But then, was falling asleep beside her—after traveling for days with no chaperone—really any better in the eyes of others?

Cook cleared her throat before swiftly scooping up the spoon from the ground, moving to rinse the utensil, and changing the topic. "I heard the duchess was confined to her bedchamber and half the servants were let go."

Ah, yes. Her father hadn't wasted any time in handling matters. And Louisa seized the change of subject with both hands, "Papa and that woman are leaving for London soon. I'm afraid some rumors might start soon about our family and the duchess."

"Never mind that, dearie," Cook said, shaking droplets from the spoon, "so long as you and your brother are all right."

"I believe we shall be," Louisa murmured.

"Me too," Leo said, nodding. "I never liked her to begin with."

Loui's brows lifted. "You didn't? This is the first time I'm hearing this."

Her brother shrugged. "You never asked me."

"Well, I never liked her either. I wonder what Papa saw in her." She smiled at her brother, warmth creeping into her heart. "But thank you for taking my side."

"Of course," Leo said, eyes bright. "You are my family."

Louisa cocked her head, studying the child. "Papa is your family as well." In fact, he was the head of the family!

"Yes, but you are closer to my age than him."

A loss. She stared at Leo at a complete loss. This boy's reasoning truly stumped her at times! Before she could formulate a response, a voice cut through the air.

"Ah, my lady! There you are!"

Louisa turned her head to find Tabitha, one of the chambermaids, hurrying toward her, a folded piece of parchment clutched in her hand. "A letter just arrived for you."

Louisa's stomach twisted. "Oh? A letter for me?"

She took the parchment from Tabitha. Her fingers brushed against the wax seal—no crest, no initials. Who could it be from? A face suddenly swam in her vision. A cold face with a warm freckle beneath his eye. Could it be from Oliver? If this was the duke, the man certainly had mettle, sending her a letter with her father still in residence.

She broke the seal and unfolded the paper, and her eyes widened at the bold sentence scrawled there.

She blinked and then scowled.

What on earth did this mean?

OLIVER HAD MADE few rash decisions in his life. In fact, he could only recall one: saving Lady Louisa that day when he'd discovered his father had ordered her kidnapping and she was being held in the cottage he considered his refuge.

Determination welled in his being. And he knew it wouldn't let go until he had completed his mission. Her look of horror surfaced in his mind again, and he pushed it aside. Not the time. Not the place. Not with the task that lay before him.

But he couldn't rid himself of it completely. He could shove it from his mind, but he couldn't drag it from his heart or yank it from his bones. And a memory without bounds would turn into a nightmare with no end.

Oliver stood at the base of the imposing mansion, its dark silhouette grim against the moonlit sky as he stared up at the wall he needed to scale. His chest tightened with the force of his racing heart, determination and trepidation colliding in his veins. Would she be there? Would she be waiting for him? Or would she have a servant waiting for him? Or worse, her father. He shook his head, dismissing the doubts.

He had to try.

If he didn't, he would regret it for the rest of his life, and he still wanted to live a long one. He had no desire to become the kind of man who stared out of windows, penning tragic poetry about lost chances.

"Are you sure you want to do this?" the devil murmured at his shoulder, so damn close that Oliver nearly shuddered. "I didn't mean to encourage you to *this* extent."

He cast Helgate a flat look and pressed a finger to the man's shoulder to add some distance. "You cannot take it back the moment before it happens."

"Right, but looking at this wall . . . I fear for your life."

"That is why I brought you long," He unfastened his cloak and handed it over. "If I fall, you can catch me."

Helgate snorted and took the garment, shaking it out before draping it over his shoulder. "The things you say with that cold face."

Oliver arched a brow. "Afraid you can't catch me? And here I thought you considered yourself a man of impeccable skill."

"I am, which is precisely why I intend to remain standing. So don't expect miracles if you fall."

"Where is Miles?" Oliver asked, ignoring his friend's unhelpfulness.

"He's in the shadows over yonder." Helgate gestured off to their right.

Oliver glanced over, and a man, cast in shadows, stepped forward to give a nod. Oliver inclined his head, and the phantom retreated into the shadows once more.

"Why did you want him here, anyway?" Helgate muttered. "He's going to hound me about this forever."

"Which is why I requested his presence." He sent his friend a quirk of a smile. "To keep you in proper bounds."

A shocked look crossed Helgate's face. "And what proper bounds are those?" His friend jabbed up the residence. "Who is determined to scale such a wall without even a vine in sight? What about *your* proper bounds?"

"I've conquered prisons worse than this."

"Don't remind me," Helgate snapped, wiping at his brows. "*I* almost perished. God, wasn't that situation similar to this?"

Oliver tugged off his gloves, stripping them finger by finger, and tossed them to Helgate. Bending down, he removed his boots, knowing he would need the grip of all his limbs to climb the wall successfully. He didn't listen to Helgate's griping. His friend was just worried, naturally so. But he took on this mission with the same seriousness as anything else he had ever undertaken, and not even the smallest sliver of doubt, could be allowed to enter his mind.

"Here, don't forget this," Helgate said, handing him over a small box. "You went through all the trouble of procuring it on that barman's guidance. Don't squander your pitiful purchase."

Oliver stared at the black, velvet-covered jewelry box. This was an apology. An apology . . . hell, he didn't know anymore. He'd bought the bauble on a whim, thoroughly annoyed at himself for doing something so out of character.

"Helgate." Oliver turned to his friend solemnly. "If I fail or, for whatever reason, don't survive the night, take care of my mother."

"If you die tonight," came Helgate's hard resolution, "I die tonight."

Oliver tossed his stockings and boots aside, the icy cobblestones biting into his bare feet. He ignored the cold. "Don't let Miles hear you say such things. He will kill you himself."

A slap landed on his shoulder. "Don't curse me, old chap. I shall be here for you. The moment I hear shouts, screams, or rifles fired, we shall barge in."

"If I enter successfully, you may leave," Oliver tossed over his shoulder, preparing to climb. He flexed his fingers before running them along the cold stone, the rough surface scraping beneath his touch. This was good. There were no vines or trellises to aid his ascent, so the climb would test his endurance, but it would be worth it. He hoped.

"Crazy fool," Helgate muttered.

He took a deep breath and started the climb, fingers searching for crevices, toes gripping ledges. The stone of the wall bit into his skin, but he ignored the discomfort, channeling all his focus on every inch he had to gain.

In his mind, he'd already climbed this wall a thousand times. This was the one thousand and first time, and it would be the last.

He reached a narrow ledge, pausing to catch his breath. The wall loomed above him, and he could see the faint light from Louisa's bedchamber window. The closer he got, the more his heart pounded, but he couldn't allow it to distract him.

He required extreme calm.

It didn't help that he could feel Helgate's hawk eyes boring into his back.

Oliver clenched his jaw forged on, muscles straining, fingers and toes aching. He narrowed his thoughts on Louisa—her kindness, her strength, the way her eyes softened when she spoke of her brother.

Her heart.

With a steady breath, he reached the balcony ledge, his fingers curling around the stone as he hauled himself up. Once perched atop the ledge, he paused for a breath, then swung his legs over, landing lightly on the other side. He peered back over the ledge, nodding down at Helgate before he turned and padded over to the glass doors.

The curtains weren't drawn completely shut, and a sliver of light spilled onto the balcony. Through the gap, Oliver spotted Louisa reclining on her bed. Her profile was bathed in the soft glow of a candle, tracing the delicate curve of her cheek and the soft fall of her hair hanging over her shoulder. She looked like an angel—as ever—beautiful, untouchable, and also very much lost in thought.

Helgate's words in the tavern echoed in his head.

Dear God.

He was in love with Louisa Talbot.

The truth struck him with the force of a fist to the gut. Oliver stood frozen, staring at her through the glass, dumbfounded. He had denied it earlier, fought against it, even, but the moment his gaze fell on her now, everything inside him shifted. He *knew*. He loved her. Completely. Madly. Recklessly. Loved her. This angel—so fierce, so clever—had undone him in every possible way.

As if she could sense him, Louisa turned. Her eyes widened the moment they met his, her entire body jerking in fright.

Confound it!

The last thing he wanted was to startle her.

For one breathless moment, he hesitated. Then, slowly, he tapped lightly on the glass, hoping she recognized it was him.

She did. Her eyes widened further, and relief flooded him when she sprang to her feet and rushed to the door. She flung it open, shock, disbelief, and confusion, flashing across her features. "Oliver? What are you doing here?"

"We need to talk," Oliver said softly.

"Could this not have waited?" She held up a hand. "Wait, is this how you entered the last time?"

He shook his head, motioning to his bare feet. "No, that time

I picked the lock of your side door on the ground floor, but with Talbot in residence, I didn't want to take the chance of being heard or seen."

"So tonight you took the chance of dying?" Her gaze darted to the balustrade and back.

Oliver shrugged, drinking in the sight of her, unable to look away. "I have something important to tell you. After that, I'll leave."

She stepped aside. "Very well, come inside before your feet turn blue and fall off!"

A hint of a smile touched Oliver's lips. "Well, I wouldn't want that." The knot in his chest slowly started to loosen. He'd fully expected to be chased away, but instead, she'd invited him into her chamber. He inwardly cursed as his gaze fell on the bed, flashes of her atop him raiding his mind.

He hadn't thought this through.

The moment the door shut behind him, he jerked, turning to face her, and any words died on his lips.

Chapter Twenty-One

LOUISA'S BROWS FURROWED. The duke stared at her in silence, his expression unreadable, as if the very air had been stolen from his lungs. Her own breath faltered as well. She studied his face, tracing every small line with her eyes, searching for any sign of change in the short time they had been apart.

Within the far reaches of her mind, in some obscure corner, she understood this line of thinking was a bit skewed. But that faint awareness was overshadowed by part joy and part relief that he hadn't just left without a word. That even if this was his final goodbye, she would cling to his presence for as long as she could.

"I thought you would be on your way to London by now."

"I couldn't leave."

"Why not?" She hated the hopeful flutter in her heart. "What was so important that you had to tell me?"

He hesitated, then reached into his jacket pocket and removed a black jewelry box. Her stomach flipped. Surely he hadn't come to . . . to . . . propose! No. That was absurd. And the Duke of Mortimer may be many things, but not absurd. She need not have stretched her imagination that far, however.

"I came to apologize."

"For what?" He had nothing to apologize for. Unless . . . Her heart sank. Had he truly been part of her kidnapping? Could she forgive him if he had been in some way? Did she want to know if he had?

No, she didn't.

She lifted her hands, shaking her head, a silent plea for him not to say another word, but his words were faster.

"I shouldn't have left the way I did earlier."

She froze, searching his face. "Then, you . . . didn't come to apologize for being part of the kidnapping?"

His brows drew together. "What do you mean?" Then his shoulders went rigid. "You don't think I helped kidnap you?" When she said nothing, he cursed, dragging a hand through his hair. "Of course this would be what you imagined."

"I don't mean to accuse you . . ." Louisa felt wretched for a variety of reasons. All the melancholy she'd experienced in the kitchen came rushing back. "Honestly, I do not know what to imagine." In her heart, she wanted to launch herself into his arms, hold him tight, and forget about the world. If only all the uncertainties that came with the past, present, and future hadn't coiled around her heart like venomous vipers.

"I didn't." His fingers gripped the box in his hand, knuckles whitening. "I had no part in what happened to you back then. I . . ." His voice trailed off.

An impression of familiarity suddenly filled Louisa, and as she observed the duke, the image of a young man she'd been thinking of so often lately swam across her mind, overlapping with his.

She nearly gasped.

Good God.

Could it be?

"But you were there," she said slowly, now almost certain that she was right. "You're the young man from my dreams. . ." She lowered her gaze, attempting to grab hold of the memory she'd once believed only a dream that would always stubbornly leave the moment she tried to grasp at it. Her protector in the shadows.

"Yes," he said simply, solemnly.

Her gaze shot up to meet his again, her heart racing. Her

throat tightened, and she held her breath, waiting for his next words.

"I am the one who let you go."

The breath left her lungs in a rush. Let her go? He made it sound so simple, so insignificant. His eyes, however, held unfathomable gloominess—like a man walking to the gallows. Let her go?

No.

He hadn't merely *let* her go. He had *saved* her.

Those coiled vipers, the chaos, her heart, finally settled.

"You rescued me, Oliver," Louisa said, her voice quiet but firm. "You took me from that place and handed me over to my father's men."

He shook his head. "I didn't hand you over. Not directly."

Indeed, had her father known that the son of his enemy had aided him, the course of events might have taken a rather different turn. Although, knowing her father, perhaps not. However, the important thing here was that Oliver had saved her from that nightmare. No wonder she had always felt safe with him, despite their families being at odds. She had trusted him implicitly. At first, she had thought it was because she didn't give any credence to the feud between the families, but now . . . she knew that was not the case.

He'd saved her.

She had been dreaming about him for ten years.

"You still saved me."

He merely stared at her, unblinking.

"Are you not going to say anything?" Louisa pressed. *"It's a pleasure, Louisa—"*

"Your father must have been livid after I left."

Ah, her impossibly handsome, inscrutable duke. "My father was beyond furious, and I took quite the verbal beating for defying him, but I could not condone what he had done. This might be ten years too late, but thank you for defying your own father back then."

"You do not hate me?" he asked softly.

Louisa blinked at the man. "Why would I hate the man who helped me?" *Oh.* "If this is because of what my father said about blood, I do not share his view."

He let out a visible breath. "That is a relief." The gloominess left his gaze. "I don't want you to hate me."

Silly man, I could never hate you. I love you.

Louisa nearly coughed at her own thought, almost the same as when Leo had blurted out her sleeping arrangement with this "gardener"!

"What?" He stepped up to her. "Is something wrong?"

She cleared her throat, shaking her head furiously before pointing at the jewelry box in his hand. "You brought me a gift?"

"This?" He nodded. "Someone suggested women enjoy baubles as an apology gift."

She held out her hand, her whole body suddenly thrumming with interest. "Oh? Let me see?"

He placed the box onto her palm. "It's nothing much."

Louisa didn't comment. It wasn't "nothing much" to her, but rather, his gift was everything. Even if he didn't know it. She slowly opened the lid, and her jaw promptly dropped.

"This . . ."

"Do you not like it?" he whispered. "I shall exchange it for something else if you don't."

"No, I . . ." Her gaze lifted to meet his, her gaze burning. "This is a ring!" Louisa burst out. A *ring*! Not some bauble! Definitely not "nothing much"! A gold ring with bright three bright rubies set next to each other.

He nodded. "The jeweler said it's the latest design."

"I hate to ask this in such a direct manner, Oliver, but this . . ." Her eyes narrowed. "Are you proposing to me?"

The color seemed to drain from the poor man's face. "No. What? No."

She pointed at the ring. "*No?*"

"I mean . . ." A curse. "Do you wish for me to propose to

you?"

Lawks, why hadn't she seen it before? The man was as clueless as a lamppost when it came to matters of romance. His approach to everything had always been upside down, inside out.

"No! Of course not!" She didn't want him to propose if he didn't want to propose. Besides, there were still so many things that needed their attention. Her father, for one—he would never approve . . .

Urg!

Louisa didn't want to think about that now. Her gaze fell to the ring. She started when a big hand covered it softly, swallowing up her whole hand and the box.

"Louisa, all you need to do is say the word. I gave you the proverbial key to my house before. I didn't know what I even meant by it at the time, not fully, I suppose, and I know I'm not the sort of man you must have hoped for, but if it means anything, I am the most helpless when it comes to you. I have no power in the face of your presence . . . For what it's worth, you hold it all."

Louisa's breath caught. "Are you saying . . .?" Did he mean what she thought he did?

His gaze never wavered. His lips parted—

"Well, I hate to break up this touching scene," a shrewd voice came from the door.

Louisa jerked, her head whipping toward the interruption.

Camilla!

The shadow that refused to fade!

And then her heart nearly stuttered to a stop.

In Camilla's hand was a pistol, and it was pointed straight at them.

"But I need to borrow your lover for a bit."

NO STRING OF curses could suit the depth of Oliver's fury.

Of all the moments to be interrupted in his whole entire life, this was the bloody worst. He was already struggling to breathe out the words in his heart, but nothing sobered a man up like a pistol pointed in the direction of the woman he loved.

He stepped so that his body shielded Louisa and said coldly, "Borrow me? You have some nerve on you, madam."

"Would I have built an empire if I didn't?" She gave a laugh that sounded more like a cackle. "The moment I saw the way you looked at my stepdaughter, I knew still had a chance."

"You were acting earlier," Louisa accused. "Playing along with Papa. You never had any intention of listening to him."

"Listening to him? Do you mean being escorted to Bow Street without putting up a struggle of any sort? Do not make me laugh, child. All I had to do was wait for either you or your lover to take a step toward the other."

"Papa dismissed all your people."

The duchess scoffed. "There will always be one or two you never expect who slip through the cracks."

Oliver scowled, every muscle taut, poised for action. "And what do you mean to do now?"

"I mean to retrieve my ledger and the betting book."

The woman had more than nerve, she was downright mad. "I don't have them," Oliver said.

A small hand gripped the sleeve of his shirt. The touch was light, barely there, yet it sent a sharp current through him. He drew steadiness from that small gesture.

"Oh, I know," the pistol shifted two inches and settled solely on him, "but you will take me to them."

Ah, bloody hell. This woman wasn't just downright mad, she had clearly lost all sense entirely.

So had someone else.

Louisa suddenly stepped in front of him, placing herself directly in the line of the pistol. "No, he will not."

Oliver let out a foul curse.

"So brave for a child," the duchess cooed. "But so naïve."

Oliver gritted his teeth. "The books are on their way to Bow Street as we speak. If that is your desired destination, I do not mind taking you to your ledger."

The duchess's smile slipped. "You lie."

"Whether I am lying or not, it's the only destination I shall ever escort you to."

Oliver calculated the distance between him and the woman. Three strides—no, four—and he would be able to wrestle the pistol from her.

Four steps . . .

He could risk two, but not four.

The betting book, strictly speaking, *was* on its way to his contact at Bow Street. The Talbot ledger, however, was not. Helgate still had it in his possession so that he could copy its pages, as he had done with the Havendish ledger. Also, Oliver would never send them both as a pair. This way, if there were trouble on the road, and something happened to one, they would still have the other. Quite frankly, these books had a way of getting themselves "lost", if the betting book was anything to go by. It was the most damnable thing, and he wasn't about to tempt fate by sending everything off to London at the same time.

"Well then," the duchess said, cutting through the hush left in the wake of his words. "I shall just have to exchange *you* for the ledger. I doubt Bow Street will have trouble handing over two books for the price of one duke."

An oath shot through his mind. This woman was determined to take him. He could only pray that Helgate and Miles hadn't left, and that they protected Louisa in his stead. "I will come with you—"

"Oliver!"

"—so long as Louisa remains unharmed."

The duchess laughed mockingly. "How sweet the two of you are. Your father is going to love *this*, Louisa. Such ill-fated, doomed love."

"It is only ill-fated or doomed if we decide that it is," Louisa snapped, her whole body stiffening. "You, on the other hand, will lose everything you hold dear soon enough."

"You never did approve of me," the woman said to Louisa, a bitter edge to her voice. "I've always been curious. What was it about me that put you so on edge?"

"Your face," Louisa answered without any hesitation. "I clearly saw two."

"Ah, well, you cannot win all hearts." She motioned with her pistol to Oliver. "No harm shall befall your Juliet. However, I cannot leave her here like this, and now that I've seen your hopeless affections for each other, how can I bear to part the two of you?"

Oliver ground his teeth.

Damn it, he didn't want Louisa near this woman and the aim of her pistol. Her eyes blazed with a cold, ruthless determination. She would shoot. The way her fingers tightened around the grip, the slight shift of her weight, the dead aim—it all made his blood run cold.

Louisa stood close to him—so close the sweet scent he so loved tickled his nose—her shoulders squared, her chin raised defiantly, but he could feel the subtle tremor that coursed through her body.

She was afraid, but she was also committed.

Oliver's mind raced for a way to get out of this without Louisa getting hurt. He couldn't stand by and let this woman gain a victory. Not after everything they had endured, not after the secrets they had unearthed and the truths he had yet to confess.

He had to take a risk.

A four-step risk.

His muscles coiled, ready to leap, to knock the weapon from the duchess's hands. But before he could move, Louisa's arm shot out and she called, "Camilla! Catch this!"

Oliver barely had time to process what she was doing before he saw his black-velvet jewelry box sail through the air.

The duchess's gaze flicked towards it, and Louisa shot past him like a cannonball, arms outstretched.

"Louisa!" Oliver lunged forward. Everything happened so damn fast. He reached out, his fingers grazing Louisa's arm as he tried to pull her back, to shield her, to take the risk himself. But it was too late. The duchess's lips twisted in a snarl.

Too late.

A shot fired, the blast echoing off the walls of the chamber.

Time seemed to slow to the pace of a snail, the world narrowing down to the sharp crack of one shot, the acrid scent of gunpowder, and the crippling fear gripping him.

"Oliver!"

He snatched the wrist of the duchess in a grasp that could have suffocated death, and yanked, the sound of a loud crack, and even a louder cry of pain, following in the wake of the shot.

The pistol fell to the ground with a thud.

Oliver kicked it away immediately and flung the woman's hand away from him. He'd snapped a bone in her wrist, but didn't bloody care. She could be grateful he hadn't done more.

"Oliver?"

He glanced at Louisa, their eyes meeting, and the look on her face had the blood seeping from his. He staggered toward her. "Were you shot? Where are you shot?"

"No, you fool! I'm not the one who was shot! You are!"

He glanced down, assessing himself. Sure enough, his arm was bleeding. He pressed on the wound. "It's nothing."

"Do not lie to me! That is certainly something!"

"Louisa!" Leo cried before Oliver could respond. The boy rushed into the chamber, only to be yanked back by Talbot, who had a pistol in hand. His eyes took in the scene with one sweep.

Ah, well.

It seemed Oliver was going to die tonight after all.

His limbs grew leaden, the life draining from them as relief replaced the heart-rending fear that had gripped him moments ago. The pain from the wound hadn't reached him yet, but the blood, hot and thick, seeped through his fingers, staining his shirt.

"Talbot," Oliver began before frowning. The world tilted around him, and his knees buckled. They hit the floor a second later.

Damn it.

Why the hell was he so dizzy from a mere flesh wound?

"Oliver!" He caught the blur of Louisa's skirts as she dropped to her knees beside him. Her hands were on him, frantic and trembling, he thought, attempting to staunch the flow of blood. "Send for a doctor!"

Darkness crept at the edges of his vision.

The last thing he saw before the world faded to black was Louisa's face, pale and stricken, her eyes wide with fear and something else—something that looked a lot like heartbreak.

He should have worn a black shirt.

A loud crash sounded in the distance.

I love you, angel.

And then, there was nothing.

Chapter Twenty-Two

F EAR GRIPPED LOUISA'S heart.

Her hands covered his, pressing down hard.

She had never felt like this, never known this kind of desperate, raw terror. Not even when she'd been abducted. Her breaths came in shallow gasps, each one harder to draw as the blood seeped through both their hands. Each drop seemed to drag her deeper into the dread that threatened to consume her. It was as though she were bleeding out alongside him.

You better not die tonight, Oliver Cavanagh!

"You fool!" she scolded the unconscious man. She pressed harder on his arm. "How could you not know you've been shot?"

She glanced over at the duchess, who had lost consciousness after Oliver snapped her wrist. At least they did not have to worry that she might run away. Louisa had half a mind to shoot the woman for good measure. But that would mean letting go of Oliver, and there was no way she could do that—not for anything. The world would have to crumble before she . . . no, not even then.

"Leo," her father said, "go wake the butler, if he hasn't been woken already by the noise. Have him send for the doctor."

Leo cast her a worried look but nodded, darting from the chamber. Her father stepped up to them, securing his pistol in his waistband. "Let me see."

Louisa hesitated, not daring to move. "Are you going help him or kill him?"

Her father scowled, his voice thick with disbelief. "Do I look like a murderer, Louisa? Let me see the wound."

She parted her lips to respond, but before she could speak, two figures burst into the chamber, pistols drawn. Louisa's eyes widened. "Mr. Helgate?" Her gaze shifted to a cloaked figure behind him. She couldn't catch even a hint of a face. "And Miles, I presume? What are you doing here?"

Helgate strode over to kneel at her side. "We heard a shot." He reached out to the wound. "How bad is it?"

Louisa granted him instant access, her gaze meeting her father's. She had hoped to keep this part of their adventure, where she had met more dangerous characters—*and stayed over at their cottage*—from him. Unfortunately, one glimpse at his frosty gaze, and she understood her father had already pieced together the bulk of it. He must already know something of Mr. Helgate and Miles, or he wouldn't have been angered to the point of not saying even one word.

"It's a flesh wound," Mr. Helgate announced, sighing.

Louisa let out a breath of relief. Thank God. "Help me move him to the bed."

"No," her father said, rising to his feet. He motioned to Mr. Helgate. "Take him and leave this house."

"Papa!"

"Do not argue with me, Louisa. Or would you have me nurse a man back to health who climbed up to my daughter's balcony?"

"He saved my life!"

"Which is why he is still alive."

"And which is why *I* shall care for him. Papa, you should look after your wife—she seems in need of care as well," She glanced at Mr. Helgate. "Please carry him to the bed. A doctor has been summoned."

Mr. Helgate nodded, and after quickly binding the wound with a piece of cloth he'd torn from his own shirt, he brought

Oliver to her bed under the cold gaze of her father. What a nerve-wracking predicament, but Louisa could be just as stubborn as he could. She glanced at the door, only to find the phantom, Miles, had disappeared again.

Her father sighed heavily and bent to pick up his wife, casting a warning glare at Mr. Helgate. "I'll be back shortly."

The moment he left, Mr. Helgate turned to Louisa with a hard face. "What happened? It's a flesh wound, but he is out cold."

Louisa stared at Oliver worriedly, noting the sweat forming on his brows. She curled her fingers through his. "I don't know. He just collapsed." She glanced at Mr. Helgate. "Will he be all right?"

"He's sturdy, he'll be fine. It's your father I'm more worried about."

"Louisa!" Leo rushed back into the room, slowing as he reached the bed. "Is your gardener going to die?"

"No, Leo," Louisa said, her heart aching at his pinched features, and she repeated Mr. Helgate's words, "He is sturdy, he'll be fine. It's our father I'm worried about more."

"Leave Papa to me," Leo announced bravely, yet at the same time rushed over to Mr. Helgate, clutching his jacket in a small fist. "Where is your friend?"

Mr. Helgate cast a quick look at the door. "He is not good with people, so he likes to keep to the shadows."

Louisa's gaze caught on the jewelry box disregarded on the floor and briefly left Oliver's side to retrieve it. She set it aside when she caught sight of the blood coating the palms of her hands.

All this for what? A book? A ledger?

She cursed Camilla to perdition.

"What are you doing in Ashford?" she asked Mr. Helgate, desperate for something, *anything*, to distract herself from Oliver lying bloodied on her bed.

"We had some business here," Mr. Helgate said. "Also, I had

a feeling that the best time to take care of that business would be right after you left Brighton."

Louisa didn't ask any further. She'd rather not know.

A groan came from the bed. She smoothed Oliver's furrowed brow. "Shall you stay?" she asked Helgate.

"He is not staying," a sharp voice once more came from her father, who filled the doorway. "Neither is Mortimer." His gaze had firmly settled on Mr. Helgate. "What I would like to know is how a man such as you is not only acquainted with my daughter, but also my son."

Mr. Helgate curled his lip in annoyance. "I'm not in the mood to answer a question you already know the answer to."

Louisa and Leo shared a look.

Leo lifted his chin. "I met Mr. Helgate in Brighton."

Dear Lord, Leo! Can you say that without clutching at the man's tailcoat?

"Brighton?" The duke's face clouded over. "And when were you in Brighton? No, don't answer that." His gaze fell onto the man on the bed. "It all ties back to one man, does it not?"

"Papa." Louisa inhaled a fortifying breath. "I know about your strife with Oliver's family, but he is not his father. I am in love with him and shall not be apart from him."

If his face had been stormy before, it now crackled with fury. "I forbid the match."

Louisa crossed her arms over her chest. "I forbid you to forbid the match."

His eyes narrowed. "I forbid you to forbid me to forbid the match."

Louisa pinched the bridge of her nose.

Her father wouldn't yield on this. His anger toward the Cavanaghs ran too deep. "Oliver, back then, was the person who helped me return my family, Papa."

"What?" Her father's face went blank. "Did he tell you that? Lies!"

"No, it's not a lie," Louisa maintained her stance. "I remember him. In my memories, he was always too vague to recognize, but the moment he confessed, I recalled his face—but when he was young. That is not a lie."

"And so what if he did help you? They should never have taken you in the first place! What about everything else that family has done to us?"

"And what of you, Papa? What have you done to that family? Oliver has only ever been kind to me and Leo when he probably has every reason to resent us because of this feud. I don't care for it either. He is not the true enemy."

"It doesn't matter, I still forbid the match."

"*I give my permission*," Louisa said sharply. Firmly.

"I give my permission, too."

Louisa's head swung to her brother, followed by her father's deep scowl.

Leo.

She glanced back at her father, whose face was twisted with frustration, his fists clenched tightly at his sides. He was the head of the family, his word law, but it seemed he faltered when both his children stood against him, united in their rebellion.

"I won't change my mind," he bit out, but said nothing more.

Well, they were at an impasse, for she wouldn't change her mind either.

Her gaze drifted back to Oliver.

Now all you need to do is wake up.

OLIVER OPENED HIS eyes to find himself in a soft bed surrounded by sweetness. What had happened? Camilla had fired a shot, her aim finding his arm. A flesh wound, he thought, nothing more. Then blackness had taken him. Damn it. Awareness of the chamber slowly settled in. His eyes shifted to where a soft hand held his.

"Louisa?" He grimaced at the gruffness of his voice.

"No, it's Leo," the youthful voice of Louisa's brother came.

"Leo?" What happened to Louisa? Had she been hurt, too? No, then Leo would be her, not him.

"Do not look so disappointed," the boy said, a hint of a pout in his tone. "Louisa is—"

"Here." She suddenly breezed into the room, straight to him. The bed dipped as she settled onto the mattress. "You can go now, Leo."

Leo let go of his hand, giving it a small pat, and spoke to his sister. "Father said since I have chosen to defy him, you and I should swap rooms and I must stand guard all night."

"Then can you stand guard outside? I wish to discuss something with Oliver."

"Very well," Leo said reluctantly. "I shall return in a bit."

Oliver's eyes clung to Louisa, unwilling to lose sight of her, afraid if he blinked, she might disappear. There was no sign of her being injured, too. The tension in his body eased.

Her gaze returned to his with concern. "Does it hurt?"

Oliver took stock of his body. His arm stung, but other than that, he wasn't any the worse for wear. "It's bearable," he muttered. "Were you worried?"

"I want to punch you for asking me that!" Her scowl brought him up short. "You had everyone worried. Even Mr. Helgate."

Oliver furrowed his brow. He and Miles must not have left after all, and then come when they heard the shot. "Miles came as well?"

"If you are referring to the cloaked gentleman, then yes, but he slipped away after Mr. Helgate confirmed you were still alive."

Christ. "Your father?" If Helgate and Miles heard the shot, Talbot would have, too. The fact that he was still alive and in her bed meant they had persuaded him somehow to show a wealth of leniency.

"You heard what Leo said, he took responsibility for you."

"And Talbot allowed it?"

A small smile formed on Louisa's lips. "Leo and I have discovered he is quite powerless to completely oppose both his children. Also, I might have mentioned that you saved and protected me on multiple occasions." She lifted her right hand. "The ring fits perfectly, thank you."

Oliver blinked at the hand that waved before him, and for a moment, words failed him.

She wore the ring.

Accepted the ring.

His ring.

He had bought it as a suggestion from the barman and recommendation from the jeweler, but the sight of his purchase on her finger made his gut clench in pleasure. Then he recalled their rude interruption.

"Louisa." Her name came out softer than he intended, but it had the desired effect. Her eyes, which had been fixed on the ring on her finger, lifted to meet his. There was a flicker of surprise there, softened with something else—something that made his heart pound. The words in his soul tore from his lips. "I love you."

She blinked at him, and he reached out to press his hand against hers, which was still suspended in the air, and locked his fingers in hers.

"Lawks, you . . ."

He squeezed her hand. "And if you don't believe me, I shall prove myself until you do."

"I do . . . believe you . . ."

"You do? Are you sure?"

She suddenly laughed, her eyes crinkling into crescents as she laughed. "Why do you sound so surprised?"

"I don't know," Oliver muttered. "My mind is still a bit muddled." And he was very much afraid that he was dreaming.

She locked her fingers with his and leaned in until their faces were almost touching. "You know, you are precisely the sort of man I swore I would avoid at all costs."

He knew. "You are not avoiding me right now," he said softly.

"No," she murmured back. "Because I fell in love with you anyway."

Dear God. Sweeter words he had never heard before that moment. He wanted to draw her into his arms, hold her, kiss her, *love* her. "How long before your brother returns?"

She smiled. "I cannot say."

He swore.

"Do not tell me you have wicked things on your mind, Oliver Cavanagh," she teased.

"When it comes to you, Louisa, I don't believe I possess very many proper thoughts."

"Well," she murmured, her lips suddenly grazing his. "We might have a moment or two still."

Oliver captured her lips in a tender, lingering kiss. He expressed, or tried to express, all the things he struggled to put into words—a silent promise of his sincerity. No obstacles existed here. He hadn't fallen in love with a Talbot. He'd fallen in love with an angel.

He broke the kiss reluctantly. "Your carriage would be most welcome right about now."

A grin split her face. "Oh! I received a note earlier from Theodosia." She retrieved a piece of paper from the table beside the bed. "*On our way to Gretna*, she says. Shall we join them?"

Oliver thought he'd heard wrong. Did she mean what he thought she meant? "Join them?"

She nodded. "We'd have lots of time in my carriage, and we'd get to experience the thrill of elopement."

"Louisa," Oliver said slowly, not wanting to imagine meaning in her words that she might not intend, "is this your way of proposing to me?"

"Well, you did give me a ring. It's on the right hand now, but I would very much like to move it to the left hand. That is, if you accept."

"I accept," Oliver said instantly. "The part about the ring. Not the elopement."

Surprise lit her gaze. "You do not wish to elope?"

Oliver shook her head. The idea didn't sit well with him at all. "No, I would like to share such a day with family and friends."

"Friends, certainly, but you do realize that with family we would be placing Cavanaghs and Talbots together in a confined space."

Oliver chuckled. "Well, one does need entertainment at a wedding, does one not?"

"There will be scandal enough with Camilla's activities exposed, along with Lord knows who else."

That's right. They wouldn't be able to escape some form of scandal. But the fact that this book, this investigation, had brought him to Louisa, and her to him, was something he wanted to cherish and celebrate.

"Are you certain you wish to expose her, and not have your father handle her according to his wishes?"

Her brows furrowed. "Would *you* be happy with that?"

"It's not my family who will suffer for this," Oliver pointed out. "My mission is to dismember her organization. How they are dealt with is not my concern. So, I'll follow your direction."

A slow, sultry smile played on her lips. "And here I thought you weren't romantic."

He really wasn't. But for her, he could most certainly try. A thought suddenly occurred to him. "How is the duchess? I think I snapped her wrist."

"Oh, you did, but it's nothing she doesn't deserve. The doctor already treated her injury after he treated yours."

He nodded. "A graze."

Her eyes narrowed. "You still collapsed."

His ears heated. "It happens." What else could he say? It was deuced embarrassing.

She scoffed, laying her head on her chest. "The sound of your heartbeat is strong."

That is because it's beating for you.

And it would beat so, forever.

Until his dying breath.

Epilogue

London, three weeks later

"DEAR LORD, THIS cake..." Theodosia murmured, chewing.

Louisa grinned. She was back in London in the Talbot townhouse, enjoying tea and cake with her friends, Theodosia, Harriet, and Selena. "What do you think? I am considering this orange flavor for our wedding."

Theodosia swallowed, then said, "*Oh?* You plan to bake your own wedding cake? Do you think that is wise?"

"I suppose you are right," Louisa said, mind racing. She didn't want to spend days in the kitchen. "It might not be enough for the guests. I must prepare the recipe for Cook instead."

"A wedding your father still doesn't approve of," Harriet pointed out.

"Oh, he will come around," Louisa said darkly, stabbing her fork in her otherwise untouched slice. "He doesn't have a choice. It's time to put the feud between the Cavanagh and Talbot households to rest."

Selena cleared her throat and set her plate aside. "One thing,"—she swallowed, pointed to the cake—"a bit too much salt."

Louisa's head snapped to her own slice. Taking a small bite, she barely managed to swallow before recoiling and setting her plate aside. Lawks! This... "How on earth did this happen? I swear I added the right amount!" Her gaze swung to Theodosia and Harriet. "Why didn't you say anything?"

Harriet arched a brow. "It's *not* some form of savory cake?"

"No!" Louisa exclaimed, aghast. Her eyes suddenly widened, horror filling her. "Dear Lord, I baked two!"

Theodosia set her plate down calmly. "I hesitate to ask this," she said, lifting her teacup, "but where is the second one?"

Louisa bolted upright. "I sent it to Oliver's house."

Her three friends stared at her in mute disbelief.

"No!" Her hands flew to her head. "I sent it to Oliver's house!" How could she have made such a mistake? She wanted him to taste a masterpiece, not a devil-piece! She could just imagine that usually stoic face scrunching up in shock.

Selena snagged her wrist and tugged her back onto the sofa. "It's too late now. He has probably already tasted it. There is nothing you can do about it."

Louisa groaned and slumped against the cushions. "Urgh!"

Her friend was right. There was no undoing this nightmare.

Harriet, ever the voice of reason, steered the conversation back on course. "Have you decided where you shall marry? You might be the only one of us who will have a normal wedding."

If marrying your family's nemesis was normal, then yes. "We shall be wed beneath the weeping willow tree at Ashford in two months."

Selena laughed. "You truly have no fear of your father."

"Why should I have fear? Besides, it was Leo's idea," Louisa said. She had to give the little brat his due, he had some good ideas. "And besides, my father is powerless in the face of his children."

Power truly had its limits. It all but disappeared in the face of love.

"I still cannot believe you are marrying a duke," Theodosia mused. "Didn't you say you vow never to marry a king, prince, or duke?"

"I've learned a lot since then," she smiled, still dancing in the clouds herself, "and changed my mind."

Harriet lifted her teacup in salute. "Well, that is what life is all about."

Selena, however, remained a touch brooding. "I still cannot believe the head of the secret women's club was your *stepmother*," she muttered with a scowl. "I wasted so much energy on nothing."

"Imagine if you'd been accepted into their club," Theodosia said with a sly smile. "You would soon be an infamous criminal."

Selena scoffed. "By association."

Theodosia sipped her tea. "Of course."

Harriet turned back to Louisa. "What is going to happen to your stepmother? The gossip columns are surprisingly silent on the matter."

Louisa waved a hand, unconcerned. "Oh, do not worry, they shall explode soon enough after my wedding." Oliver had handed over the power to her, and she had decided, much to her father's relief, to deal with the matter after she wed. He still wished to keep the scandal quiet, but to do that, he would have to remain married to Camilla. And he wasn't prepared to accept that.

Neither were Louisa and Leo.

She'd learned a lot of things since she got embroiled in this tangled mess—the book, Oliver, her stepmother, and even those infuriating Fury brothers. For one, she'd learned that not all threats came with snarling teeth and drawn blades—some arrived wrapped in silk. Therefore—her second lesson—a lady should always keep her friends close at heart, and known enemies close at hand. That being said, known enemies could become allies, and allies enemies. And lastly, sometimes rough and tough had more honor than the elegant and esteemed.

Life truly possessed a wicked sense of humor.

And Louisa?

Well, she was learning to laugh along with it.

"Where is the duchess now?" Selena asked, drawing her from her thoughts.

Louisa smirked. "Oh, she is confined in one of my father's houses here in London. Not even a rat can enter or leave that residence without him knowing." Oliver had also stationed guards outside the garden, the streets, and everywhere else he could manage. Why, she imagined there was a person of his beneath every lamppost in St. James's.

Harriet hummed, tapping her chin. "She must be quite livid."

Livid? Louisa recalled the woman's string of curses upon regaining consciousness. If there was a single resident who hadn't heard the full scope of the woman's wrath, they were surely deaf. But rather than annoyance, each curse, each shattered vase, each cry of indignation, filled Louisa with immense satisfaction.

She needn't worry about Camilla anymore.

But she missed Oliver.

She missed their time in the country.

Her father had kept a hawk-like eye on her ever since they'd announced their engagement. No, ever since that night when he'd discovered Oliver in her bedchamber. As it was, he still refused to allow her betrothed into his residence.

"Let's forget about that woman," Louisa said, dusting off her skirts. "We should head to Bond Street."

Theodosia gave her a knowing look. "You wish to sneak a visit with a certain duke, don't you?"

"You've caught me." She did want to see Oliver. Had to see him. It was as if an itch had formed in her heart and it wouldn't be soothed until she could leap into his arms. Bond Street had become a term she would use since she returned to London. It was code to meet Oliver, since her father's ears were still too sensitive to terms like *Oliver, Mortimer, Cavanagh, betrothed,* and even *duke.*

"It's broad daylight," Selena said. "You will no doubt be spotted if you call on your betrothed."

"Is that so wrong?" Louisa asked, half-exasperated.

"No," Harriet said, clutching her breast. "I think it's romantic."

Louisa leaped to her feet. "Then shall we go buy ribbons in Bond Street?"

Theodosia rose, too, chuckling. "Very well, I am also curious about this Mr. Helgate I know nothing about. You mentioned he was there, as well, didn't you?"

"He should be," she said thoughtfully. "Though I cannot know if he will be there right this moment."

"Nevertheless, I cannot let you let you go alone. What if I miss out on more theatrics?" Theodosia looked at the others. "What about you two?"

Harriet shook her head. "I shall return home. Leeds and I are meeting Leonora and Dare for dinner tonight, Ophelia and Avondale might also join us, and I still have some things to prepare."

"I shall skip as well," Selena said, rising along with Harriet. "I suddenly have an urge to feed Warrick and my brother some cake. Can I perhaps have two slices to take with me?"

Theodosia laughed, and Louisa nodded with a grin. "Take it all."

The day had started out sweet, turned a bit salty, and it would soon turn sweet again. Life was good.

In another drawing room not so far away

OLIVER PULLED A face.

The cake on his plate looked innocent enough—fluffy, golden brown, with a light dusting of powdered sugar on top. A vision of perfection. His angel's perfection.

And a deception of the highest order. Because the moment it touched his tongue, his taste buds staged a violent rebellion.

It was as if the entire Atlantic had been reduced to powder form and baked into this one unsuspecting slice. His mouth puckered. His throat clenched. His soul briefly left his body.

He glanced at Helgate, who was valiantly attempting to maintain his composure. A twitching eye. A stiff jaw. The faintest tremor in his fingers as he reached for his glass. A losing battle.

Then there was Miles. Silent, stoic, Miles. A man who faced down danger without so much as a blink. And here said, jaw working methodically, his chewing mechanical—but his eyes, dear Christ, his eyes were *watering*.

Helgate gulped his sherry down in one go. He exhaled sharply, then forced a tight-lipped smile. "Delicious."

"The sherry or my wife's cake?"

"She's not your wife yet," Helgate muttered, placing his empty glass back on the table. He nodded toward Oliver's plate. "And I don't see you stuffing your mouth with what's left on your plate."

Oliver cleared his throat. "I am pacing myself."

Miles coughed. Or perhaps choked. It was hard to say.

Helgate lifted a brow. "Pacing yourself or preserving yourself?"

"Same thing."

Miles, still chewing, placed his plate before Helgate without a word.

Helgate recoiled. "Absolutely not."

"You said you would do anything for me."

"Yes, I'd die for you but not bloody this. It's atrocious." At Oliver's look, he quickly amended, "Atrociously delicious."

"It's only a tiny bit over-salted," Oliver remarked.

"A *tiny* bit?"

Miles grunted and reached for his sherry as well. He, however, had the grace to take only a sip before he placed his glass down. "I look forward to your wedding."

Helgate scowled at the man as if he'd just declared war. "Ever the diplomat."

"Better than being ever the one who spews his thoughts left and right," Oliver said dryly, leveling a look at his friend.

Helgate, who seemed to think his knack for being blunt had

been called upon for more exercise, jabbed a finger at the cake on the table. "Old chap, this cake could double as a salt lick for cattle."

"I heard you sent the Talbot ledger to Maxen Fury," Miles interjected smoothly, steering the conversation away from the dangerous waters of dessert critique.

Oliver inclined his head. "Only the pages Helgate copied."

Helgate folded his arms across his chest. "I still don't know if that was the best move to make."

Oliver shrugged. Honestly, he didn't either. He did not that he didn't want to make enemies of those seven Furys. Not when he just found his angel. She came first. He'd protect her at any cost. "Someone is going to absorb those routes, might as well be the devil we already know rather than any of the duchess's henchmen or club members who remain at large."

Helgate gave a slow nod. "Use one evil to eradicate the other."

"Precisely." It will give them more power, but the authorities wouldn't have to tread lightly in bringing *them* down. At least that was Oliver's way of thinking. "And didn't you tell Maxen Fury you had your eye on them now? Go wild, old chap."

Helgate's lips twitched, but before he could respond, a knock sounded on the door. Oliver turned, expecting a footman. Instead, it was Louisa and Lady Theodosia.

"*Louisa.*" Oliver leaped to his feet, striding over to her, fingers grasping hers. She'd already tugged off her gloves, the touch of skin sending ripples to all the places that shouldn't be awakened in public. "I didn't expect to see you today."

She grinned. A beautiful, breathless grin. "Is it a delightful surprise?"

"Always."

Lady Theodosia cleared her throat.

Right.

Louisa's gaze shifted to his guests, her gaze falling on the cake.

Hell. Damnation. Christ.

"Well, gentlemen," her angelic voice asked, so ever sweetly, "what do you think of my creation?"

Oliver quickly sent his two friends warning looks.

Helgate, in a rare moment of discretion, cleared his throat and rose to his feet, though his expression remained carefully neutral. "It's unforgettable."

Miles rose a beat later, stiff as a plank at finding himself in company, but nodding.

Oliver also followed with a nod.

"Unforgettable?" Louisa echoed, tapping her slipper against his boot. "Is that the collective perspective,"—her bright eyes met his—"my dear betrothed?"

Oliver shot a quick glance at Lady Theodosia, who snorted, then at his friends, who were suddenly riveted by the table's legs, their eyes glued to anything but the cake.

"Unforgettable," Oliver repeated, every ounce of tact he'd cultivated over the years failing at that moment. "It's the perfect word to use. It certainly stands out," he said, trying to sound as diplomatic as Miles had.

Lady Theodosia laughed. "No need to keep up appearances, Mortimer. The cake is a horror the likes of which I've never before experienced."

Louisa sighed, then twisted her lips into a smile, blue eyes sparkling. "You don't need to spare my feelings. I made two, and I've tasted the other one."

"Thank God," Helgate muttered. "It will take a whole barrel of sherry to wash my palate of the salt. Miles, where is that bottle?"

Lady Theodosia stepped forward. "You must be Mr. Helgate. I'll have a sherry as well."

"Ah, you've heard tales about me, then."

Lady Theodosia grinned. "Only terrible ones."

Oliver, sensing an opportunity to escape with his angel, slid his fingers between hers. "Why don't you take a moment to get acquainted while I steal my betrothed away. We need to discuss cake."

Lady Theodosia snorted. "Cake my arse."

Oliver didn't tarry. He squeezed their entwined fingers, then pulled her from the drawing room to the morning room.

Louisa laughed. "Shall I kiss the saltiness away?"

God. "Please do."

She grabbed the lapels of his jacket and kissed him, and all the saltiness truly did melt away. It never failed to do so. Both his hands cupped her face, his tongue seeking hers, an urgent request for more.

Loud laughter and a curse came from the other room.

This was his future.

Laughter and curses of friends and family. A sense of home. A belonging that filled his body like nothing else ever had and never will again.

And Louisa. Most of all, Louisa.

All his promises were hers.

He promised she would be safe ten years ago, and then he promised he would get her brother back, now he promised to protect her all his life.

He couldn't wait.

The End

About the Author

Award-winning and bestselling author Tanya Wilde developed a passion for reading when she had nothing better to do than lurk in the library during her lunch breaks. Her love affair with pen and paper soon followed after she devoured all of their historical romance books!

When she's not meddling in the lives of her characters or pondering names for her imaginary big, white greyhound, she's off on adventures with her partner in crime. Wilde lives in a town at the foot of the Outeniqua Mountains, South Africa.

You can connect with her at www.authortanyawilde.com.

Website – www.authortanyawilde.com
Instagram – instagram.com/tanyawilde
Facebook – facebook.com/groups/843373666456177
BookBub – bookbub.com/authors/tanya-wilde

9 781967 169764